RED HOOK

The Weird of Hali

Novels by John Michael Greer

The Weird of Hali:

I – Innsmouth

II – Kingsport

III – Chorazin

IV – Dreamlands

V – Providence

VI – Red Hook

VII – Arkham

Others:

The Fires of Shalsha

Star's Reach

Twilight's Last Gleaming

Retrotopia

The Shoggoth Concerto

The Nyogtha Variations

A Voyage to Hyperborea

The Seal of Yueh Lao

Journey Star

The Witch of Criswell

RED HOOK

The Weird of Hali

Book Six

John Michael Greer

Published in 2023 by
Sphinx Books
London

British Library Cataloguing in Publication Data

A C.I.P. for this book is available from the British Library

ISBN-13: 978-1-91257-396-7

Typeset by Medlar Publishing Solutions Pvt Ltd, India

www.aeonbooks.co.uk/sphinx

From Brooklyn Heights I look across the river
To gray Manhattan, where the towers rise.
Despite our boasts, they cannot scrape the skies:
They rise and fall, the skies rise up forever.
Brownstone and concrete, brick and iron beams
Weigh down the land and bridge the surging deep,
But only for a while. Time turns in sleep
And shrugs aside the rubble of our dreams.
And you, the children of those distant years
Whose feet will someday dance upon the green
Where once stood our proud towers, shed no tears
For us, and for the things that might have been.
The things that matter stay when all else passes:
Night on the river, wind amidst the grasses.

> —"Looking Across The East River"
> by Justin Geoffrey

CONTENTS

Chapter 1: The Letter from Red Hook   1

Chapter 2: The Witch of Arkham   17

Chapter 3: The Face in the Water   32

Chapter 4: A Breath of Cool Air   47

Chapter 5: The Companion of Night   65

Chapter 6: The Silence of the Stars   78

Chapter 7: The Empty Circle   94

Chapter 8: The Night Ocean   111

Chapter 9: The Isle of the Manhattans   130

Chapter 10: The Silver Key   147

Chapter 11: The Fungi from Yuggoth   166

Chapter 12: The Toad God's Daughter   184

Chapter 13: The Place Outside The Portal   204

ACKNOWLEDGMENTS   223

CHAPTER 1

THE LETTER FROM RED HOOK

Justin Martense didn't expect any mail at all that day, though the little town of Lefferts Corners still had some semblance of postal service. Every week or two, when the weather was good enough, a truck from Kingston made the long winding trip up into the Catskills to drop off what mail there was. Old Letty van Kauran, who added the duties of part-time postmaster to those of Lefferts Corners' unpaid mayor and general fount of good advice, saw to it that each letter got to its addressee, but Justin could count on going from one month to the next without so much as a single letter reaching him. So far from the big cities and the routes that linked them, the few gas stations still in business pumped locally distilled ethanol and recycled cooking oil when they had anything at all, and life was settling back into a rhythm that the waning era of freeways and smokestacks had only briefly interrupted.

That rhythm occupied most of Justin's thoughts as morning slid toward midday and Lefferts Corners drowsed in yet another unusually hot August. Papers sprawled over the kitchen table of the old farmhouse: deeds, bank statements, forms from the county records office, and more, everything he needed to finish wrapping up eleven years of his life. Lean and pale, his unruly hair the color of ripe barley, Justin leaned over the table, ran a finger down a handwritten list, made certain that he had everything, and began putting the papers in order. The eyes that scanned each paper were of different colors, one ice blue, the other dark brown.

Methodical noises from the other side of the spacious kitchen wound up with the doleful sound of the oven door closing. "There we go," said Rose Wheeler, pulling off oven mitts: a slender woman, seemingly in her thirties, with black hair, red cheeks, and a ready smile. A windup timer chattered under its breath as she set it. "The Hasbroucks are coming at five, right?"

"Local time," Justin said without looking up. Rose chuckled, headed for the sink. Notions of timeliness had gotten noticeably casual in that corner of the Catskills, where cell phones and the internet were fading memories, and clocks were mostly antiques no one in Lefferts Corners knew how to repair any more.

Water splashed in the sink as Justin finished getting the papers in order. Then, in the silence that followed, a knock sounded at the door.

Justin glanced up at the clock, noted that it wasn't quite quarter to twelve, pushed back his chair and headed for the kitchen door. A glance through the window showed a familiar face, and he opened the door. "Hi, Sam. What's up?"

Sam van Kauran was a stocky middle-aged farmer, mostly bald, who lived two miles further out Maple Hill Road. "Hi, Justin. Letty asked me to drop off a letter." He fumbled in a pocket, got out an envelope with a handwritten address and handed it over.

Startled, Justin still managed to hold up his end of the usual conversation about the weather and the year's prospects, and to offer the expected beer and listen to the expected reason why Sam had to hurry home instead. Only when Sam had gone back out to the road, climbed into his battered pickup, and started the engine did Justin sit down again and consider the letter.

The plain white envelope had his name and address on it in a hand he knew he ought to recognize, but the return address was a complete riddle: General Delivery, Brooklyn, NY 11231. He opened the envelope, pulled out the single sheet of cheap paper inside, unfolded it and read the brief handwritten message:

> Justin,
> *I'd like to take you up on that offer.*
> —Owen

Justin stared at the message for a moment, trying to make sense of it.

"What is it?" Rose asked. "If you don't mind my asking."

"Not at all." He showed her the letter, and she gave it a puzzled look, then glanced at him. "That's Owen Merrill's handwriting, isn't it?"

"Yeah," said Justin, who'd recognized it as soon as he'd opened the letter.

"What did you offer him?"

"None that I can think of." He read the letter again. "I wonder—"

Then he remembered, with terrible clarity, the one time he'd made such an offer and Owen had accepted it. The two of them had been walking down a dirt road at night in the far western end of New York State, with the dark mass of Elk Hill looming above them, thunder rumbling in the distance, the clouds beyond the hill lit by a greenish glow that had no natural origin. "If we both get out of this in one piece," he'd said, "I owe you one, big time." Owen's response whispered in his memory: "I may take you up on that one of these days."

"Is something wrong?" Rose asked.

Justin glanced up from the letter to her worried face. "I don't know," he said. "I'm going to have to talk to old Mrs. Typer right away."

"Not before lunch, I hope."

That got an unwilling grin. "Of course not."

Boots sounded on the three steps up to the kitchen door a moment later: Arthur Wheeler and the three farmhands they had that season, all four of them in well-worn jeans and tee shirts, and well splashed with water—they'd obviously taken the time to wash off the dust of the morning's work at the pump beside the barn. Arthur crossed the kitchen to give his wife a hug and a kiss, while the farmhands grinned and headed for the big table. Justin gave the letter another uneasy look, then put it into his shirt pocket and followed them.

* * *

Terry Hasbrouck was a first cousin of Justin's on his mother's side and Sylvie Hasbrouck a third cousin once removed on his father's: nothing unusual in a town like Lefferts Corners, where most people were related one way or another. Terry had the lean Martense build and the barley-colored hair, Sylvie was dark and plump but had the mismatched Martense eyes. They greeted Justin like the old friends they were, then sat at the table and sorted through the paperwork Justin had assembled.

"Damn shame about the porphyria," said Terry, while Sylvie went through the farm's financial records, one finger tracing line after line.

Justin shrugged. "It was going to happen sooner or later."

"Oh, I get that." With a sudden grin: "I remember Aunt Beast sitting you and Bobby and Trish and Sylvie down and explaining it all, while the rest of us pretended not to listen." Justin grinned too, savoring the same memory.

Sylvie looked up from the papers then. "Thank you, Justin. This is really helpful."

"You're welcome." He paused, trying to decide how to ask the necessary question, but they forestalled him. Terry glanced at his wife, she nodded fractionally, and then he turned to Justin and said, "We're good with it if you are."

"I'm glad to hear that." Justin stood up, shook hands with both of them. There would be papers signed to satisfy the county, but in Lefferts Corners the handshake settled the deal.

A little more conversation, a few more pleasantries, and then Terry and Sylvie said their goodbyes and left. Like most of the younger people of Lefferts Corners, they'd made the leap back to horsedrawn vehicles while their elders were still clinging to cars and pickups. Their trim little one-horse carriage, Amish make from Pennsylvania but painted a jaunty blue, sat in a shady patch by the side of the road, a mare standing patiently by with her face in a nosebag. Justin watched them cross to the carriage, and thought about the farm he'd just sold.

He'd expected to feel—what? Sad, because the eleven years he'd spent working the farm had been good ones; relieved, because he'd wrapped up those eleven years neatly enough now that the family illness had shown up more or less on schedule, and managed to do the right thing and keep the farm in the family; uncertain, because once his summer plans with the Wheelers were finished, he had no idea what he was going to do with the rest of his life. As he watched Terry and Sylvie drive away, though, none of those feelings surfaced. Instead, something tense and wary gathered in his deep places, circled endlessly back to the letter in his pocket.

Another half hour or so passed before the sun dipped behind the great rolling peak of Tempest Mountain to the northwest, sending blue shadows across the rumpled landscape below. Once those shadows spread far enough to hide Maple Hill Road from the sun, Justin let Rose know where he was going and headed out the door.

He had a wagon and two good Morgan geldings in the barn, and a battered blue compact with a full fuel tank in the garage, but the evening was pleasant, a cool breeze had picked up, and Susan Typer's house was only about a mile closer to town.

His shoes struck a leisurely beat on the road's shoulder, bare dirt now that the county couldn't afford gravel any more. Jays squabbled overhead, and cows glanced up at him incuriously as he passed one farm after another.

From one of the houses, a faint familiar whisper of music came: drone of a mountain dulcimer playing a tune Justin knew well, "The Desrick on Yandro." Dulcimers hadn't been a Catskill instrument back in the day, but they'd come back into fashion nationally just short of a decade back, for the first time since the 1960s folk revival. A couple of local crafts-people learned how to make them, and once electricity got scarce, rural counties started losing internet service, and the only music left was homemade by definition, they'd become common in Lefferts Corners. The sound reminded Justin of an absence in his life, and he hurried on.

Finally the Typer place came in sight, a trim little farmhouse painted white. Justin let his pace slow, headed for the door. Susan Typer's front parlor served as a waiting room during busy hours, but nobody sat in the overstuffed chairs that evening. Susan herself came to the door to greet him: a diminutive gray-haired woman in a flower print house dress. They said the usual things, and then Justin followed her to the back parlor and settled in the usual armchair.

"I hope it's not the porphyria again," Susan said as she perched in her own chair.

"No, thank the Black Goat," said Justin, and saw her quick little smile, acknowledging the reference. "I need to get a message fast to a friend who's spending the summer in Kingsport, Massachusetts. Someone I know may be in trouble."

"Why, that's no problem at all," said Susan. "Moon's three days past full and the sky's good and clear, so it'll be on its way tonight. Who needs the message and what should I say?"

Justin had written both those out on one of the last sheets of an old notepad, and handed the slip of paper to her. She read it, nodded, and said, "Plenty of witches around there these days, too, and that means it'll be easy as pie." The note went into her purse, and they spent a quarter hour talking about local doings and a few moments settling the fee before Justin excused himself and started homeward again.

Halfway home, the absurdity of it all sank in, and he started to laugh. Fifteen years back, he'd used cell phones and the internet to contact people hundreds of miles away; ten years back, though he'd been to Elk Hill and learned a few things about the Great Old Ones, he'd still relied on the same technologies as his neighbors. Now taking a message to a witch who'd send it through the moon's beams was just as ordinary as typing a text message had been, and not for Justin alone. Worshippers of the Great Old Ones weren't quite a majority in Lefferts Corners yet but it was getting close. The Starry Wisdom church down on Corey Avenue in town—it had been the First Church of Christ decades back, then an antiques store, and then one of Lefferts Corners' many empty buildings before the Starry Wisdom folk bought it—was busier of a Sunday than any other church in town.

His laughter faltered after a few more paces, though. There were still people in Lefferts Corners who reacted to talk of witchcraft with disbelief or dread, and off in the unknowable distance, the enemies of the Great Old Ones waited. Justin had tangled with them at Elk Hill, and come through the experience alive through no strength or wisdom of his own. Every last person who attended services at the Starry Wisdom church, or went to one of the local witches for healing and counsel, or coupled in the fields to invoke the Black Goat of the Woods and make the crops flourish, knew that they lived on borrowed time—that the enemies of the old gods of nature could descend on Lefferts Corners at any moment and force a bitter choice between abandoning everything they had and a fight to the death that could only have one ending.

And Owen—was he facing those cold and ruthless men again, as he'd done so many times before? Maybe a message carried by moonlight would say.

Maybe. Justin pushed the thought away and kept walking.

* * *

He didn't expect a response for a day or so, the vagaries of witchcraft being what they were, but another neighbor on his way up Maple Hill Road from town dropped off the answer a little after ten the next morning. Justin unfolded the sheet of paper, read:

> Dear Justin,
> I was able to reach a witch in Kingsport last night easy, and get a reply after not much more than half an hour. Laura Merrill says that her husband went down to New York City a month ago, and no one's heard from him in weeks, not even the Starry Wisdom Church down there. She said he was in a place called Red Hook looking for something hidden underground. The witch I talked to thought Mrs. Merrill was really worried about him. Sorry not to have better news to pass on.
>
> Sincerely,
> Susan

Justin read it a second time, and then turned away, only half hearing Rose's worried voice from the other end of the kitchen. Owen really was in trouble, then. All at once the cryptic nature of the letter he'd gotten made perfect sense. If Owen knew or guessed that someone else might read the letter before it got to Lefferts Corners, a message that only Justin could interpret could have been the one sure way he could send for help.

In his mind, images of his first meeting with Owen and the days that followed it circled endlessly: the long harrowing drive that brought Justin to Dunwich in the mountains of northern

Massachusetts, that first conversation they'd had in the town's one restaurant, and the way that Owen's calm acceptance of his impossible story had given him the first flicker of hope he'd felt since the Martense family curse tightened its grip on him. Then, beyond all expectation, Owen had gone with him to Chorazin, flung himself into the mystery that surrounded Justin's family and its terrible heritage, and brought them both through it alive and sane. There was a road—

Justin sank into a chair at the kitchen table.

—and at the end of it, uniformed men with assault guns, a horror from the deeps of space, a goddess trapped under a silent hill, a stone door as old as time—

He let his face sink into his hands.

—and Owen's hand reaching out to grasp his, hauling him up out of water and mud onto firm ground, when every other solidity had gone spinning away into the chaos of a flamelit night.

"I owe him my life," he whispered, eyes still shut. "I told him that in Chorazin."

"Justin?" Rose's voice broke into the spinning thoughts. He glanced up as she put a hand on his shoulder. "There's something really wrong, isn't there?"

"Yeah." He handed her the note from the witch, watched her eyes narrow, then widen.

"You think he needs your help," said Rose.

"That's what the letter was about." He drew in a breath. "I'm going to want to talk with you and Arthur a little later. This changes—a lot of things."

He had work to do, so did she, and so did Arthur, who'd taken over managing the daytime fieldwork now that Justin couldn't be out in sunlight. All in all, it was after dinner before the three of them could sit down in the parlor in privacy. Justin handed Arthur the letter and the witch's note, explained the conclusions he'd reached, and was about to say what he was planning to do about it all when Arthur said, "You're going after him, of course."

"I have to." With a little shrug: "I have no idea how long it might take, so our plans may be out the window."

Arthur raised an expressive eyebrow. "You're planning on doing this all by yourself?" When Justin, startled, didn't answer at once: "Justin, don't be a sap. Owen's my friend too, and I've got almost as much reason as you do to want to help him. What's more, I know something you don't." Justin gestured, and he went on: "Red Hook's a neighborhood on the west side of Brooklyn, right on the water across from Governor's Island. I had rooms not that far from there when I was taking classes at the Pratt Institute."

"I bet it's changed a little since then," Justin pointed out.

Arthur grinned. "While Rose and I were Emerson Slater's prize exhibits? No doubt." Then, serious again: "But there ought to be a place to tie up a boat not too far away. So we can sail the *Keziah Mason* there, and do whatever we have to do. Once we've got Owen, we can pop back up here, pick up Rose, and Bob's your uncle."

"Arthur Wheeler," Rose said then, "if you think I'm going to let the two of you run off by yourselves to New York City, think again."

Arthur turned to face her. "We've got to help Owen."

"Of course you do," she replied at once. "But you're going to take me with you." With a sudden bright smile: "After all, someone's got to keep you two hotheads out of trouble—and if it comes to it, I'm a better shot than either of you."

Justin and Arthur glanced at each other. "I'm good with it," said Justin.

Arthur glanced at them both, nodded. "I won't say I'm happy, but—" He shrugged. "How soon do you want to go?"

Justin considered that. "Tomorrow evening. If I drive all night we can get to the marina before the sun comes up. I can't imagine that Bill'll have any trouble keeping things running for a few days before Terry and Sylvie take charge."

"That's true enough." Arthur turned to Rose and asked, "Will that work?" When she nodded: "Let's do it."

* * *

Now that the family illness had made sunlight Justin's enemy, the small hours of the morning were his favorite time, when silence wrapped the world and he could walk in the open air without risking blisters or worse. He'd taken to doing chores in the dark hours, though that was a stopgap, no way to run a farm for more than a little while. The cattle and horses slept restlessly in their stalls when he went by, or blinked awake and gave him uneasy looks, though the barn cats came padding over as usual to wreathe about his ankles and beg for treats.

That night, though, he had other tasks facing him. He'd expected to have weeks more to pack what he meant to take aboard the *Keziah Mason*, and load the rest into boxes to be left in the attic until he figured out what he was going to do with his life and sent for them. Now he had less than twenty-four hours to take care of the same task, and that meant filling boxes as fast as he could. Fortunately he'd never been one to collect things he didn't need. He'd gotten all the boxes but one packed and labeled by the time the moon hung low in the western sky.

That last box was for his few keepsakes—things he'd gotten in his childhood and treasured ever since, gifts from people he wanted to remember, an assortment of photos in frames. Just over half of the latter were of his son Robin, a thin boy with hair more colorless than blond, a lean high-cheekboned face, pale intent eyes: by himself, most of them, in various corners of the farm, or playing the dulcimer he'd taken up two years before and adored; the others with Justin, with Arthur and Rose, or with Aunt Josephine, whose face and hands were covered with coarse white hair and who had the mismatched Martense eyes. Justin smiled and wished the boy was there to be hugged, but Robin was spending that summer with his mother, and probably wouldn't be back to the world humans knew until the leaves started to turn.

Robin's pictures got wrapped in scraps of old blankets and stowed safely. Other photos followed them: Justin's parents, both missing and presumed dead after a cat-5 hurricane veered without warning and hit the Florida town where they'd retired; Aunt Josephine, who'd mostly raised Justin, and who was two years in the ground after one too many heart attacks; an assortment of friends. The last of them made him stop for a moment, draw in an unsteady breath.

The photo was ordinary enough, four adults and three children standing more or less together on a sidewalk by the harbor of the little Massachusetts town of Kingsport. Justin was one of the adults, with Robin standing in front of him, and next to them stood Owen, broad-shouldered and sandy-haired, a wry smile on his face. Next to Owen was his wife Laura in her wheelchair—she had tentacles in place of legs, and three decades of walking and standing on boneless limbs had taken their toll—and next to her was their daughter Asenath, six years old then, who had her mother's curly brown hair and olive complexion, but four ordinary human limbs. Her sandy-haired younger brother Barnabas, three that year, stood close by his mother's chair, looking away from the camera.

Off past Asenath, finally, was a woman in her thirties with a mop of disorderly mouse-colored hair, and a thin pale face Justin knew better than he knew his own. That she stood as far as possible from Justin made his smile falter and then turn bleak.

Jenny. Justin repeated the name silently, feeling an overfamiliar sense of frustration. Jenny Chaudronnier. He'd fallen in love with her in Chorazin, and ever since—could it really have been eleven years?—he'd had to deal with the hard fact that she didn't return his feelings. It wasn't that she loved someone else; that would have been easier to face. It was that the whole world of emotions he felt for her was a foreign country to her. He'd scarcely encountered the word "asexual" before meeting her, though he'd become painfully familiar with it afterwards.

There had been difficult conversations between them. Once he'd said bitter things in anger, and though he'd regretted them the moment they left his lips and done his best to make amends, the gap separating him from Jenny widened thereafter into a chasm. It could never have turned out any other way, he told himself; she was the daughter of the toad god Tsathoggua by a human woman, a sorceress at home in a world he could never enter.

He'd fled from her into other relationships, one with a pleasant young woman from another Lefferts Corners family, one with an equally pleasant older woman from Chorazin. Those had unraveled after a year in one case, two years in the other, and he knew the reason perfectly well. He hadn't really wanted them, he'd wanted Jenny, and the difference finally became too great to bear. All in all, it had taken him nearly seven years to come to terms with the fact that things weren't going to change, and once that happened he looked back on the years he'd spent mooning after Jenny and hated the self he saw reflected there: a besotted young idiot too clueless to take no for an answer.

That spring, when he'd gotten the usual letter inviting him to spend the summer in Kingsport, he'd sent back a polite note and gone sailing with the Wheelers instead. That left a gaping Jenny-shaped hole in his life, but it felt as though he'd turned a running sore into a clean wound. It helped that he had friends, family, the comfortable landscape of Lefferts Corners, and a farm that had been in the family since 1783, to distract him from the memories of his folly.

And now—

Justin tried to dismiss the thought, put the photo all anyhow in the box, and made himself go on with the packing: clothes and other necessities for the trip down to Red Hook, now that the rest was done, stuffed into a pair of garish orange duffels. He finished before dawn, grabbed an hour of sleep, then dragged himself out of bed.

As an initiate in the Starry Wisdom church, if only of the first and lowest degree, he had a morning meditation to do, and the themes of the meditation changed according to the cycles of the secret calendar. That morning, and for weeks to come, the meditation focused on letting go of the habit of trying to force the world to make sense. He'd long since understood the point of it intellectually, and knew well enough that human thoughts had no more in common with the things they signified than a child's stick-figure drawing of a horse had in common with the surging, sweating reality of a horse at full gallop. To get from that knowledge to the point that he could let the world make as much or as little sense as it wanted, that was a harder thing, and most of two months trying to make that happen had gotten Justin no results he could sense.

Still, he trudged his way through the meditation. Once it was done, he took care of the last few details before the trip: a fast note to Terry and Sylvie letting them know that he'd been called away by an emergency, and they'd need to take over the running of the farm sooner than anyone had expected; a note asking Susan Typer to send another brief message to Laura Merrill; and a letter to Laura following up the note, to be sent by way of the Starry Wisdom Church's slow but secret network, telling her what he meant to do, and asking her to find a home for Robin if something happened to him.

In the letter to Laura went another letter in a smaller envelope, labeled *To Robin, in the event of my death*, in which he poured out his feelings for his son and tried to offer what consolation he could. It wasn't the first time he'd written such a letter. Each time he'd done it he'd felt cold and sick, imagining Robin having to read the thing. This time was no different, and he was glad when he'd finished it and could turn his mind elsewhere.

Those went out right after breakfast with Bill Hasbrouck, the oldest of the farmhands, who'd known Justin since second grade and who'd handled errands in town since the porphyria showed up. A check made out to cash went with Bill, too, to go to the bank and get funds for the trip—there had been another currency reform the year before, the third in five years, and for the moment the new dollars seemed to be holding onto their value. Then, once Justin was sure everything was ready, he went back to bed and slept until dinner.

After the meal, it was time to load the car. Three rifles went into the bottom of the trunk—Arthur's long brown .30-'06, Justin's .30-'30, and Rose's precise little lever-action .243, with the scope she never needed to use. Duffels went atop them, and a cooler full of food and an assortment of other necessities atop those. The three of them worked together with an efficiency born of long practice. An hour, maybe, saw the car loaded with everything they'd need, and then Justin said his goodbyes to the farmhands and headed for the garage. Rose and Arthur were standing by the passenger side of the little blue compact; beyond them, evening's fading light trickled in through the open garage door. Justin faced them and said, "You're sure."

Neither of them said a word. Rose smiled, and Arthur motioned with his head toward the driver's seat. Looking at them, Justin remembered the way he'd seen them first: gray stone statues in a small-time tourist trap a dozen miles from Lefferts Corners, where they'd been on display for nearly a century. Though he'd been there to see them restored to life, and gotten to know them as friends and housemates thereafter, now and then he thought that they'd kept something of the unyielding nature of the stone they'd been, and this was one of those times.

He grinned and got in. Arthur climbed in next to him; Rose settled in back, extracted a half-finished sock from her knitting bag and busied herself with it. The engine whined at Justin and then growled to reluctant life.

Long blue shadows lay over the Catskills as he pulled out onto Maple Hill Road, turned left and eased the gas pedal down. He didn't let himself look back at the farm, and spared only a brief glance off to the right a mile further on, where the first dim lights of what was left of the town of Lefferts Corners glimmered in the middle distance. A memory haunted him: a few words he'd exchanged with Owen on the way to Lefferts Corners all those years ago. "If I could," he'd said, "I'd settle down in Lefferts Corners and never go anywhere else again." He'd meant it at the time, too, and got what he'd wanted, only to spend eleven years figuring out that it wasn't what he'd wanted after all.

Ahead, Maple Hill Road sank into shadow. Justin clicked on the headlamps and drove on into the gathering night.

CHAPTER 2

THE WITCH OF ARKHAM

The eastern sky was turning gray with dawn when they came in sight of the little town south of Kingston where the *Keziah Mason* was moored. In the middle distance, the Hudson swept southward, a moving darkness edged with silver. Nearer, the pale glimmer of streetlights reminded them that they'd reached one of the places where the twenty-first century everyone expected hadn't quite finished fading away. Justin woke his two passengers, who had been asleep for many miles, then dodged another round of potholes in the road and headed for the marina.

The marina gate was locked when they got there, but a gangly young man in a tee shirt and jeans came out from the office to let them in and wished them a sleepy good morning. Once the car was safely in the parking lot behind fences topped with barbed wire, and they'd made sure the *Keziah Mason* was fit to sail and hauled their gear aboard, Rose busied herself getting everything stowed belowdecks and Arthur went to work filling the tank for the onboard diesel with oil that smelled of french fries. Justin, who had the only legal identification among them—even in Lefferts Corners, the state department of motor vehicles wasn't quite ready to hand out ID cards to a couple who'd been born in the 1890s and spent most of a century turned to stone—walked through the gray morning to the little public library six blocks back from the waterfront.

That was a gamble, but he'd remembered correctly that the library opened early that day; hours were shifting everywhere now that electricity was expensive and daylight was cheap. The rundown brick building had its doors open, and the three tired computers on a table up against one wall still had balky but effective access to what was left of the internet. Lacking a library card, he had to sweet-talk the librarian into giving him fifteen minutes of computer time, but before that interval was up he'd written down half a dozen phone numbers on a slip of paper, thanked her, and headed back down the hill toward the Hudson.

The marina had a land line that renters could use—that was becoming common again now that cell service had gotten so bad—and he dialed the best prospect first. "Yeah," said the voice on the other end in a thick Brooklyn accent once Justin explained his business. "We got plenty of empty slips these days. How long's your boat?" Justin told him. "No problem at all. Lemme get you on the schedule." They settled the details, and then Justin went back out onto the dock with the welcome news that they'd be moored at the Gerritsen Street Marina on the shores of the Red Hook neighborhood itself.

Breakfast was cooking by the time he got to the *Keziah Mason*, and he settled into one of the bench seats in the dining nook belowdecks as bacon, eggs, and pancakes hit the table. Once their plates were empty, Arthur sat back with a pleased sigh and said, "Ready to go?"

Rose simply smiled, and Justin said, "No time like right now."

He and Arthur went topside into the cool air. Above, clouds burnt red with morning, but the sun hadn't risen over the mountains. The marina around them was dead silent. It had few boats these days, and the swelling daylight made the buildings of the little town look even more ramshackle than they'd been a year before, but then Justin had spent years watching the slow unraveling of the world he'd known in childhood, and expected nothing else.

He went to the wheel beside the hatch, started the diesel engine belowdecks. As Arthur stepped onto the dock and started loosing ropes, the engine whined, roared, and settled into a steady purr. Justin grinned, glanced forward to judge the angle he'd need to slip past the cabin cruiser moored ahead.

The *Keziah Mason* was a little over thirty feet long, a sturdy deepwater sailboat with berths for four, its hull broad in the middle and tapering from there to a long lean bow and a rounded stern. Mahogany decking long since gone silver with salt air and sunlight gleamed in the morning, and the cabin trunk, the long low porthole-dotted shape that ran forward from the cockpit and covered the main cabin belowdecks, would need a new coat of white paint soon. Still, Justin decided, she looked ready for the voyage they'd planned, and more than ready for a run down the Hudson to a Brooklyn marina.

Rose came up through the companionway and perched on one of the seat locker lids as Arthur climbed back aboard. A little deft work with the engine, the wheel, and one remaining rope, and the sailboat slid gracefully forward past the cabin cruiser, setting the dark water swelling. Justin turned to port, the marina slid behind, and the great green sweep of the Hudson River spread before them, reaching south and north to the edge of sight.

Little traffic moved yet on the water: a tug churning upstream with barges in tow, a makeshift ferry chugging from shore to shore now that the nearest bridge wasn't safe to cross any more. A brisk breeze came from west-northwest, rippling the water as it passed. As soon as the current had the sailboat in its grip, Justin shut off the engine. Rose took the wheel and Justin and Arthur went to work raising the sails, twin white triangles against the harsh blue of the sky.

Wind filled the sails and the boat began picking up speed. Arthur looked forward and aft, made sure that everything was as it should be, then grinned and ducked belowdecks. He was back a few minutes later with three glasses and an open bottle. Golden liquid splashed into the glasses. Some quirk of the changing climate had given Lefferts Corners bumper crops of dandelions the past three years, and Rose had roasted the roots for medicine, picked greens for salads, and gathered blossoms to brew the best dandelion wine in town.

"To Keziah Mason," Arthur said then, raising his glass. "Her namesake may not go as far as she did or as fast, but who's counting?"

Justin laughed, and glasses clinked together. He sipped the wine, caught himself before downing the glass and reaching for more. No you don't, he reminded himself: too much alcohol can bring on an attack. It annoyed him that he had to be careful about such things now, but he'd known since boyhood that the time would come sooner or later if he lived that long.

He compromised by drinking the glass slowly, savoring it, and promising himself more later on. Arthur finished his glass, motioned with the bottle to the others, and when they both shook their heads poured himself another glass.

"Hey," said Justin. "Save some for Owen."

That got him a broad grin. "Rose packed a bottle just for him. With any luck we'll be opening it in a day or two."

"That's the spirit," said Rose, her eyes on the river ahead.

The morning brightened and the *Keziah Mason* sped along. Then the rising sun and a dip in the mountains to the east conspired to send sunlight streaming onto the river. Justin grimaced, gathered up the glasses, and headed for the companionway and the shade of the cabin.

* * *

After driving all night he was more than ready for sleep, enough so that he skipped his morning meditation. The berth he always took, a little cubbyhole of a space aft of the dining area, was ready—Rose, true to form, had made it up neatly with sheets and one of her patchwork quilts. An oval of sunlight splashed in through the one porthole the space boasted, but Justin pulled the little curtain across it, settled atop the covers and was sound asleep in moments.

He woke to the slow swaying movement of a sailboat under way, glanced bleary-eyed at the curtain over the porthole. A glance out through it once he'd sat up confirmed his guess: from the *Keziah Mason*'s shadow on the water, it was well past noon. He didn't have to ask where to look for lunch, and two robust chicken salad sandwiches on homebaked bread and a bottle of the previous autumn's cider made their appearance from the refrigerator.

Once those had been polished off, he sat back, pulled open the curtain covering the porthole near him, and watched the Hudson's eastern bank slide past, dotted with buildings that were even more rundown and desolate than they'd been the last time he'd come that way, signs of the closing age. Everyone he knew who'd learned something of the Great Old Ones, and something of their enemies, had wondered for years whether the long slow unraveling of the economy was just the ordinary workings of history, the sort of thing that had happened to a hundred civilizations before, or whether someone else had taken a hand in the process—or a tentacle. No one knew. Even Jenny, when the subject had come up one evening the last summer he'd spent in Kingsport, had admitted her ignorance.

The day brought Justin no new answers. Watching the riverbank slip by, he thought he recognized some of the scenery, and it meant that New York City was still a couple more hours further south. Considering that, he thought of something he had ample time to do, something that might just give him some of the guidance he needed.

Once he'd washed the plate, the bottle, and his hands, he went back to his berth, opened one of the lockers beneath the bed, and got out a little packet in a wrapper made of quilted black silk, tied shut with a narrow ribbon. The wrapper was a gift from Tcho-Tcho friends in Buffalo, and what was inside was a gift, too, though it came from far stranger hands.

He went back to the dining nook and put the packet on the table. A quick motion untied the ribbon, unfolded the quilted cloth. Inside was a length of tattered silk, and inside that was a deck of cards with faded images on them. They'd been cheaply printed more than a century ago, or so Jenny told him once, but they'd spent most of that time being shuffled and dealt at intervals by the Great Old One Shub-Ne'hurrath, the Black Goat of the Woods with a Thousand Young, in one of her many temporary human forms.

Sallie Eagle, as the Black Goat had called herself then, had dealt out one three-card spread after another and interpreted them all without a moment's pause. Justin had met witches since then who could do the same thing, but that was for the talented, not for him. Sometimes, when he dealt just three cards, he could catch their meaning, but sometimes they were utterly opaque to him and sometimes he misunderstood them completely. He muttered a prayer for help, dealt out three cards face down, and turned them over one at a time.

The first card had a crude image of some kind of animal with a mane and big curving fangs. The Lion meant bad news, a sudden shock, the unexpected and unwelcome. He nodded slowly, hoping the other cards would be as clear.

The second card showed a ship under full sail underneath a crescent moon. The Ship meant changes, new directions, a voyage, and as the middle card of the reading it located all these things in the present.

The third card showed a crossroads with a sign standing by it pointing in four directions. One of the roads curved away toward a rising sun. The Crossroads spoke of a choice, and on the right side it hadn't yet arrived and might have to be looked for. One road led toward better things, but the others weren't so promising. He frowned, wondered why the cards were telling him only about things he already knew: the unexpected news about Owen, the voyage down the Hudson, the uncertainties that waited for him once they reached Red Hook.

Then, a sudden shift, and he knew what the cards were trying to say to him. The Lion meant that something really had gone wrong for Owen in Red Hook, something no one had expected. The Ship meant that the choice he'd made, and the Wheelers had made with him, might well take him to places he had no way to anticipate. The Crossroads said that what he was about to do could actually have some effect on the situation.

He nodded slowly. Other questions waited, but he made himself shuffle the cards again, wrap them in the bit of silk the Black Goat had used to cover them and then in the Tcho-Tcho wrapper, and tie the ribbon shut. Once the cards were safely stowed in the locker, he went back to the bench seat and settled onto it, gazing out the porthole again at the Hudson's eastern shoreline as another long-abandoned factory slid past.

The slow pace of the river got him thinking of Arthur's joke. Keziah Mason, the sailboat's namesake, had been the most famous witch of Arkham's colonial days, and stories about her doings still found listeners in the old Massachusetts town's gambrel-roofed houses and narrow streets. They said that the old witch had a familiar who looked like a rat with a human face; they said that she traveled through space, and maybe through time as well; they said—and here the court records of Essex County offered unnerving corroboration—that she'd drawn strange curves and angles on the walls of her cell in the Salem jail in some sticky red fluid and vanished without a trace, leaving the jailer stark staring mad.

These days, to be sure, such stories evoked more fondness than fear, now that Arkham had become home to so many of the worshippers of the Great Old Ones. Families from fallen Innsmouth lived there; young people from Dunwich and Chorazin came there looking for opportunities those little mountain villages didn't provide; Tcho-Tchos had moved there from the big refugee community in Buffalo, and of course there were also students attending what little was left of Miskatonic University, which resided now in the old brick campus downtown and taught more classes on strange lore than on conventional academic subjects.

No, you couldn't get many shudders out of an Arkham audience any more with stories of Keziah Mason, not when witches practiced their craft openly there, and the old witch's famous familiar, Brown Jenkin, had more than a score of descendants in Arkham alone. Asenath Merrill had one, a bright-eyed little creature she'd named Rachel, but then she was training to be a witch herself. She was crazy about Keziah Mason—half the stories about the witch that Justin knew, he'd heard from Asenath—and it had been the girl's idea to name the sailboat after her, though Arthur had laughed his great golden laugh and adopted the idea with his usual enthusiasm.

That memory led in directions Justin didn't want to go. He chased it from his mind, and tried to turn his attention to the eastern bank of the river, with limited success.

* * *

The companionway hatch opened then, surprising Justin out of a shallow doze. "We're almost there," Rose called down. "Arthur says you should come topside if you can."

"Sure thing." Justin went to his berth, took from the cupboards beneath it a jacket and a broad-brimmed hat: black, both of them, to blot out as much sunlight as possible. Black cotton gloves from the jacket pockets went onto his hands.

So armored, he hauled himself up the companionway steps into the cockpit.

Rose hadn't exaggerated. To starboard, the waterfront towns of the Jersey shore huddled against the river's edge, dotted here and there with tall buildings that had seen many better days. Boats slid up and down the Hudson, and the sun blazed down from high overhead, so that it was easy for Justin to keep his hat angled to shield himself from its rays. It was to port, though, that the real spectacle unfolded.

To port, Manhattan rose up from the Hudson's edge, mile after mile of crowded buildings, with one great cluster of sky-scrapers rising from midtown, another equally massive group further south, and buildings twenty and thirty stories tall scattered everywhere, all but inconspicuous among so many giants. Though he knew only a little about architecture, Justin caught something of the jumble of historical eras spread out before him: brick buildings from the nineteenth century by turns sober and gaudy, the Art Deco fussiness of the Empire State Building and its peers, the stark brutality of Bauhaus glass and steel, the jumbled confusion of styles that followed, and then something like silence. It had been years, Justin recalled read-ing somewhere, since a new building of any size had gone up in New York, or anywhere else.

He stood staring at Manhattan for a good long while. He'd seen New York City many times before, passing through or passing by, and knew its feverish sleepless energy. For that matter, the view from the Hudson was familiar enough, now that the roads were so bad that the water route made more sense, the way it had done in years gone by. Still, something seemed different. It took Justin some minutes to notice how few of Manhattan's skyscrapers had more than a scattering of lights in them if they had any at all, how few cars or buses moved on the streets he could see. The city felt tired and old, pushed to the edge of exhaustion by too many centuries of fre-netic life. In it, or maybe through it, he could sense the closing of the age that had sent those towers soaring above what had once been a forested island close to the ocean.

The wind freshened and changed its angle as the presence of the Atlantic made itself felt. Justin took the wheel while Rose and Arthur changed the set of the sails. The massive buildings of downtown Manhattan slid by, the Brooklyn Bridge soared to port in the middle distance, and the Statue of Liberty stood pale and elegant further still to starboard. Then Governors Island, low and ringed with trees, loomed up ahead. A glance at the chart and another at the compass helped Justin keep the proper course; the *Keziah Mason* rounded the western end of Governors Island and, with another adjustment of the sails, headed in toward the Brooklyn shore.

"There we go," said Arthur then, pointing a little south of their course.

Justin had already spotted it: the low unmistakable profile of a small marina, dotted with a handful of shapes that had to be boats, wedged between two decrepit piers. The wind stayed brisk, and so it wasn't until the marina was close by and room for maneuvering between buoys had gotten scarce that the sails came down, the diesel belowdecks grumbled to life, and the *Keziah Mason* slid gracefully into port.

Tying up temporarily at the outermost dock was a familiar drill, and once it was done Arthur started up the main dock to the marina office, little more than a shack with vinyl siding perched on the shore, just inside the gate in the chain link fence topped with razor wire that shut the marina away from the street. He didn't get far, for the shack's occupant had already noticed them and was on his way down the dock to meet them, clipboard in hand: a stout bullet-headed man in cargo pants and a ragged t-shirt with a picture of Godzilla on it and, below that, the caption **I 8 N Y**. "Youse the *Keezar Mason* outta Kingston?" he asked.

"That's us," said Arthur.

"Sweet. Lemme get you signed in here." A pen scratched over cheap paper, money changed hands, and then the man handed over a ring with keys on it. "Okay. You wanna tie up at twenty-six, right by the end of the second pier." He gestured vaguely northward. "Gate's open twenty-four hours but you gotta have the key to get in. Office hours are eight to six daily, and there's a phone in the office you can use if you need to—lots of folks have trouble with their cell phones here any more, don't ask me why. You want electricity, lemme know; it's not cheap, not these days, but I can get it for you. Fuel, that's not cheap either, but we got biodiesel and stove fuel. Here's the rules." He handed over a blurred photocopy on blue paper. "Most of the other boats got people living aboard 'em, so don't make any more noise than you gotta. I'm Pete Mazurewicz, by the way."

"Pleased to meet you," said Arthur, and introduced himself and the others. Rose, once hands had been shaken, asked: "Can you tell me where I can find the nearest grocery?"

"Sure thing. The street there, it's Gerritsen Street. Go three blocks and you get to the Mazour Grocery. Two more blocks and you're on Van Brunt—that's the main drag, and you still got a bunch of stores there. Watch the tides, though. If we get a wind outta the south and a high tide, you're gonna have water all over the streets."

Rose thanked him. He made sure they had no more questions, and headed back toward the office. Once he was gone, the three of them looked at each other, and Arthur said, "Well, let's get the old lady where she should be."

It took some finicky work with the diesel engine to handle the incoming surge of the tide and slide the *Keziah Mason* past a tired-looking ketch as she rounded the pier. Still, they got her tied up properly, and then went belowdecks and gathered around the table for a council of war.

"So what's the plan?" Arthur propped his elbows on the table.

"Good question," said Justin. "Owen's got to know that I'd get here as soon as I could, and I'd be willing to bet he knows I might not come alone. So he's going to be looking for me, and maybe for other people he knows, if he possibly can. The question is where he's hiding."

"And from what," said Arthur.

"I've got my suspicions," Justin replied.

"And if those people are involved," Arthur went on, "there are things we don't dare risk. I'd thought about suggesting that we get in touch with the Starry Wisdom Church here in town, but the other side would have to be idiots not to expect that, and watch for it."

Justin nodded uneasily. "And Laura said they've got no idea where he is anyway," he said. Arthur met his gaze, said nothing.

"It seems to me," said Rose after a moment's silence, "that the first thing to do is for Arthur and I to walk around the neighborhood a little, pick up some groceries, maybe visit some of the other stores on—what did he call the street, Arthur?"

"Van Brunt."

"Thank you. If you're right, Justin, and Owen or someone who's helping him is watching for us, that's a likely place to do it."

"True," said Justin. "I'm trying to figure out if I can risk going with you."

"Probably not," she told him. "It won't do Owen a lot of good if you end up flat on your back with another attack of porphyria."

He nodded, conceding the point. She slid off the bench seat, pulled open a cupboard and got out a pair of sturdy canvas shopping bags she'd made, then another. "Wish us luck."

"All the luck in the world," said Justin.

She said something cheery and headed topside. Arthur got up and glanced down at Justin. "I know," he said. "In your place I don't know if I could stand it."

"You didn't grow up with porphyria in the family." Justin motioned with his head toward the companionway. "See you soon." Arthur slapped his shoulder, and left the cabin.

* * *

They were gone for hours: probably a good idea, Justin admitted, but it made him feel bored and useless. He glanced at the thickening hair on the backs of his hands, and remembered Aunt Josephine, who'd spent more than half her life staying out of the sun, and who'd been covered pretty much head to foot with coarse white hair by the time of Justin's first memories: they'd called her Aunt Beast, after a character in a children's book, and she'd always laughed at the title. With a sudden grin, he recalled summer evenings when he and the other children who gathered at her house played in an inflatable pool in her backyard, and she'd put on a bikini to spare her clothes a good soaking and sat outside with them, looking for all the world like a sasquatch at a beach party. Would he look much the same in a decade or two? It seemed likely enough, if he lived that long.

He went to his berth, tried to nap, dozed off and on for two hours or so before the thin mattress got too uncomfortable to bear any longer, then got up and tried another card reading, this time to figure out where Owen was. The cards that turned up were the Book, the Eye, and the Clouds. The Book meant a secret; the Eye could mean that he was watching someone or something, or that someone or something was watching him; the Clouds in the right hand position, with the dark side toward the other cards, meant obscurity and uncertainty—but did that mean that he wouldn't see what he was looking for, or that someone else wouldn't see him? He spent something like half an hour trying to extract meaning from the cards, and succeeded instead in losing himself in deeper and deeper uncertainties. Finally he put the cards away and sat staring out the porthole at the waters of the harbor and the derelict pier close by, trying to think of some better way to find Owen, and failing utterly.

The sun slid west and finally neared the ragged skyline of the Jersey shore, where low clouds had begun to gather. As the last of the sunlight guttered, Justin breathed a sigh of relief and climbed out through the companionway hatch. Though there was nowhere he could go and nothing he could do that mattered, it felt good to get out under the sky again.

He perched on the cabin trunk and looked around. If the other boats in the marina had people living aboard them, they showed no sign of it. The tired-looking ketch not far from the *Keziah Mason*, the two battered cabin cruisers further off, the dozen other assorted sailboats and motorboats tied up at intervals to the docks, and what looked like a jerry-built houseboat on a catamaran hull on the far side of the marina close to shore: all of them looked as though they'd been abandoned for years. He shook his head, turned toward the Upper Bay.

The moment he did so, it felt as though someone was watching him. He dismissed the feeling as just nerves, but it didn't go away, and after a moment, as casually as he could, he glanced back over his shoulder.

Someone was walking away from the gate, as though he'd been looking through the chainlink fence a moment earlier. Justin couldn't see the figure with any precision as it strode away into the gathering evening, getting little more than a sense of dark clothing and a broad-brimmed hat, but something about the rhythm of the long swinging stride stirred a memory he couldn't track down.

The figure vanished into dimness, and Justin turned back to look at the harbor. It seemed like only a few moments later that he heard familiar voices and the rattle of the gate opening, and glanced back to see Rose and Arthur starting down the long dock with full grocery bags.

"We didn't find Owen," Arthur said as he handed Justin his two bags. "But we must have walked through half of Red Hook, and if he's watching he probably saw us." He climbed aboard, took Rose's bags and then helped her onto the *Keziah Mason*. She looked dazed, and shook herself when she got aboard.

"Are you okay?" Justin asked her.

"Why, of course." Forcing a smile: "I'm just not used to being someplace quite so crowded. I'm sure I'll get used to it, but ..." She let the sentence trail off.

They climbed down into the cabin, and Rose busied herself getting the groceries put away where she wanted them. "Did you see somebody walking up the street from the marina just now?" Justin asked them. "Kind of tall, with the same sort of hat I've got?"

Arthur and Rose both gave him blank looks. "No," Rose said. "Gerritsen Street was empty from the time we turned off Van Brunt."

That was when the memory finally surfaced, and Justin knew he hadn't seen that long swinging stride. He'd heard it, sounding like drumbeats on the floor of the Starry Wisdom church in Chorazin, announcing the arrival of a power far more than human.

Shaken by the recollection, Justin listened to a rambling account of Rose's and Arthur's peregrinations, lent a hand to the labors that set dinner in motion. He'd been mistaken, he decided. Maybe it was a trick of the evening light, maybe it was someone who'd ducked into one of the buildings just before Rose and Arthur started down Gerritsen Street; he wasn't sure, but almost anything seemed more likely than the alternative—

Which was that Nyarlathotep, the soul and mighty messenger of the Great Old Ones, had come to Brooklyn and interested himself in the fate of Owen Merrill.

CHAPTER 3

THE FACE IN THE WATER

Justin woke the next morning as the first faint light of dawn came seeping in through the porthole by his berth. Half an hour or so trying to get back to sleep had no effect worth noticing, and finally he got up, washed and dressed, fumbled through a Starry Wisdom meditation that felt even more pointless than usual, and boiled water for coffee on the galley stove. The low faint rhythm of Rose's snoring came from the door forward, unmingled with any other sound, and once the coffee was made Justin filled a mug with it, poured the rest into a thermos, and climbed out through the companionway hatch to the cockpit.

A thick fog had come flowing in during the night, and the light of the dawning day came filtered through pallid vagueness. As he sat there in the cockpit, watching the fog drift slowly past, it was hard for Justin to convince himself that New York City surrounded him. The water of the harbor rose and fell in slow swells, dark and smooth as glass; the fog eddied and swirled so close that the bow of the *Keziah Mason* was a blur from where he sat and the nearest boats were little more than guesses. Great Cthulhu himself in all his might could have gone wading through the Upper Bay, Justin thought, without anyone being the wiser. He sipped his coffee, watched the fog form beads of moisture on the railing, wondered how soon Rose and Arthur would wake and what they should do next.

A faint plashing noise aft of the boat caught his attention, and he turned, blinked, stared. A human head framed with wet brown hair rose out of the water and gazed up at him. From the shape of the face, through the brown of the eyes, to the olive skin with the green undertones that told of Deep One ancestry, it looked for all the world like a younger version of Laura Merrill.

He stared at the head in total silence for a time, his mouth open, then managed to say aloud, "You've got to be a hallucination."

The head laughed, and it was almost Laura's laugh, too. "I feel like one sometimes," it said. "But not this morning. You're Justin Martense, aren't you?"

"Yeah," he said, nonplussed. "How'd you know?"

"Laura's told me a lot about you." Then, taking mercy on his bafflement: "You have no clue who I am, do you? I'm Belinda Marsh, Laura's sister."

"Okay," said Justin, remembering some of Owen's comments about his in-laws. "Are you here looking for Owen?"

A quick nod sent her hair swirling in the dark water. "I couldn't bear sitting around doing nothing when he's probably in trouble."

"I get that," said Justin. "God, I get that."

"I know. Laura got your message." A half-embarrassed shrug brought shoulders briefly to the water's surface. "That was why I finally decided to swim down here from Kingsport. There's a lot I can't do, since I can't let myself be seen by most humans, but I thought that if there was someone else looking I might be able to help."

"You're on," he said. "We need all the help we can get."

Belinda's face lit up. "Thank you, Justin." Then: "You've got Rose and Arthur Wheeler here with you, don't you?"

A motion of his head indicated the cabin door behind him. "They're asleep below."

"Well, don't wake them for me." She surfaced a little further, so that head and neck and shoulders rose out of the dark water. Justin could make out a golden torc around her neck, and dim moving shapes further down: tentacles, he guessed, recalling something Owen had said. "I need to find a place to stay underwater, and get everything settled there. I'll come up here tonight." When he agreed: "Okay, good. See you this evening."

"I'll look forward to it," Justin said.

That got him a sudden bright smile, and then she plunged back down into the water. Tentacles showed briefly below the surface, water surged and roiled, but after a few moments the slow swells resumed and the fog flowed past as before.

Justin watched the rippling water where she'd been, shook his head, and sipped more of his coffee. Fragments of conversations he'd had with Owen tumbled through his mind. Laura and Belinda, they were from the little town of Innsmouth on Massachusetts' north shore, abandoned now to the rising seas after one too many assaults from the enemies of the Great Old Ones. Like nearly everyone else from Innsmouth, they had Deep Ones as well as humans in their ancestry—family on both sides of the shoreline, Laura liked to say. Their father had mated with the Black Goat of the Woods, though, and so Laura and Belinda had been born with tentacles: Laura had just two in place of her legs, and how many had Owen said Belinda had? Justin couldn't remember. For those who worshiped the old gods of Earth, it was nothing out of the ordinary, just one of the things that happened from time to time.

He emptied his mug, went below for a refill. Rose's quiet snoring was still the only sound in the cabin, but a sheet of paper was sitting on the dining table. Justin gave it a startled look; he was sure the table had been clear when he'd made the coffee a quarter hour before. He went over to the table, picked up the sheet, and found a few lines on it that looked for all the world as though they'd been made with an old-fashioned mechanical typewriter. They read:

```
Justin -
Red Hook Library Branch 3pm today
lecture on Brooklyn history & folklore
you should be there
```

Justin read this twice with a puzzled frown, then set the sheet of paper back on the table. It didn't bother him that there was no natural way the message could have gotten there; that simply meant that it had gotten there in some unnatural way. The question that mattered was whether to follow its advice. It might be a message from Owen, that was clear enough, but it might also be something far less welcome.

After a moment, he went back to his berth and pulled out the black silk packet. There were plenty of ways to use the cards, some simpler than others, but the simplest of all was one he'd learned from a hundred-year-old initiate in Dunwich, and that might give him the clue he needed. He took the cards back to the table, struggled to clear his mind as he unwrapped them, then shuffled once, cut the deck, and drew one card.

He turned it over to find the crudely drawn image of a rider on a horse, and grinned. The Rider meant good news, and also a message from far off; it could also mean the prompt arrival of someone looked for. The answer seemed clear enough, and he put the cards away.

* * *

The Red Hook branch of the Brooklyn Public Library turned out to be a low brick and concrete building on Wolcott Street. It had two stacks of sandbags near the front door, waiting for the next round of tidal flooding, but other than that it seemed almost unaffected by the decade and a half of wrenching changes just past. As Justin ducked through the front door out of the sunlight, he found people browsing in the stacks and plenty of books on the shelves.

It had been a risk for him to go out in daylight, but he'd discussed the note with Rose and Arthur and gotten them to agree; the thought of spending another day cooped up in the cabin of the *Keziah Mason* was more than he could bear. Hat, jacket, and gloves kept most of the sun's rays off him, and he'd stayed in what shade he could find. He'd expected to be surrounded all the way there by bustling crowds, but that hadn't happened.

There had been a few crowded blocks on Van Brunt Street, but nothing like what he recalled from visits to other parts of New York City in past years, and far more of the blocks were half-empty. Cars were scarce, too, and most of them had little cardboard signs in the front windscreens with a dollar sign on them: unlicensed taxis, he guessed. Half a dozen blank walls had garish flyers encouraging the locals to apply for jobs out west; Justin considered those, wondered what that was about, and kept walking.

On the way to Van Brunt, he'd paced down lonely blocks on Gerritsen Street past crumbling brick buildings with windows that gaped empty to the wind, and vacant lots overgrown with weeds where scurrying shapes he couldn't quite make out watched him pass. All in all, the walk left him wondering whether the unraveling he'd watched in Lefferts Corners had gotten its grip on Brooklyn as well, or whether something else was involved.

The clock on the wall told him he'd gotten to the library half an hour early, so he shed hat and gloves, picked up the latest issue of the New York *Times* from the periodicals rack, settled in a chair with a clear view of the door to the meeting room, and pretended to read while watching the people come and go. He half expected Owen to come strolling in through the library doors at any moment, but that didn't happen, nor did anyone who might be carrying a message from Owen approach him.

When the clock showed five minutes to three, Justin put the magazine away and went into the meeting room. The chairs there had gaudily colored plastic seats and backs, and if the light fixtures overhead had only half as many fluorescent tubes as places for them, Justin didn't mind. He settled onto a bright orange chair, got out a pen and a notepad he'd bought as protective cover on the way there, and waited with an eye on the door for Owen's appearance.

Owen didn't appear. Instead, the room filled up with people of every age and color, and then a plump and matronly librarian accompanied a lean old woman in a rumpled brown skirt and jacket to the podium at the front. "Hi, everybody," the librarian said, and chattered her way through an introduction as the old woman turned toward the audience, peered at them through gold-rimmed glasses. "Mrs. Ruth Frankweiler," the librarian said finally, and Justin applauded with the rest.

"Thank you," said the old woman, and smiled. "You know, I bet that each of you walked at least a short distance on the way here, the way I did. I wonder how many of you wondered as you walked what this corner of Long Island looked like before this city of ours rose here, when the Leni Lenape had their villages all over what we now call Brooklyn and spent their summers digging for oysters and clams on the beaches of Coney Island. Try to imagine it."

Justin tried. He didn't get far at first, but Mrs. Frankweiler helped, describing Brooklyn as it had been back when the Leni Lenape called it "the sandy place," when dense oak forests swept southeast from Red Hook up Park Slope and then down again to the Flatbush lowlands beyond, when wolves howled on moonlit nights and ospreys circled over the beaches of the Upper Harbor. She described Henry Hudson's voyage, and then the early days of the Dutch colony, when scattered farm towns dotted the landscape: Breukelen, the Broken

Valley; t'Vlache Bos, the Wooded Plain; Boswijk, the Town in the Woods; 's Gravensande, the Count's Beach—names that time rounded down to Brooklyn, Flatbush, Boswick, and Gravesend.

"Gravesend, that was the strange one," said Mrs. Frankweiler then. "It wasn't settled by the Dutch, but by an English noblewoman, Lady Deborah Moody, and for exactly one hundred twenty years after it was founded, the people didn't permit a single church to be built there."

Instinctive caution kept Justin's reaction from showing in his face, but his pen darted across the notepad: *Gravesend, Lady Deborah Moody, no churches*.

"A very odd thing in those days, you must admit. Still, Lady Moody was quite as odd, and she ran with some even odder people. The pastor of the Reformed church in Flatbush wrote scandalized letters back to the Dutch West India Company talking about her theological improprieties. I went to Amsterdam some years back and read them. Quite colorful, really. He claimed that she worshiped strange gods, spent her time searching for underground treasure, and had dealings with Agatha Sleght, the famous witch of old Greenwich Village."

Justin blinked in surprise, for he knew plenty of Sleghts in Lefferts Corners, one Dutch family of the many that moved to the Catskills when the English took Nieuw Amsterdam from its founders. His pen darted across the notepad, writing: *Agatha Sleght*.

"But Lady Moody died in 1660, and after that Gravesend turned little by little into an ordinary farming and fishing town. Oh, others kept up the habit of digging for treasure; Brooklyn had many more hills than it has today, not all of them natural, and most of them were excavated by someone looking for treasure. There was supposed to be a golden pedestal with a base of onyx buried in a cavern somewhere under Brooklyn. Brought here before the Indians, the story went, from somewhere across the sea."

Just then two more men came into the room and found seats in the back row. Justin glanced back, hoping that one of them was Owen, but was disappointed again. The glance left him feeling uneasy; the newcomers wore nondescript clothes, but they looked and moved like soldiers, and something about them set Justin's teeth on edge.

"But those days didn't last once the English arrived," said Frankweiler, and went on at once to talk about the day that Nieuw Amsterdam changed to New York, as though witches and golden pedestals had never been mentioned at all. An assortment of harmless stories followed. Mrs. Frankweiler finally wound down, and everyone applauded. She asked for questions and got a flurry of aimless inquiries. When those ran out, the librarian came up, called for another round of applause, and escorted Mrs. Frankweiler back out into the main room of the library.

People began filing out. Justin waited as long as he could without being conspicuous, then got up and turned toward the door. The two men who'd come in late were gone by then, and Justin felt a surge of relief. That was when he realized why they'd set his teeth on edge: something about them reminded him all too precisely of the members of the Radiance negation team he'd faced on that terrible night at Chorazin.

He let himself move with the last of the audience out into the main room of the library, drifted over to the stacks, and looked at random books for a time, while keeping a sidelong eye on what was left of the crowd. Once the people who'd come for the lecture had left, Justin put on his best clueless-newcomer expression, and wandered over to the librarian's desk, where the same woman who'd introduced the speaker was now sitting.

"That was a great talk," he said. "I'm kind of new in town and I didn't know any of that."

The librarian dimpled. "Thank you. Mrs. Frankweiler's a wonderful speaker."

"Is she a local historian?" Justin asked.

"Well, not exactly. She lives in Connecticut, but you won't find anyone who knows as much about New York City's history. She's even written a book." Justin made the appropriate noises, and the librarian beamed and went on. "It's quite a story. There was a big scandal here in Red Hook in 1919 with police raids, tunnels going from the harbor to secret pools underground, wild rumors about black magic, that sort of thing—and one of her great-grandparents was involved in it somehow. So she researched it and got the book published, and we have it. Let me see—" Fingers set her keyboard rattling, and then she looked crestfallen. "Oh, it's checked out. I can put a hold on it for you if you've got your library card."

Justin deflected that, thanked the librarian, went to a free table and spent a little while noting down what he'd learned: *Ruth Frankweiler, 1919 scandal, tunnels from harbor to underground pool, police raid*, and more. Once that was done, he put on hat and gloves and headed out into the hot sultry afternoon. He'd wondered for a cold moment if the men he'd seen would be waiting outside, but they were nowhere in sight. Relieved, he set off along the cracked and tilting sidewalks toward the marina.

* * *

"Tunnels," said Justin, and sipped at his soda. Around him, the familiar cabin of the *Keziah Mason* curved protectively. Evening showed golden through the portholes, and the cool of the harbor seemed to radiate up from below. Pots and pans clattered in the galley; Rose, working there, whistled a mountain tune that had been old when Nieuw Amsterdam was founded. "Do you remember what the witch wrote?"

"Yes," Arthur said. "What's more, I remember the scandal your lecturer talked about."

Justin gave him a startled look. "Seriously?"

"It was all over the papers." Arthur leaned back against his side of the dining nook. "Let's see—1919. May, I think, because I'd just gotten back from Paris. I'd gone to visit a sculptor friend of mine, a fellow named Boris Yvain, for the first time since the war, and I was back here a couple of weeks or so when the story broke. The cops got the goods on a man-smuggling operation here in Red Hook, and there was a tunnel in from the harbor involved, I'm sure of it. So there were raids, but—" He shrugged. "Some buildings collapsed right in the middle of it all, and a lot of people died. Afterwards there was a big fuss, the police blocked the tunnel, and an odd bird named Malone wrote letters to every paper in the region insisting that the whole Red Hook neighborhood was full of black magic and devil worship."

"Malone," said Justin after a frozen moment. "Thomas F. Malone?"

"That could have been the name," Arthur replied. "Why?"

"Family history. If it's the same guy, he killed a relative of mine in 1921. Aunt Josephine used to say that the Malone I'm thinking of had been involved in some kind of trouble about immigrants and devil worship in New York City before he came out to Lefferts Corners."

"Might have been the same fellow, then. His letters were pretty lurid."

"The one I'm thinking of," said Justin, "died in a hospital for the criminally insane."

Rose finished her work in the galley, came aft. "There we go," she said. "If Laura's sister comes to visit tonight we've got dinner enough for all." She pulled down a folding seat, settled on it. "Any notion yet why the note said you should go to the talk?"

"Maybe." Justin leaned forward, propped his chin on his hands. "Laura said Owen was looking for something in the Red Hook area. Mrs. Frankweiler talked about buried treasure here in Brooklyn, and a town that's part of Brooklyn now where the people wouldn't have a church for more than a hundred years. Then there's this business about tunnels from the harbor going to an underground pool here in Red Hook, and people yelling about black magic and devil worship—and that usually means they've caught somebody worshiping the Great Old Ones. I think whoever put the note here wanted me to find out about that." With a sudden grin: "And now I know there are newspaper stories from May of 1919 that can tell me a lot more. So I'm thinking that a trip to the main branch of the Brooklyn Public Library might be in order."

"Maybe," said Arthur. "But I'm not happy about those two men you saw."

Justin nodded. "I know—but we knew coming down here that there'd be danger."

Arthur nodded, frowning, and then glanced at his wife. "Rose—"

"If you think you're going to talk me into leaving," Rose said to him, "think again."

He met her level gaze for a minute, and then sighed and said, "I'd be a lot happier if you were somewhere safe."

"Of course," she said. "But you aren't leaving until Owen's found, so neither am I." Then, with a bright smile: "What's more, I learned something really useful from the women who live on the other boats."

"I didn't know there was anyone on the other boats," Justin said in surprise.

"Oh, yes—there's all kinds of fees and regulations if you live aboard officially, so a lot of people do it without letting the city know. But I found out that there's a knitters' gathering not much more than a dozen blocks from here, tomorrow at four. If you really want to know what's going on in a town, you need to listen while the local knitters gossip."

Justin and Arthur looked at each other, nonplussed. "I don't think I'd ever have thought of that," Justin said after a moment.

"Of course not," said Rose. "Men usually don't." Then: "Speaking of which, the sun's down, and I'd be willing to bet Miss Marsh is waiting for someone to show himself topside before she comes out of the water." She took a bath towel from one of the lockers, set it on the table. "And she'll probably need this."

"Oh, probably," Justin agreed. He knew Rose and Arthur well enough to catch the unspoken message: they needed private time to talk. "And it'll be nice to get some fresh air now that it doesn't come with sunlight." He unfolded himself from the dining nook, picked up the towel, and went to the companionway stair.

* * *

Evening streamed over New York City as he clambered up into the cockpit and shut the companionway hatch behind him. Seagulls flew overhead, calling to each other in high mournful voices, and the deep intricate murmur of the city played a bass to their treble. A handful of lights flickered on in Manhattan's dark towers. All at once Justin found himself thinking of Mrs. Frankweiler's lecture earlier that day, and tried to imagine Manhattan Island as it had been when the only settlements there were a handful of Native American villages. Had it been dotted with vanished hills like Brooklyn, not all of them natural? The Brooklyn Public Library might tell him that, he guessed, or it might not. He sat on one of the seat locker lids, tried to guess what his next move should be.

He was deep in thought, trying to figure out which of the leads he'd gotten at the lecture was worth following up first, when a soft plashing sound broke his concentration. He got up from and looked over the *Keziah Mason*'s stern. As he'd expected, a familiar face framed in floating brown hair smiled up at him out of the water.

"Hi," said Belinda. "Is it safe for me to come aboard?"

Justin looked around, made sure that nobody was within sight. "Yeah."

"Thank you." Tentacles slid up out of the water, wrapped around the bars of the ladder. She pulled herself up out of the water in a single deft movement, slipped over the stern and settled on one of the seats, where she toweled off in a quick flurry of tentacular motion.

Tentacles she had in plenty. Two flowed out from each shoulder in place of arms, and eight more descended from what would have been hips in a human woman. Exactly how they merged with her torso was no mystery, since she wore nothing but the golden torc he'd seen earlier. That didn't startle Justin—none of the folk of Innsmouth, children of Dagon that they were, could be talked into wearing anything in the water—and he had his own reasons for being used to tentacles. When she extended one of her arm-tentacles, he took it in a gentle grip as though it was a hand. He wasn't surprised to find that, as Laura's did, it felt like ordinary human skin and flesh stretched into an unhuman shape.

"If you'd like to come belowdecks," Justin said then, "dinner's just about ready."

Her face lit up. "Thank you. I don't get to eat land food anything like as often as I'd like."

Justin made a little extra noise opening the companionway hatch, then called down it, "Our guest is here," and stood aside to let Belinda enter first. Thinking of Laura's problems with her tentacles, he'd wondered how well Belinda could walk, but eight tentacles seemed to be that much more robust than two; she moved with a quick sinuous grace that impressed him.

He followed her down the companionway, reached the cabin as she was introducing herself to Rose and Arthur. "Can I get you a blanket or something?" Rose asked her.

"I'm fine," said Belinda. Then, seeing Rose's expression: "I'm sorry—I spend so little time among humans these days I'm forgetting my manners. Of course, if you like."

Moments later Belinda had a blanket wrapped neatly around her for modesty's sake, and settled comfortably on one of the dining area's bench seats. Since Rose and Arthur always sat together on the other bench seat, Justin settled next to her once he'd helped serve the meal. Dinner and casual talk followed, and it wasn't until the plates were looking distinctly empty that Arthur brought the conversation back around to serious business. "Justin told us," he said, "that you came here to help try to find Owen."

She nodded. "I was visiting my sister in Kingsport when Justin's message came. I'd been trying to work up the nerve to come down here and see what I could do, but I wasn't quite brave enough to do it on my own. Once I knew there were other people looking for him, it was easier." She glanced down at her plate. "Though I'm not sure what I can do."

"I've got one idea," Justin said. "Back in 1919 there was a secret tunnel running inland from the harbor here in Red Hook. I don't know what the odds are that it's still there." He turned to Arthur. "Didn't you say the police blocked it up?"

"That's what the papers said," he replied, "but I read something a few years later saying that the authorities thought it had been opened up again, or that there was another they missed."

"So that's one thing you could look for," Justin said to Belinda. "I don't know for a fact that it has anything to do with Owen, but it's possible. Laura said he was looking for something underground, and I've learned a few things that make me think that might be connected."

Belinda nodded, taking this in. "I'll see what I can find," she promised. "It'll take some looking. The shore below the waterline is the most unholy mess, with all kinds of wreckage heaped up everywhere, and around by where the Gowanus Canal empties out, the water's unbelievably foul. The Deep Ones off Jamaica Bay told me that there used to be shoggoths living in Gowanus Creek and the bay it empties into, but the water got so bad they had to leave."

"There are Deep Ones near here?" Arthur said, eyebrows rising.

"Oh, yes. Just a few hundred of them, not much more than a village, but it's been there for a long time, and you know how Deep Ones are."

"As it happens, I don't," said Rose, smiling. "How are Deep Ones?"

"Stubborn," said Belinda. "If they've been living or herding fish in a certain place for long enough, it'll be a dry day in R'lyeh before they go anywhere else. The village off Jamaica Bay was there when the Ice Age glaciers made Long Island, and it'll probably still be there when the seas finish rising and the shore's a hundred miles further inland." She paused, then said: "Would you like some fresh fish tomorrow? They've got more culls from the schools they herd than they have mouths to feed right now."

"Please," said Rose. "On one condition—that you come help us eat it."

"That," Belinda said, "I'd be happy to do."

CHAPTER 4

A BREATH OF COOL AIR

Justin walked out to the sidewalk's edge as the bus came in sight, joined the others at the stop. Sparse traffic clattered and growled down Van Brunt Street, spraying salt water: the tide was higher than usual and a steady wind blew off the Lower Bay, sending water gurgling up through the storm sewers and running through the streets a few inches deep. The bus lurched to a halt, sending water surging across the sidewalk. Justin climbed aboard and found a seat away from the sun as it pulled away from the curb and drove off.

Arthur and Rose had tried to talk him into staying aboard the *Keziah Mason* while Arthur went to the library. They were probably right, too, but the trip to the Red Hook branch had gone well enough that Justin wasn't minded to listen. He wanted to do something to help find Owen, and as long blue shadows flowed across the wet streets of Red Hook, giving him plenty of shelter from the sun, the risk of an attack of porphyria seemed far away.

Getting to the Brooklyn Public Library's main branch was easy but slow, since the only bus that ran through Red Hook had a roundabout route and didn't run on time. Still, it got him there eventually. The route wandered through neighborhoods that looked a little more like the New York City he was used to, thronged with people and full of life, though even so there

47

were more empty buildings and fewer cars than he remembered. Here and there, too, he saw the garish posters announcing plenty of jobs out west.

Finally he left the bus in sight of the improbably ornate triumphal arch that marked Brooklyn's heart, and plunged into crowds from which the music of a hundred languages rose dancing to the skies. Arthur's directions led him straight to the library nearby. Had the soaring stone Art Deco facade been a little less Euclidean and the flanking pillars and the great bronze doors ornamented with something a little more eldritch, Justin thought, it could have passed for the temple-tomb of Great Cthulhu in lost R'lyeh.

Once through the doors, though, he encountered not the dead yet dreaming corpse of a Great Old One but welcome dimness and the memorable scent of old libraries. It took Justin a few minutes to get himself oriented, but with the help of a sign on a wall near the front doors, he found his way through the ornate hallways of an earlier era to the Brooklyn Collection on the second floor. There a tall brown-skinned librarian with her hair in long elegant braids beamed in answer to his question, and showed him how to access the library's immense collection of old Brooklyn newspapers.

He searched issues from May of 1919 without result, but June was a different matter. The front page of the Brooklyn *Daily Eagle* from June 9, 1919 shrieked *HORROR IN RED HOOK*, and went on in lurid detail about the collapse of three old houses in Parker Place, the death of eleven policemen and thirty-seven prisoners, and the alleged degeneracy of the Red Hook neighborhood and the immigrant families who lived there. Justin rolled his eyes but kept reading, hoping to find information that might help lead him to Owen.

That article had nothing to the point, but later articles filled in details Justin could use. The police had gone into Red Hook after accusations of children being kidnapped for sacrifice had circulated for weeks, though three other papers had looked into

the claims and found them baseless. The raids had focused on
two blocks on Parker Place, and had arrested scores of immigrants, some of whom wore ornate robes and miters and had
been celebrating the festivities of a religion Justin knew well
when the police kicked down the doors.

Three articles mentioned rumors about a secret tunnel leading from beneath a pier somewhere on the Red Hook waterfront to points unknown further inland, one made a joking
reference to old stories about buried treasure in Brooklyn, and
one quoted a passage that it claimed had been found written on the wall of a church near the Gowanus Canal. It ran:
"O friend and companion of night, thou who rejoicest in the
baying of dogs and spilt blood, who wanderest in the midst of
shades among the tombs, who longest for blood and bringest
terror to mortals, Gorgo, Mormo, thousand-faced moon, look
favorably upon our sacrifices!" Justin pondered that, copied it
down on his notepad.

A few days later, the horror at Red Hook was shoved off
the front pages by stories about the wrapping up of the peace
negotiations at Versailles, and the astonishing news that two
British airmen in a Vickers aeroplane had succeeded, for the
first time ever, in flying across the Atlantic. Justin considered
winding up his researches, decided to read a few more days of
the *Daily Eagle*, and was glad he did. The June 18 issue had a
story that claimed to connect the events in Red Hook with "the
shocking deaths of Robert and Cornelia Suydam." Justin knew
he'd seen the names earlier in his search, and a little more
exploration turned up accounts that soon had him filling page
after page of his notepad with details.

Robert Suydam, or so the papers claimed, had been a long-
time resident of the Flatbush neighborhood, a quiet and schol-
arly old man who belonged to an old Brooklyn family and who
had written well-regarded books on medieval superstitions.
Sometime in the early months of 1916 he rented a basement
flat in Parker Place, in one of the shabbier parts of Red Hook,

and began holding nocturnal meetings there with a congregation drawn from the whole range of Red Hook's immigrant communities. In 1917, Suydam's relatives tried to have him committed, but his calm and cogent response to the judge's questions forestalled them; in the winter of 1919, an announcement in the *Daily Eagle* proclaimed his engagement to a much younger woman, a distant relative of his who'd assisted him in his studies; on June 8 the wedding was celebrated, and that night, as three Red Hook houses collapsed on police and their prisoners, Suydam and his bride were found dead in their stateroom aboard a Cunard liner bound for Paris.

The aftermath, though, was the thing that set Justin's pen moving as fast as he could drive it. A tramp steamer came alongside the Cunarder and presented a document from Robert Suydam urging whoever it might concern to deliver his body into the hands of the bearer and his associates. The Cunard captain reluctantly complied, and Suydam's corpse was carried away, leaving his bride to be embalmed and brought home—passenger ships of any size in those days, Justin gathered, normally had a crew member aboard trained to function as an undertaker.

Then, the morning after the police raids, Suydam's body was found three stories under Parker Place by an underground pool, at the end of a secret canal that ran west to the Upper Bay. Though he'd been dead only a matter of hours, his corpse was so completely decayed that it had to be identified from dental records.

Justin got as many details of the underground canal as he could, and paged ahead further. The June 28 issue of the *Daily Eagle* was mostly full of stories about the signing of the Versailles Treaty, but in the back pages he found a letter to the editor that caught his eye instantly. It ranted about the evils of immigration, tunnels under the streets of Red Hook, strange rites of devil worship, and naked creatures of unimaginable shape that perched on golden pedestals. There was

something almost poetic about the letter's paranoiac ravings—
"cosmic sin had entered," the writer insisted, "and festered by
unhallowed rites had commenced the grinning march of death
that was to rot us all into fungous abnormalities too hideous
for the grave's holding." There was plenty more of the same
shrill sort.

It was the name at the foot of the letter that settled things,
though. Thomas F. Malone, the prim old-fashioned font said,
late of the New York Police Department. Justin contemplated
the name for a long moment, and then began to nod. He
knew the name well, and so did every other Martense around
Lefferts Corners. Thomas F. Malone had come to the Catskills
in September of 1921, in an otherwise pleasant autumn, and
shot and killed four men—George Bennet, William Tobey,
Arthur Munroe, and Jacob Martense—insisting to the last
that he'd done nothing of the kind, that all four of them had
been slaughtered by evil cannibal apes. He'd ended his days,
as Justin had told Arthur, in a state institution for the criminally insane, but the Martense family remembered, and every
Martense thereafter grew up with the lurking fear that another
plausible murderer would come from outside and leave more
corpses and bitter memories behind.

* * *

Further reading in the papers turned up nothing more of use.
Justin considered his options, and decided to try to find the
book by Ruth Frankweiler that had been checked out at the
Red Hook branch. When he looked it up on one of the catalog
computers, annoyingly, both copies at the main branch were
checked out too. He gave the screen an uncharitable look, and
then set out to find books on Brooklyn legends and folklore.
That proved more successful, as the library's Brooklyn Collection seemed to have a copy of everything about the borough
that had ever seen print, but his search for references to

underground canals and golden pedestals got him nowhere. He found books aplenty on Lady Deborah Moody and the early days of Gravesend, but those that mentioned her interest in buried treasure said nothing about what she was looking for or where she went looking for it. He was almost ready to give up the quest and head back to the *Keziah Mason* when his eye strayed across a name he remembered: Agatha Sleght.

That book mentioned only what Ruth Frankweiler had said, that Lady Moody had been accused of dealing with the famous witch of Greenwich Village. It took Justin close to half an hour of searching before he finally found more, and that was only a few paragraphs in a volume of New York legends, but he copied nearly all of it onto his notepad. The Sleght family had arrived early on in the days of Nieuw Amsterdam, and settled in Red Hook when that was a few farms on the edge of Long Island's trackless forests. How a daughter of the family ended up leading a hermit's existence on the flank of a long-vanished hill east of the tiny farm town of Groenwijk, where she was sought out secretly by the local people for charms and healing herbs, the encyclopedia didn't say, and the only one of the legends about her it saw fit to repeat was a story that she had consorted with the Devil and born him a monstrously deformed daughter.

The book had two more things to say about Agatha Sleght. The first was that she was still living beside the hill at the dawn of the eighteenth century, when Groenwijk had become the village of Greenwich and the people who sought her help spoke English instead of Dutch. The second was that she was dead by 1718, when a squire from England named Joseph Hyde built his country house atop the hill. Joseph's grandson Matthew had an entry of his own, to judge by a cross-reference in boldface. All Justin found out about him when he turned to **Hyde, Matthew**, though, was that he had been born in 1739, succeeded to the estate in 1768, was said to have murdered a local band of Indians by giving them poisoned rum, and still haunted the streets of Greenwich Village at night, a shadowy figure in a cloak and a broad-brimmed hat.

That was all Justin could find, and when another hour of searching the catalogue and the bookshelves turned up nothing but endlessly repeated stories about alligators in the New York City sewer system, he decided to call it a day. A glance at the first clock he passed gave him hope that the worst of the heat had passed, but when he went out through the bronze doors and descended the steps toward the great ornate arch the sunlight crashed down over his head and bounced back up from the pavement. Glare splashed off glass windows and cars, making the jacket and broad-brimmed hat he wore next to useless, and before he got to the bus stop that would take him back to Red Hook, pain surged through his bowels and his skin felt as though it had caught on fire, as an attack of porphyria hit him hard.

He stifled a profanity, got onto the shady side of the street as quickly as he could, made himself look around. Anger at his own stupidity twisted in him. A café not far away had sidewalk tables in full shade; he braced himself against the pain, headed that way, got seated. The waitress, a plump Hispanic woman with a broad smile, came over to take his order, and said, "You don't look like you're doing too good."

"I'll be fine," Justin said, and ordered a tall soft drink to get sugar into his system: something he'd seen a dozen relatives do in similar situations. The waitress gave him a dubious look but went away and returned with the soft drink. Justin thanked her, paid, and took sips small enough not to trouble his stomach while he waited for the edge of the pain to blunt.

The waitress was back when the drink was half done. "You sure you'll be okay?"

She wasn't just being polite, Justin realized; she was actually concerned. That and a renewed stab of pain in his belly pushed him past an easy denial. "Well, sooner or later," he admitted. "It's a hereditary thing—I get sick when I take too much sunlight. I just have to figure out how to get back to the place I'm staying in Red Hook."

The waitress considered him, and Justin recognized the look: it was the same any of the Martenses and Typers and Hasbroucks in Lefferts Corners would have aimed at an outsider who might need help and might have some other agenda. He submitted patiently to the look, and was rewarded by a little smile and the words, "I know somebody who can probably help you. Not to get you back to Red Hook—I can call a cab for you if you've got the cash—but a doctor."

"I can cover a cab," Justin said. "Does the doctor treat this kind of thing?"

"Oh, Dr. Muñoz treats anything. He's really good. My youngest had a heart condition, and he came to visit every week for a whole year. She's fine now, and he didn't charge the way other doctors do. Pay what you can afford is what he said, and he meant it."

The pain in his belly settled the matter. "I think I'd like to see him. Where's his office?"

"Oh, he lives down in Red Hook. That's why I thought of him. Gimme a minute." She headed inside, appeared a little later with a beer for one of the other patrons, then came over to Justin. "Here you go. I've called the cab, and called him too. Tell him Lisa Herrero sent you."

She handed him a napkin with an inky scrawl on it and hurried away again, leaving Justin to decipher the message: *Dr. Muñoz 27 Parker Place #301.* The address seemed familiar, though he couldn't place it at first. It wasn't until he'd given the waitress a five dollar tip and was standing at the curb waiting for the cab that the memory surfaced: Robert Suydam had celebrated the rites of the Great Old Ones in a basement flat on Parker Place. Coincidence? He knew he had no way to tell.

* * *

As he'd half expected, the car that pulled up for him wasn't a licensed cab. It had a piece of cardboard marked with a dollar sign in the front windscreen and another passenger already sitting in back, and the young man behind the wheel had enough of a resemblance to Lisa Herrero that Justin guessed he was a close relative. "Parker Place?" the driver said. "No prob. We got one stop west of the canal and then we're there."

Justin got in, tried not to worry as the cab whipped a tight U-turn through the middle of the traffic and sped down what looked like a random assortment of streets while the driver took two calls on a balky cell phone. The other passenger, whose immense handlebar mustache made the rest of his face fade into irrelevance, turned to Justin and said, "Some kinda convention in town, or what?" When Justin gave him a baffled look, he went on: "The hat and stuff. Not five minutes ago I saw this other guy wearin' a big black hat like yours headin' up Flatbush."

"Really tall?" Justin asked.

"Oh yeah." A sharp turn nearly landed him in Justin's lap, and he hauled himself back onto his side of the seat. "I bet he played basketball when he was in school."

The thought of Nyarlathotep taking a jump shot made Justin choke. "I've seen him," he said after a moment. "Sunlight makes me sick —that's why I wear this. I don't know about him."

The man with the mustache grunted a response, and the taxi rattled onto a bridge over a narrow waterway lined with old warehouses and rundown docks, along streets where seawater still pooled in low spots. It occurred to Justin then that the waitress might be setting him up for robbery or worse. Though he'd spent years in Europe and had friends with doctorates, Justin knew perfectly well that to the New Yorkers he met he was just one more rube from the Catskills, and more likely than not a lamb ready for fleecing. He thought about telling the driver to take him to the marina instead, but the pain in his belly argued against that. A bad attack could have him flat on his back for a week. If there was any chance he could avoid that and keep looking for Owen, he was going to try it.

Two more blocks and a sharp turn later, the taxi pulled up in front of an old church with a sign in front reading *Red Hook Community Center*. The man with the mustache paid up and climbed out of the cab, and the moment the door slammed shut, the cab driver floored it, zigzagged through a maze of narrow potholed streets lined with machine shops and row houses, and finally jolted to a stop.

Parker Place turned out to be a little rump-end of a street three blocks long, set at an odd angle to the rest of the streets in that part of Red Hook, and lined on both sides with run-down brick buildings four stories tall. Justin paid his fare, got out, and watched the cab drive off. He was maybe eight blocks from the marina, he guessed. The front door of 27 Parker Place had sheets of metal bolted crudely but effectively over it, and the intercom next to the door looked as though it had stopped working about the time Nieuw Amsterdam became New York, but Justin pressed the buttons anyway.

The loudspeaker crackled, and a soft hollow voice spoke out of it: "Hello?"

"Hi," Justin said. "Lisa Herrero sent me. I'm the guy she called about."

"Of course." The lock buzzed, and Justin went in. The elevator had a sheet of paper taped over the door saying OUT OF ORDER, and from the faded ink and the yellowing of the tape, the sign had been there for years. Fortunately the stairs weren't hard to find. He got to the third floor, found the door marked 301, and knocked.

The door opened to reveal a short elderly man neatly dressed in a cream-colored linen suit. Dark eyes regarded him through gold-framed glasses; a precisely trimmed beard edged a fine-boned face. "Please come in," he said. "You are?"

"Justin Martense."

That earned Justin a quick smile. "An old Brooklyn name, though I suspect you come from elsewhere. I am Dr. Muñoz." They shook hands; Muñoz' felt unexpectedly cold and dry, and the skin had a curious coarse texture. "Please have a seat. The rash on your face—it is perhaps porphyria? Yes? I thought so. Nothing else gives quite that color."

Justin, impressed, let himself be led into the room, settled on a comfortable chair while the doctor bolted the door and took another chair facing his. The space around him looked like a gentleman's study rather than a doctor's office, with mahogany furniture, ample bookshelves, and two landscapes in oil on the walls that Justin, no connoisseur of art, was still sure had been painted well before the twentieth century dawned. A coffee table between the two chairs had an assortment of books on it, one of them lying carelessly open. An air conditioner in one window labored gamely, but yielded only a faint breath of cool air.

*   *   *

"Now tell me about your porphyria," Muñoz said, picking up a notebook and a pen. "You have had symptoms for how long?" A series of gently probing questions followed, extracting from him every detail of the family illness, and the circumstances of the attacks he'd suffered.

"That must be difficult for you," Muñoz said sympathetically. "To have to flee the sunlight, after so many years when it was your friend. I understand. Years ago I was ill for some time, and I could not tolerate the least heat or excitement; I lived in rooms in Manhattan then, and had to have machinery to keep my rooms quite cold. Fortunately a friend found a cure for my illness." With a reminiscent smile: "I have never liked cold since then." He got to his feet. "Now I shall need a few drops of your blood, and then I think I can do something for you."

He went into the adjoining room—Justin got a brief glimpse of glassware and machinery through the open door—and returned with a needle and a pipette. A quick motion, almost painless, pierced the pad of one of Justin's fingers; a red line slid up the pipette; then Muñoz neatly bandaged the finger and vanished into the next room.

In the minutes that followed, as low nameless sounds came whispering out of the laboratory, Justin spent a while looking at the nearest bookshelf for want of anything else to occupy his thoughts. He didn't recognize any of the books at first; some, ancient volumes bound in leather with metal hasps, had nothing on their spines at all, while others had titles such as *Marvells of Science* and *The Works of Borellus*. In the midst of them was a big volume with old-fashioned German blackletter script on the binding. It took a few minutes for Justin to puzzle out what it said, but when he did he drew in a sudden sharp breath. The upper lines, he was sure of it, spelled out *Unaussprechlichen Kulten*, and below that was the name *F. W. v. Junzt*.

That was promising, and not just because Justin had read the same book more than once in English translation. Still, he knew better than to go rummaging in the private library of anyone who had a book by Friedrich von Junzt on his shelves; besides, he knew just enough German to order bock at a Munich biergarten and find the restroom afterwards. He sat back, wondered how long Muñoz would be. After a while, when the low sounds from the laboratory showed no sign of reaching a conclusion, he sat forward again and considered the open book on the coffee table: a slim hardback, apparently of poetry. The open pages displayed a sonnet:

LOOKING ACROSS THE EAST RIVER
From Brooklyn Heights I look across the river
To gray Manhattan, where the towers rise.
Despite our boasts, they cannot scrape the skies:

They rise and fall, the skies rise up forever.
Brownstone and concrete, brick and iron beams
Weigh down the land and bridge the surging
deep,
But only for a while. Time turns in sleep
And shrugs aside the rubble of our dreams.
And you, the children of those distant years
Whose feet will someday dance upon the green
Where once stood our proud towers, shed no
tears
For us, and for the things that might have
been.
The things that matter stay when all else
passes:
Night on the river, wind amidst the grasses.

Justin frowned. The style seemed almost familiar, but the shift in the last two lines from bleak historical vision to nature poetry seemed jarring. He shrugged, and heard the noises from the laboratory fall silent at last.

"Here we are," said Muñoz, returning at last from the laboratory. "You should drink this now." He held out a beaker half full of a colorless liquid. "This afternoon I have no other calls, so I can make up some pills for you and have young Esteban bring them to you in the morning. You are staying here in Red Hook?"

"At the Gerritsen Street Marina."

"Ah, excellent. But the medicine will not do you any good in the beaker, you know."

Justin allowed a rueful laugh. The thought of downing a cup or so of liquid all at once in the middle of an attack made him queasy, but he decided to risk it and took a good swallow. Pain spiked in his stomach and then unraveled. He gave the beaker a startled look, and finished the liquid. By the time he could hand the beaker back, the pain in his belly was almost gone.

"It is simply a matter of assisting the body to do away with the excess porphyrins," said Muñoz, and went back into the laboratory with the beaker. He returned a moment later. "That is not something your modern physician knows how to do, but the ancients—ah, they understood so many things that we have lost! To remove something that is in excess, to add something that is lacking, even to maintain life despite the most serious impairments, or restore it when it has departed—I will not say that these were child's play to them, but they could do them." Then, seeing Justin's expression: "But I ramble. If you can keep your exposure to sunlight modest, that will help complete the process. How are you doing?"

"I feel—well, a lot better," said Justin. "How much do I owe you?"

The doctor's gesture dismissed the question. "Pay what you can afford. It is my pleasure to be of service." Justin stood, and Muñoz shook his hand, gave him a business card, said the usual things, and retired discreetly to the laboratory. Justin watched him go, then went to the desk on one side of the room and left three large bills on it.

A few moments later he was descending the stair to the door, shaking his head. A strange old man, he thought, with his talk about ancient medicines and restoring life. Still, the medicine Muñoz had given him seemed to have done him a surprising amount of good. An assortment of subtle discomforts he'd long since given up noticing made themselves apparent by their absence.

At the door, he glanced at the business card in his hand. It read:

León Muñoz, M.D.
General and Family Practice
27 Parker Place #301, Brooklyn NY 11231

He pocketed the card, stepped out into the blazing heat.

He got back to the marina without incident, let himself in through the locked gate, headed down the docks to the *Keziah Mason*. The sun was still well above the low skyline of the Jersey shore when he climbed aboard the sailboat, and Rose and Arthur hadn't returned yet—still looking for Owen, he guessed, and hoped they'd have better luck than he had. He unlocked the companionway hatch, climbed down through it, took off gloves and hat and jacket with a sigh, and only then noticed the sheet of paper sitting on the dining table. He picked it up, found that it had another typewritten message on it:

Justin –
Stay off the streets
They know who you are
They're looking for you

He stared at the note for a long moment, then put it in one of the cupboards beneath his berth with the other note and Owen's letter.

* * *

After a few moments he got out the cards that had been Sallie Eagle's, shuffled and dealt three cards: the Moon, the Crossroads, and the Cat. He pondered them for a while, trying to make sense of them and failing utterly. The Moon meant something important had been revealed; the Crossroads in the middle position warned him that he faced a crucial choice soon; the Cat suggested that he would encounter someone who could be a source of help or the opposite, depending on details Justin couldn't yet be sure of. The whole pattern meant something, but what? He could not tell.

He put the cards away, considered the options, and lay down on his berth to rest: Dr. Muñoz' medicine had taken away most of the symptoms of the attack, but a heavy tired feeling he knew well from after earlier attacks still weighed on him. He had almost settled into a comfortable doze when footsteps on the deck above told him that Arthur and Rose had returned.

"No Owen," Rose said, as she stowed packages of various kinds in the galley cupboards. She didn't look quite as shaken as she'd done the first time she'd gone into New York, but Justin knew her well enough to tell that it was still a strain for her. "Though I can tell you one thing we didn't know before, which is that we're not the only ones looking for him."

Justin, who was sitting at the table by then, gave her a startled look. "The ladies at the knitting circle were talking about it," she went on. "Three different women had met people who were either asking for Owen by name or describing him, and telling different stories about why they want to find him."

"That's not good," said Justin.

"No," Arthur agreed. "What's more, he's not the only one they're looking for."

"I know," said Justin. "They're looking for me." In response to his raised eyebrows: "I found another note when I got back here. Let me get it." He unfolded himself from the bench seat, went to his berth, returned with the latest typewritten note.

Arthur read it, nodded. "I found out more directly. After I dropped Rose off at the community center—it's in an old church over by the Gowanus Canal, a pleasant-looking place with some fine stonework—I went to run some errands, then headed to the library to see if that book by Frankweiler was in, and stopped at a bar for a cold beer on the way." Rose made a clucking noise of disapproval but softened it with a fond smile. "About a minute after I sat down at the bar, a fellow sat next to me and told me a rigmarole about how he was looking for a friend of his who'd come down here from the Catskills, one eye blue, one brown, name of Martense. Of course I played dumb and started talking about a cat I had in college who had eyes like that, and kept at it until he interrupted me. So we went back and forth a little, until he decided I didn't know anything and I was sure I knew what I needed to know, and he left."

"You're good," said Justin.

Arthur shrugged, dismissing the compliment. "I did field intelligence when I was in the Army, and learned a few things." Then: "The fellow was lying through his teeth, of course. He's no friend of yours, and all he knows about you comes out of somebody's file cabinet."

Justin nodded, thinking of the cold competent men he'd faced below Elk Hill eleven years before. "Well," he said, "we'll deal. At least they don't know about you and Rose."

"Here's hoping," Arthur replied.

"There we are," said Rose, who had finished in the galley. "We ought to be able to do something really nice with Miss Marsh's fish. Speaking of whom, Arthur, did you—"

"Sure thing." He lifted up a flimsy bag. Justin gave him a questioning look, and he handed the bag over. In it were two cheap cotton muumuus with maritime-themed prints on them, one seahorses and seaweed, the other fishes and waves.

"I know I'm old-fashioned," said Rose, "but I couldn't stand the thought that the poor thing doesn't have a stitch to wear." With a worried look at Justin: "I hope she won't mind. I know you've said that some of the other kinds of people in the world have their own habits."

"You know," said Justin, "I think she'll like these."

He was right, too. "That was really sweet of her," Belinda said, beaming, once she'd climbed aboard and toweled off the sea water. "I used to wear muumuus all the time when I lived in Innsmouth." She wriggled into the muumuu with the seahorses on it, settled it with a fluid gesture of her tentacles, and smiled. Justin smiled also, gathered up the fish—four fine haddock on a cord that appeared to be braided from seaweed—and headed belowdecks.

"I have some news," Belinda said, once Arthur was busy cleaning the fish and the others had settled at the table. "I think

I've found the underwater canal. It's about half a mile south of here, and it's mostly blocked with stones but not completely. I think there's a way through."

"You didn't try?" Rose asked.

Belinda looked down at the table. "I probably should have, but it's really risky to go into sea caves alone, and this is kind of the same thing." Looking up: "I wondered if one of you would be willing to go with me. I can borrow an artificial gill from the Deep Ones."

Arthur considered that, eyebrows rising; Rose shot him a minatory look. Before either of them could speak, Justin said, "Sure. I'm a pretty good swimmer, and I need to stay out of the sunlight anyway."

Belinda's face lit up. "Thank you. The Deep Ones say there'll be fog tomorrow morning, so no one'll be able to see us leave here."

"Let's do it," said Justin, trying to sound more confident than he felt.

CHAPTER 5

THE COMPANION OF NIGHT

The Deep Ones were right about the fog. It came in somewhere in the small hours, gray and clammy, muffling the sounds of Red Hook and the greater city beyond. By the time Justin climbed on deck the fog had begun to thin beneath the summer sun, but the other boats in the marina were still vague blurs and the buildings of Red Hook no more than a guess.

He'd found a worn but wearable pair of swim trunks in a collection of old clothes he kept aboard the *Keziah Mason*, and Arthur had gone digging in the forward lockers and come up with a diver's mask he used for checking the hull from beneath when he didn't want to pay to have the boat hauled out of the water. That didn't seem like much in the way of gear for venturing into an abandoned canal under the streets of Red Hook, but Justin had made the offer and he wasn't about to back out. He'd already gone up to the marina office to let the manager know to expect a messenger from Dr. Muñoz, so he had nothing else to keep him. Still, a few moments passed before he went to the stern, climbed halfway down the ladder, and splashed a bare foot back and forth in the water: the signal they'd arranged.

Belinda surfaced after a minute or so, smiled up at him. "Good morning. I've got the artificial gill and a few other

65

things, and made sure the mouth of the tunnel's still open, so everything should be fine. Ready?"

It would have been the simple truth to say no, but he silenced the thought the moment it surfaced. "Sure," he said, and got the diver's mask settled over his eyes.

"Good. I'll be below." Tentacles sculled, and she vanished from sight. He drew in a breath, straightened, stepped off the ladder and plunged straight down into the dark surging waters of the harbor.

Shock of the water's chill left him dazed for a moment. By the time his mind cleared, he was a dozen feet below the waves and a shape that had to be Belinda was swimming over to him. Something pressed against his mouth; he let it slide between his lips, waited until two of her tentacles fastened cords around the back of his neck. When he drew in a first tentative breath through the mouthpiece, the air came through cool and salt-tinged, though it had an acrid edge of oil and industrial chemicals as well.

A pulsing, buzzing sound rang in his head, and recognizable words came out of it: "Nod if you can understand me." He nodded, and the buzzing went on. "You're breathing okay? Good. Don't try to talk—you have to learn how to do it—and don't breathe any deeper than you have to, or you'll float upwards."

He nodded again. The diver's mask gave him clearer vision than he'd expected. He could see the hull of the *Keziah Mason* rising above him, a dark shape etched against the shimmering of the water's surface. More to the point, he could see Belinda clearly in the wavering light, her body just a few feet from his face: the human head and half-human body, the three slits on either side of her ribcage that fluttered open as she breathed water. She wore the golden torc around her neck, a belt of twisted gold links around her waist with obscure shapes hanging from it, and nothing else; Justin could see with perfect clarity her small round breasts and the cleft of her sex. He tried to avoid looking at these or too obviously away from them, hoped that his blush wasn't as visible as it felt.

"Okay," the buzzing in his head said. "Follow me." She darted away in a flurry of sculling tentacles, and he swam after her as best he could.

Their route took them under the boats and docks of the marina, and then south and southeast along the shores of Red Hook, dodging an impressive assortment of underwater wreckage. Justin had expected the angular rusting shapes of disused refrigerators and washing machines, the litter of discarded toilets and bathtubs, the heaps of broken lumber from buildings demolished and dumped into the harbor, and the rubble of long-collapsed piers, but he wasn't sure what to make of the cars that had apparently been driven straight off this or that pier into the water, or the two apparently intact buildings that rose out of the murk, one of them with an illegible sign still visible above its door. He shook his head, swam on.

They'd gone the half mile she'd mentioned, or close to it, when the buzzing voice sounded again. "Okay," Belinda said. "Now we go down to the bottom." She swam down at an angle, glanced back to see if he was following, plunged further into murky water.

Ahead of him, soaring black shapes rose up out of the darkness like the pillars of some roofless and abandoned temple: pilings, he guessed, from a pier that had toppled into the harbor long before. He could only just see their dim shapes around him when a light blinked on below, and then another. Following them, he caught up with Belinda, who was sculling gracefully in the murky water. A few feet below her, barely visible, stretched a surface of ooze, crumpled beer cans, and random refuse spread over what looked like the pier's wreckage.

"Do you see the gap in the stones?" Belinda asked. A golden object in one tentacle, the source of one of the lights, turned and splashed its pallid glow on the sea wall near them. The wall had a broad opening in it—Justin thought, looking up, that he could make out a brick archway—but the space below the arch had been filled long ago with huge ragged stones. A second look showed that several of the stones on one side had been forced out from within, leaving a tunnel into blackness.

He nodded, and she gave him one of the golden objects: a Deep One flashlight, he guessed, though it didn't look anything like the human equivalent. It had an oddly shaped strap on it, which he realized after a moment was meant to fasten it onto one side of his head. Once he had it in place, he swam with her toward the gap in the stones.

* * *

The gap was bigger than it looked, as though something larger than a human being had made it, and Justin found it easy enough to maneuver after Belinda. The winding passage beyond it was edged on three sides by great ragged stones and on the fourth by slimy bricks. Twenty feet or so of careful swimming, and they were past the rocks. He'd worried that the roof of the canal might have caved in, but the lights showed a tunnel of rough but sturdy brickwork some ten feet across with an uneven bottom and an arched ceiling, reaching away in a line not quite straight into unguessed distances.

Belinda turned toward him, and the buzzing voice sounded. "Does this look like the tunnel you read about?" He nodded, and she motioned ahead. Side by side, they swam on.

Just as the newspaper stories had said, the tunnel went on for something like a mile under the streets of Red Hook: northwest toward the high ground around Parker Place, Justin thought, though he couldn't be sure. Here and there great pits pierced the floor of the tunnel, and a light pointed down into them displayed nothing but unbroken blackness; here and there, too, an old doorway high up opened onto the canal. Back before the seas started rising, Justin guessed, those doors would have been above water level most of the time, and there would have been ample room at low tide to take a rowboat or a barge up the tunnel to whatever lay at its far end. Now it looked as though even the lowest tides left only a few inches of air between salt water and brick. He and Belinda stayed well below the arched ceiling, probed this way and that with the beams from their lamps, saw nothing through the murky water but mottled brickwork and century-old ooze.

Finally the walls widened to either side, the brick vault of the ceiling gave way to a dark shimmering surface where water met air, and a stone pier jutted out, rising up well above the water's surface. It took Justin only the briefest glance to guess that they had reached the pool mentioned in the newspaper stories about Robert Suydam. He glanced at Belinda, who turned to him in the same moment.

"Up?" she asked in the buzzing voice, and when he nodded: "Take a deep breath and let me unhook the artificial gill. I'll have to put it back in its case. It can't go out of the water without damaging the membrane."

He nodded, drew in a deep breath, paused long enough for her to take the thing back. As she put it into one of the objects on her belt, he unfastened the lamp from his head and kicked to send himself to the surface.

A few moments later he broke through into near-total blackness. The air smelled stale and fetid, tinged with scents Justin was glad he couldn't recognize, but it was breathable. Belinda surfaced next to him—he could see her face dimly in the light from the lamps. They considered each other, and then one of her tentacles motioned tentatively at the pier. He nodded, and swam that way as silently as he could.

They reached the pier together. Along one side, steps of stone rose up, starting well below the water's edge: at the old level of low tide, Justin guessed. He climbed out of the water, shoved his diver's mask down around his neck, turned to offer Belinda a hand. One of her tentacles took it, and she smiled at him as she rose up onto the stair.

As he turned to climb further, a soft tittering laugh sounded from the darkness above. He looked up, startled.

"Yes, I thought you'd come here sometime soon." The voice came out of the darkness, and it didn't sound as though a human throat had made it. "Let's have a look at you."

All at once a face peered down at them from the blackness above. It wasn't a human face either. It looked, Justin thought, as though somebody who'd never seen a woman's face had tried to make one anyway. A thick mop of stringy dark hair framed the face; the mouth went further to one side than the other, ending where a yellow tusk jutted upwards, and the larger of her eyes gleamed down at them, reflective as a cat's. The strangest thing about the face, though, was that Justin didn't need to point his lamp at it to see it. It shone with a phosphorescent glow, as though light shone on it from a moon smaller and more distant than the one Justin knew.

"Come up," said the creature. "I won't devour you." Her tittering laugh sounded again. "At least not quite yet."

* * *

Justin glanced at Belinda, saw his own unsteady nerves mirrored in her eyes, and climbed the rest of the stairs. He passed the place where the surface of the pier had been originally—his lamp showed the change from the old fine stonework to newer, rougher brick, cracked and discolored as though it had been salvaged after a fire. Wet sounds of tentacles on the steps told him that Belinda followed him up the stair, but most of his attention was on the being who waited for them.

A few further steps and more of her came into his view, and he had to make himself keep climbing. Each new glimpse thereafter was more unnerving than the last. She was wholly naked, and her head, her right arm and breast, and part of her torso looked more or less human, but the rest flowed into unexpected shapes. Her left shoulder ended not in an arm but in three long limbs of different lengths, a little like huge fingers and a little like a spider's legs, tipped with glistening claws. From there down she became wholly unhuman, a chaos of protuberances and vestigial limbs, under which two muscular froglike legs folded at unsettling angles. The phosphorescence shimmered from her whole body. Too faint to illuminate the pier or anything further off, it made her seem to hover in blackness, the sole inhabitant of an infinite void.

She watched him through both eyes as he finished coming up the stair, and then tittered again. "What, no screams? You're made of sterner stuff than most."

Justin managed a shaken smile. "Will you be offended if I say I've seen stranger?"

She smiled, baring long fangs. "No." She gestured with her one arm. "Sit. We have things to talk about."

He sat on the brick facing her, and Belinda settled next to him. One of her arm-tentacles slid around him; he could feel her dread, curled a hand around the tentacle in the hope that it would provide some comfort.

"Do you know who we are?" Belinda asked.

The cat-bright eye turned toward her. "I? No. You I've seen swimming around the edges of this little kingdom of mine—" She glanced at Justin. "—and you I've heard of, you or another like you, asking questions a good many folk don't wish to answer. I'd have left you to certain other things that live down here, oh yes, and I fancy they'd have welcomed a little fresh meat, too." She tittered. "But you—" Her gaze returned to Belinda. "—you aren't even half human, are you? Tell me."

"My mother is the Black Goat of the Woods," said Belinda. "My father's people are from Innsmouth, up in Massachusetts. Maybe you've heard of it."

"Innsmouth," the creature repeated. "Yes. A good long time ago, wasn't it? Dealings with the undersea folk, dealings with folk from the South Seas who weren't much more human than you are. I heard there was bad trouble over that." Turning suddenly to Justin: "And you. Human right down to the bone, but you don't carry on the way humans do when they see something a little—*different*." She tittered, and then all at once leaned forward with fearsome intensity. "Why are you here? Lie to me and I'll feast on your innards."

"We're looking for a friend," Justin said after a moment. "A man named Owen Merrill. He came to Red Hook a month ago, and no one's heard of him for weeks. We want to find him if he's still alive."

"Why did he come here?"

"I don't know." Meeting her unyielding look: "I don't. He studies strange things. We don't usually talk about those, and I don't know what he was looking for here."

The creature's gaze flicked over to Belinda, who said, "I don't know either. Maybe some of his friends in Arkham do, but I don't go ashore much."

That got a slow lopsided smile from her fanged mouth. "No, I fancy you don't."

"Do you know where he is?" Justin asked her then.

"I? No." The creature regarded them for a moment. "There's many a place a man could hide or be hidden here, above the ground or below it, and many a quick or slow way to die. Nor is it any job of mine to watch humans come and go." She turned to face Justin. "Your name." Justin told her, and she turned to Belinda and said, "I haven't a use for yours. I fancy no one in this town would know it."

"Probably not," Belinda admitted. "But it's Belinda Marsh." Then: "Would it be okay to ask your name?"

That got her a long silent stare, and then a little snort. "I've had plenty of names," the creature said. "Gorgo, Mormo." Teeth bared. "Lilith. Do you know those? Thousand-faced moon, friend and companion of night. How about those?" Turning suddenly back to Justin: "You know them. Tell me how."

"I read them in a newspaper article," said Justin.

The bright baleful eye glared at him for a long moment, and then she laughed her tittering laugh. "Oh, that's rich," she said. "Your friend, did he come looking for the carved golden pedestal with the onyx base, or was he after the naked thing that squatted on it?" The tittering echoed back from unseen walls.

She turned again and called out, "Erlik! Come here, child! I've got an errand for you."

Something scuttled out of the darkness. At first, stifling a shudder, Justin thought that it was a spider big enough to stand a foot or more above the bricks of the pier, but then it darted through the beam of one of the lamps and Justin saw it clearly. It was a lean black and white cat, but no cat as he'd ever thought to see outside of a nightmare. Its eight long legs, none of them quite the same length as the others, arched up and then down like a spider's; its body writhed in uneasy curves, and it had two faces half merged together on its head. Three eyes of three different shapes shone green in the lamplight, and an uncomfortably wide mouth spread between paired jaws. Still, it scurried over to its mistress and rubbed the side of one of its faces against her, making a wet purring sound.

She caressed it with her hand, murmured something to it, then glanced up at Justin and Belinda. "Go," she said. "Straight out to the harbor, and make it quick, too, or I may send something after you to bite at your heels. Come back on the third day from this if you dare, and maybe I'll have news for you. Maybe." She leaned forward again. "And tell no one about me. If you do, I'll hear of it, and whether you come here or not, no one will ever find your bones."

A gesture with her spider-limbs dismissed them. Justin got to his feet, helped Belinda rise on her tentacles. He considered thanking the strange being before him, but she had turned her attention entirely to the cat, stroking it and murmuring to it

while it rubbed one of its faces and then the other against a scaled protuberance on her lower body. He glanced at Belinda, who met his gaze with a shaken look, and the two of them hurried back down the stair to the water.

* * *

The tunnel seemed to stretch on forever as they swam as quickly as they could back the way they'd come. Finally the glow of the lamps met the heaped boulders that blocked the tunnel, and they found the gap that led out to daylight.

Once they were through and light filtered down from the water's surface above, Belinda spoke in buzzing words: "We need to talk before we say anything to Rose and Arthur." Justin nodded, and the two of them swam along the shore of Red Hook most of the way to the marina.

The space under a rundown wharf offered them a place to surface unseen. Justin waited while she took off the artificial gill, then swam up until his head and neck were above water. Her head surfaced a moment later.

"We can't tell them," she said at once. "I don't think she was bluffing."

"Neither do I," Justin admitted. "Do you think she's a child of the Great Old Ones?"

"I thought so until I saw that cat." She shuddered, then saw his expression and let out a little bleak laugh. "I know, to most people I'm just as scary—but I don't like spiders."

"I get that," he said, and got a grateful look from her. Then, following out her earlier thought: "The cat's probably not a child of the Great Old Ones."

"No. You never know with them, but I've never heard of anything like that—so there may be some other reason she looks the way she does." Then, after a moment: "But she knew what you were thinking, and that means we don't know what else she can do."

He nodded, agreeing. "What are we going to tell Rose and Arthut?"

They settled on a story, and then she looked away and said, "By the way, thanks for holding my tentacle in there. I was really scared, and that made it easier."

"Any time," said Justin. "Tell you a secret—so was I."

That got him another grateful look. He motioned toward the marina with his head, and she nodded and slipped under the water.

A few minutes later they were safe under the *Keziah Mason*. Justin took off the artificial gill again and handed it to Belinda, then swam upwards to the ladder. The day had gone bright and sultry while they'd been under Red Hook. Justin glanced around as he climbed into the cockpit, made sure no one was in sight, and motioned to Belinda, who left the water and flowed up the ladder in a quick flurry of tentacles.

He found one of her muumuus in the stowage bin, handed it to her while looking away, and she made a little snorting noise and said, "You know perfectly well what I look like."

He reddened, but faced her. "It's kind of a habit."

"I know. Humans are funny about clothes."

"You say 'humans' as though you're not one."

She shrugged on the garment, then grinned. "Laura and I are exactly eleven thirty-seconds human. We worked it out one day when we were both kids." Motioning toward the hatch: "Let's see if Arthur and Rose have any news."

Belowdecks, Arthur sat at the dining table nursing a cup of coffee. His face brightened as they came through the hatch. "Welcome back. Anything?"

"We found the tunnel," said Justin. "It goes pretty much due northwest from where the old pier was. It's blocked with rocks, so we couldn't get far, but it's there."

"Northwest." Arthur reached for something in a storage nook beside him. It turned out to be an old-fashioned paper map of Brooklyn.

"Where'd you get that?" Justin asked.

"Picked it up at a junk shop off Van Brunt Street. It cost me a pretty penny, too—now that that inter-whatever you call it—"

"The internet," Justin said helpfully.

"That's the one. Now that it doesn't work so well, a lot of people want these again." He unfolded it. "Where was the old pier?" Belinda indicated the location with the tip of one tentacle, and Arthur drew a line with his fingertip northwest from there. Roughly a mile on, the line crossed a short street that cut at an angle to the grid: Parker Place, Justin read.

"Where's Rose?" Belinda asked then.

"At another ladies' gathering," Arthur said, "crocheting, I think. It's at the same old church. It's quite a place—dancing on Friday and Saturday nights, all kinds of other things the rest of the week." He glanced up at the clock near the companionway. "Speaking of which, I should head up that way to walk her back here. Brooklyn's nothing like as rough as it was when I lived there, but—" He shrugged.

"You're old-fashioned," Justin suggested, grinning.

"You bet." Arthur returned the grin. "Set in stone, in fact." They both laughed, and then he turned to go, stopped, got something from a locker and handed it to Justin. "The fellow from the doctor's office left this at the office first thing this morning."

Justin said the usual things, and once Arthur was gone, examined the object: a brown glass bottle with a screw top and a white paper label. On the label, in the elegant handwriting of an earlier day, was this: *Take one pill daily after eating. L. Muñoz MD.*

"What is it?" Belinda asked. Justin explained about the porphyria, the waitress, and the strange old man in the apartment on Parker Place, and she nodded. "Just like visiting a witch. Are there witches up in Lefferts Corners?"

"There always have been," he said. "Since before the Martense family moved there in 1668, at least. Are there witches where you live?"

Her smile fell. "No, I live in Y'ha-nthlei these days. The Deep Ones have their own healers, and they're very good, but it's not the same." She put the smile back on, as though shrugging on a garment. "I had a great-aunt named Mehitabel Waite who was a witch, and a really good one. She used to take care of Laura and me when we were little—sore throats, sprained tentacles, all the usual little things."

"I take Robin to a witch named Susan Typer for those," said Justin. "She's a second cousin once removed one way and a fourth cousin the other way." He shrugged, laughed a little choked laugh. "That's Lefferts Corners for you."

"It sounds like Innsmouth with fewer gills," said Belinda.

Neither of them said anything for a few moments. "If you've got other things to do," Belinda said then, "I can go somewhere else until dinner."

"Only if you want to," said Justin.

Something less forced stirred beneath the smile she'd put on. "You know," she said, "if you don't mind, I'd rather stay."

CHAPTER 6

THE SILENCE OF THE STARS

They made plans in the hour or so before Arthur and Rose came back. Some excuse had to be found to go back to the tunnel, they agreed, and it wasn't too hard to find something that would serve. "Tomorrow afternoon I can tell them I've found another tunnel," said Belinda, "and ask you to come with me again. If we find out anything, we can figure out how to tell Rose and Arthur, and if not—" Tentacles traced a fluid shrug.

That raised questions Justin didn't want to think about, and Belinda was just as eager to change the subject. How they got onto the subject of Kingsport Justin was never quite sure afterwards, but before long Belinda was telling him a lively story about something Owen's daughter Asenath had done two summers back, and Justin was laughing, recalling similar memories from his Kingsport summers. When her story wound to a close, he recounted one of Robin's escapades from a Kingsport trip when the boy was five.

"I'd really like to meet Robin sometime," Belinda said when he'd finished. "Is he back in Lefferts Corners now?"

"No, he's spending the summer with his mother."

Her eyes went wide. "Oh, I envy him. Laura and I got to spend time with Mom twice when we were little, and it was the most astonishing experience. There aren't words for it."

With a sudden smile: "Literally. English doesn't have words for most of the things you meet where Mom is, and I never had enough of a head for languages to learn Aklo. Mom never minded."

"I ought to be used to the way you call her Mom," Justin said, laughing his little choked laugh. "Robin does the same thing."

"All her children do," said Belinda. "Is Robin really a shape-shifter? Laura and Owen said that, but I've never met anybody who turned out that way."

"It's true," said Justin. Recollections cascaded past his mind's eye, bringing back the complexities of raising a child who had to make a sustained effort to look human. "He can't take a lot of shapes yet—mostly it's just his resting form, which is all tentacles and eyes, and his human form. But Susan tells me he should start picking up a few more in a couple of years."

"I hope he's having a great time," she said wistfully. "I miss those days a lot."

Justin tried to think of something to say and failed. All at once memories of his Kingsport summers had come crashing back into his mind: mornings wrapped in mist and long sunny afternoons, the sea rolling restlessly out beyond the harbor, the great gray cliffs of Kingsport Head soaring up stark and irrefutable against an ever-changing sky; clambakes, beach walks, Robin and Asenath splashing in the surf while Asenath's younger brother Barnabas sat on the sand and pondered a sand dollar with narrowed eyes; cool shadows inside the Chaudronnier mansion on Green Street, with the patient clack-clack-clack of Laura's typewriter sounding from one of the parlors as she spent spare afternoon hours working on her book of Innsmouth folklore; pleasant times with good friends. He found himself wishing desperately that he could wind back the clock four years, back to the days when sunlight wasn't an enemy and he hadn't yet realized how absurd he'd been, chasing after a woman who wanted nothing to do with him.

"You're sad," Belinda said, breaking in on his thoughts.

"Just old memories," he said. When her questioning look didn't waver: "Wishing I hadn't made such a fool of myself over Jenny. I don't know if you heard about that."

"Laura told me a little about it," she replied. "She thought that was why you stopped spending summers in Kingsport."

After a moment, Justin managed a laugh. "Yeah, I would expect Laura to catch that. Chalk it up to pride, maybe. You know when you do something really stupid, and the last thing you want is to be reminded of it every single day by everything you see?"

She looked away, hard. "Yes," she said in a subdued voice. "Yes, I do."

Justin, startled, tried to figure out what to say, but before he came to a decision, footfalls on the deck above announced Arthur and Rose.

"I've got some news," Rose said once they'd greeted one another. "I talked to an old woman whose family's from someplace I've never heard of. Do you know where Kurdistan is?"

"I think part of it's in Syria," Justin guessed.

"That sounds about right," said Rose. "The woman I talked to helps run a historical society for immigrants from there. We got to talking, and so of course I asked about Owen, and she had tea with him on the eleventh of last month."

Justin's eyebrows went up. "Seriously?"

She nodded. "He was researching an organization that he said came here from Kurdistan, and wanted to know if she could tell him anything about it. She couldn't." Her smile faltered. "Or wouldn't. She thinks the organization is really bad."

"Meaning it's probably on our side of things," said Arthur. "But now we know for certain that Owen was here, and we've got a few more clues about what he was looking for. Tomorrow I'm going to head on up to the Brooklyn Library and see if I can find anything about Kurdish organizations here in Red Hook. We'll track Owen down yet."

* * *

That seemed promising, and they had a pleasant dinner together. Later, though, after Belinda had said her goodbyes and slipped noiselessly into the black water, Justin sat up late into the night, trying and failing to think of something other than the idiot he'd made of himself over Jenny. He still missed her, and it seemed unpleasantly likely that he always would, but every memory of the days he'd spent trotting after her like a lovesick puppy made him cringe—and yet every one of those was tangled up in recollections of vivid moments he'd otherwise have counted among the best of his life. When he finally dragged himself aft to his berth, he'd worked himself into a miserable mood. It took him a long time to fall asleep, and then he dreamed that he was wandering in tunnels like the ones he and Belinda had explored, while something vast and unseen gazed on him from the darkness in brooding silence.

His mood hadn't improved when he woke up the following morning, though he managed to smile and banter over breakfast, and wished Rose and Arthur luck as they headed off into the morning, Rose to another event at the community center, Arthur from there to the Brooklyn Public Library. It stung that he couldn't do more to help find Owen, even though he knew he didn't have a choice. He was deep in bleak bitter thoughts when three taps on the hull beside him let him know that Belinda had arrived.

He donned hat, jacket and gloves, and clambered out into the cockpit. A passenger ferry from Manhattan was within sight as he got there. He waited until it had vanished behind one of the big rundown piers that flanked the marina before finding a wrench in one of the bins underneath the cockpit seats and tapping three times in response. Belinda surfaced, and to Justin's surprise, his wretched mood promptly went away.

It stayed away, too, while they slipped down into the cabin, shared out the lunch Rose had left for them, made plans for the next day, talked about harmless pleasant things while the afternoon brightened and dimmed, welcomed Rose and Arthur back, listened to their disappointing news, and shared a dinner. That night, as he tried to sleep, he found his mind circling back over and over again to Belinda, in a way he recognized at once. That startled him, for she couldn't have been less like Jenny if she'd set out to make the gap as wide as possible. Maybe that's what it is, he thought. Maybe I'm finally over her, and ready to move on. And if that's what it is—

He nodded slowly to himself. If that was what it was, once they'd found Owen—he refused to let himself think about the other possibility—maybe he and Belinda could find someplace to stay together for a while and see if there was a chance for something to happen between them. The thought cheered him more than he'd expected. The one fly in that particular ointment was that the obvious place for them to go—Kingsport—was very nearly the last place on the planet he ever wanted to go again.

The next morning dawned gray. Long before Rose and Arthur, Justin woke out of more dreams of wanderings in darkness, showered and dressed, and stumbled through a Starry Wisdom meditation that went no better than usual. That done, he made a thermos of coffee and drank two cups, and then got out the cards. He shuffled, cut, and dealt out three cards as before, turning them over one at a time.

The first card showed two hands clasped. Hand in Hand meant help, friendship, some other person he could trust and confide in, and in the left hand position it meant they'd already met. Justin nodded, guessing he knew who the cards had in mind.

The second card was the Moon; its crescent hovered yellow amid crudely drawn stars. He cupped his chin with his hand, wrestled with the various meanings the card had. Was it a sign of partial success? Did it indicate misunderstanding, deception, folly? Or did it mean, since it was in the middle place, exposure or discovery? Competing possibilities warred in his mind, but none came out on top. He went on.

The last card showed jagged peaks. The Mountain meant barriers, obstacles, or powerful enemies. On the right hand side of the reading, they weren't yet in sight. There were obstacles enough in his way, Justin thought, but was that what it meant? He couldn't tell. After a few more minutes spent staring blankly at the cards, he put them away.

Later, Rose and Arthur got up; later still, once breakfast was over and Justin helped wash the dishes, the two of them headed off into Red Hook again. Justin changed into swim trunks, got the diving mask, and waited impatiently for Belinda's signal. When it came, he went up on deck at once, looked over the side, saw a dim swirling underwater shape that had to be her, walked a short distance away and plunged straight down into the water.

She swam over to him, got the artificial gill in place, and then said, "Ready?" He nodded, and they started swimming toward the tunnel. The trip there seemed quicker than before, or was it just that the route was half-familiar? Justin couldn't tell. He followed Belinda through the harbor's murky waters, came at length to the old pilings that rose like temple pillars and the dim arch mostly filled with great blocks of stone. A quick glance at each other, and they headed through the gap in the stones and reached the tunnel beyond it.

"Okay?" Belinda asked him, and when he nodded: "Here we go."

The tunnel slipped past, and a mile or so in they reached the hidden pool beneath Parker Place. Justin waited while Belinda slipped the artificial gill off him, then swam to the surface and made for the stair. When he glanced up at the looming pier in the darkness, three points of green light stared down at him for a moment and then vanished.

He clambered up onto the steps, turned to offer Belinda a hand up. Her tentacle tightened around his hand and wrist in a reassuring squeeze. Just then, somewhere above them in the darkness, a tittering laugh sounded.

"You're prompt," the not-quite-human voice said. "Come up here. I said maybe I'd have news for you, and I do, but you won't like it. No, not at all."

* * *

The same strange being sat waiting for them, luminous as before. She gestured at the brick surface of the dock in front of her, and Justin and Belinda sat. "So," she said then. "You want to find a man named Owen Merrill. So do a good many others."

"I know," said Justin.

"And you don't wish them to find him. Good. Do you know who they are?" Before he could answer: "Good. Now attend. Erlik sees a good many things, and he talks to others who sees more, much more. Now one of those others saw your Owen Merrill going down a certain stair a dozen blocks north of here some three weeks ago. Not a stair I'd send anyone down if I ever wanted to see them again, no, for it opens onto tunnels that run north of here, up toward Cobble Hill, and there are things under there, things in the sewers and the old tunnels that you wouldn't want to meet, oh, not at all."

Justin tried to process this. "I read something about alligators," he said.

Her tittering laugh echoed off unseen brick. "Alligators? No, not for many years now. I'm sorry they're gone; I liked them." Then: "If your friend knows enough, he might be fine. Otherwise he's been eaten long since. The things that live there, they're always hungry, and now that the alligators are gone they'll take meat when they can find it." She shook her head, looked wistful. "Pity about the alligators. They were so very tasty."

Justin glanced at Belinda. Her gaze met his, fell.

"But there's someone you might ask," the creature said then. "Someone who knows the tunnels as well as I do, and who knows the things that live in them a good deal better. I've just sent Erlik to see if he'll come down and talk to you. It may be a little while, all things considered, so you'll have to put up with my company for a bit."

"If you don't mind putting up with ours," said Justin, "I'm good with that."

Mismatched eyes gave him a cool amused look.

"Is it okay," Belinda said then, "if I ask you again what your name is?"

Abruptly her gaze flicked over to Belinda. "And why would you want to know that?"

"Your name?" Belinda said, flustered. "I—I think you're a child of one of the Great Old Ones, like I am. I know a lot of humans would think of me as some kind of nameless monster, but I'm a person with a name, and so are you. You don't have to tell me, but ..."

The mismatched eyes turned toward Belinda, fixed her with a terrible intensity. A silence filled the stone chamber for what felt like geological epochs, and then the creature's tittering laugh sounded, came echoing back out of the darkness.

"Trintje," she said finally. "Trintje Sleght."

A memory surfaced in Justin's mind then. "Are you related to Agatha Sleght?"

Another silence followed, less edged. "Yes," the creature said. "I'm her daughter."

Justin stared, tried to process that. "Did you know Lady Moody?" he asked.

Trintje laughed her tittering laugh again. "Good," she said. "Good. You've learned a bit more than most, I gather. Did I know Lady Moody? Not to speak of, though I'm sure she knew me. Swaddling clothes will hide plenty, and Mother and I had plenty to hide, oh yes. Not that Lady Moody cared in the least." She leaned forward, intent. "Do you know what she came here from England to do?"

"I have no idea," Justin said. "The books I read didn't say."

Trintje laughed again. "No, I fancy not. If she'd done the thing she hoped she could do, the folk who worship the Great Old Ones would have found a safe haven here in America." Her gesture embraced a continent. "There's one who dwells in darkness who might have been able to help, if certain things had been found soon enough, and certain things done with them, but—" A gesture of her spider-limbs dismissed the possibility. "It didn't work out. And the others, they turned to shedding blood sooner than anyone thought they would. Much, much sooner."

"Like at Roodsport," said Justin.

Trintje considered him. "Now that's a rare bit of lore. How do you know about it?"

"There's a town in upstate New York that was founded by people who got away from Roodsport. I've got friends there."

"So some did escape," Trintje said, nodding slowly. "And took a certain something with them, oh, I don't doubt that at all." She eyed Justin. "A bit more than most, indeed. Here, oh, they were subtler than at Roodsport, but it came to the same thing in the end. It always does."

"Until the stars are right," Belinda said.

Trintje's laugh echoed. "Oh, I gave up waiting for the stars to come round right a long time ago. No doubt they will someday, but they won't tell me when, and I doubt they'll tell you."

Silence followed. A low rhythmic sound reached Justin's ears then, faint and faraway at first, strengthening as the moments passed. "Ah," said Trintje. "Good." Only then did Justin realize that what he was hearing was the sound of footfalls on a stair.

Dim light gleamed in the middle distance, framing a door-way, and brightened slowly. Before it was bright enough to reveal anything but its own outline, a foot-high shape of night-mare darted out of the opening in a flurry of angular legs, ran over to Trintje, rubbed both his faces against her and purred. Justin felt Belinda flinch, but his attention was fixed on the doorway, the flashlight that appeared there, and the dim presence behind it.

The flashlight's beam darted this way and that, revealing the stained cracked brick of the pier, the vaulted ceiling over the pool, black mouths of tunnels reaching this way and that. Finally the beam came to rest on Justin and Belinda.

"So," said a voice Justin recognized at once. "I admit I am surprised. Good afternoon, Mr. Martense."

Astonished, he gave Belinda's tentacle a squeeze, got to his feet. "Dr. Muñoz?"

"The very one. Perhaps you will introduce me to your companion."

Belinda stood also, giving Justin a startled look, and Muñoz aimed his flashlight at the ground and came out of the dark-ness. "Miss Belinda Marsh," Justin said, and Muñoz took her tentacle in one hand and kissed it with old world courtesy. Belinda blushed.

"Please be seated," Muñoz said then, gesturing. "I understand that the two of you are looking for someone, and it is just possible I can help you."

* * *

Aboard the *Keziah Mason*, as late afternoon light spilled through the portholes, Justin finished his story. Arthur, facing him, nodded slowly. Rose simply looked baffled. Next to Justin, demurely dressed in her seahorse-print muumuu, Belinda waited.

"Do you think we can trust this Muñoz?" Arthur said then. "Just because the two of you met him in the tunnels under Red Hook doesn't mean he's on our side."

"I know," Justin admitted. "And I didn't think of trying the Outer Sign of Recognition and seeing if he knows it. Still, he had a copy of von Junzt's book in his study, right out in the open, the way some people on our side do."

"And the stair he said Owen went down ..." Rose started, then stopped, closing her eyes.

"He gave us the address," Belinda said at once.

"It's up Corlear Avenue," Justin confirmed, "eleven blocks from Gerritsen Street. Trust me, I'm not going to suggest that anyone try to see what's down there."

Arthur nodded again after a moment. "Fair enough. You're probably right that it's worth taking a chance on Muñoz. Did he say how soon he'd be able to get word to you?"

"He wasn't sure," Belinda said. "A few days, maybe."

"Okay. We can wait—and in the meantime we can keep looking. Do you two think it's worth searching the tunnels on your own?"

"I'm really of two minds about that," said Justin. "I'd like to, but Dr. Muñoz said that there are dangerous creatures in the old sewers and tunnels."

"Alligators," said Rose unexpectedly. "I read about them in a magazine." With a little smile: "Of course it was a few years ago now."

"But you're right, of course," Arthur said. "There used to be quite a few gators down there. When I was going to the Pratt Institute I knew fellows who would go down into the tunnels and hunt them. The city government went to no end of trouble to keep it out of the press, and even so you saw stories now and then. No question, probably better not to try."

So that was settled, and when Justin went out into the cockpit to see Belinda safely into the water that night, he felt more hopeful than he'd done in too many days. They said their goodbyes and she slipped into the water, and he stood watching where she'd vanished for a long while after she was gone. The night was clear, and pale stars wavered and danced in the sea's unsteady mirror. He looked up, remembered Trintje's words about the stars, and thought: when they'll come round right isn't the only thing they won't talk about.

The same hopeful mood lingered the next day, and part of the day that followed, but by then the strain of sitting belowdecks aboard the *Keziah Mason* when Owen might need his help had begun to tell. It didn't help that Belinda had to go elsewhere for a few days. A school of haddock had slipped away from the Deep Ones further north, she'd explained; it had to be rounded up and sent back where it belonged before human fishermen found it, and every hand and tentacle was needed. Justin, recalling the way folk up at Lefferts Corners rallied around when something had to be done in a hurry, couldn't argue with that, but Belinda's absence left him feeling more morose than it should have. You hardly know her, he told himself irritably, and got even more irritated when that thought didn't affect his state at all.

By the morning of the fourth day Justin was in a foul mood, but a little after the last of the breakfast dishes was washed, the manager of the marina came strolling down the dock to tell them that the same young man who'd dropped off Justin's pills had just brought another package. Justin tipped him, went below with the package and opened it on the dining table with Rose and Arthur looking on. It proved to contain an jar of blue glass with a label pasted neatly on it saying *for immediate use*. Inside, in place of medicine, was a folded letter. Justin extracted the letter, unfolded it, and read:

> My dear Mr. Martense,
> I have some news to pass on about the case we discussed, and I am pleased to say it is considerably better news than I expected. Perhaps you or a friend could come by my office this morning.
>
> > Your obedient servant,
> > Léon Muñoz, M.D.

"Oh thank God," Justin said. "I'm on my way."

"I should go instead," said Arthur. "Those fellows are still looking for you."

"It's only eight blocks," Justin protested "What are they going to do, grab me right off the street in front of everyone?"

"I wouldn't put it past them," said Arthur. "You know what we're dealing with."

A moment passed, and then Justin let out a ragged breath. "Okay," he said. "Here." He turned the letter over, found a pen, scrawled a short note to Muñoz on it, and handed it to Arthur, who pocketed it.

"Thank you, Justin. I know it's not easy." He scooped up a hat from a locker near the companionway hatch, gave Rose a kiss, and headed topside.

Justin watched him go. For all the good I've done Owen, he thought, I might as well have stayed in Lefferts Corners. Rose tried to start a conversation, but recognized his mood quickly enough and retreated into the galley. Is this the way the rest of my life is going to be, he wondered, penned and useless, like a wild thing in a cage?

A sudden dimming of the sunlight through the portholes offered some hope of a reprieve. He looked out, saw heavy clouds rolling in from the south. "I'll be on deck," he told Rose. "Just for a few minutes." She said something agreeable, and a moment later he was in the cockpit.

A crisp wind came out of the east, lifting the heat of the sultry morning. That helped his mood a little, and so did more solitude than the cabin provided. The little marina slept in the dim uncertain light, rocked by long slow swells off the Atlantic; the space aft of the *Keziah Mason* where the old ketch had been when they'd arrived had a new tenant, a nondescript motorboat rigged for deepwater fishing; gulls winged by overhead, sounding their harsh lonely cries, and the Statue of Liberty stood in the distance, a tall green shape against the Jersey shore. Justin watched the gulls go by, wondered how soon Belinda would be back, and sat down on one of the seat locker lids on the side by the dock.

A moment later something stung his shoulder, hard. His head jerked around. A shape that looked like a dart had its tip buried in him there. He tried to reach for it, but his muscles went limp and his mind, dazzled, lost track of what he was trying to do. Figures he couldn't see clearly at all leapt out of the motorboat just aft of the *Keziah Mason* and hurried toward him on muffled feet. Long before they reached him, the world around him broke into glittering shards and then faded into blackness.

* * *

Sometime later they threw him into the trunk of a car. Later he was sure of that, though at the time all he knew was that something crashed into his side, darkness followed, and what had hit him began to rattle and lurch. Whatever they'd used to drug him dazzled his mind and left his muscles limp and leaden. He tried to move, tried to think, could do neither.

The rattling and lurching stopped after a time he could not measure. Light spilled over him again, and they hauled him out of the trunk, carried him through a door into dimness. Voices spilled past him, but he couldn't make the words make sense.

Another door, another dimly lit space, and then they laid him down on a hard surface and fastened straps across him, pinning arms, legs, body. One set of hard shapes swung up to press against both sides of his head, holding it fixed in place. Another fastened around the fingers of each hand, holding the fingers straight. Someone forced his mouth open, pushed what felt like a rubber ball into it, fastened that in place.

Once they'd finished, most of them left the room. One stayed behind, though Justin's dazed mind couldn't put the fragmentary glimpses together into a face and a form. Time passed,

Justin lay in enforced motionlessness, and the one who had stayed behind paced back and forth for a while, checked the straps that held Justin pinned, then left the room, locking the door behind him. Justin heard the rattle of the lock, followed by silence.

More time passed, and the drug's grip on Justin's mind and body began to loosen. The vague dim space around him became a windowless room lit by a single bare light bulb in the center of the ceiling. He was lying on something that was pushed up against a wall, and if he strained to look off past his feet he could just see the upper end of a door. The restraints that held him gradually made sense to him: they wanted to keep him from being able to cast a spell, if he knew anything of sorcery.

He'd finally manage to think his way through this when another door whispered open up past his head. Footfalls, quick and wary, followed, and what felt unexpectedly like a child's hand touched his scalp. Justin heard the sudden hiss of indrawn breath. A moment later two small hands came to rest on the top of his head, and a strange sensation like the closing of a fist rippled through the space inside his skull.

Then the small hands left his head, the quick footfalls darted away, and the door somewhere up past his head whispered shut. Moments passed, and Justin struggled to clear his thoughts. It was important to do that, he knew, but he couldn't remember why. It was important to try to loosen the straps that held him, he knew that too, and he made a first vague effort in that direction, with no particular result.

The lock rattled again, and the door opened. Someone Justin couldn't see came in, examined him for a few moments, left again. Two more people came in a few minutes later, talking in low tones, then went out a second time, leaving the door ajar. Their voices tumbled over one another somewhere just outside the door, a vague shapeless mutter at first. A little later, as his mind cleared further, he caught scattered words he was able to follow: "still experimental," "not enough time after," "could have unexpected reactions."

Another voice broke in then, a woman's voice, cold and exact. "We haven't had an opportunity like this in four decades," she said. "We have very little time left, our allies aren't willing to wait, and the procedure's reliable enough. You have my authorization. Do it."

He heard the door swing all the way open a moment later, and made one last futile attempt to loosen the straps that held him pinned. Then a needle jabbed his arm, and darkness swallowed him.

CHAPTER 7

THE EMPTY CIRCLE

He blinked awake, knowing that something had changed.

"He should be conscious now," said a low voice off to his left: female, elderly, precise. Footfalls stirred the heavy air, and a man spoke close by, just to his right: "Mr. Martense?"

Something had changed. He felt an immense stillness around him, as though the world had gone silent forever—but he could hear the voices, a faint rhythmic beep that echoed his pulse, the soft clatter of fingers on a computer keyboard not far off.

"Mr. Martense? Can you hear me?" the man asked again.

His eyes focused. He was flat on his back in a dimly lit room, lying on something that felt like a cheap foam mattress. The man he'd heard stood by the side of the bed, leaning a little over him: short and muscular, with olive skin, black hair, an ugly scar creasing one side of his face.

He was expected to respond, he realized then. "Yes," he said aloud.

"Good," said the man. "How are you feeling?"

The question gave him the word he needed to understand the void. Feeling? He could remember feelings—love, hatred, rage, delight, misery, a thousand others—but where they had been he could perceive only a vast gray stillness that contained nothing at all. "I'm not," he said.

The man grinned. "Sorry," he said. "Of course not. What's your physical condition?"

Justin turned his attention to his body, found nothing out of the ordinary. "As usual."

"Good. I want you to listen to me very closely, Mr. Martense."

"Okay."

"You were under the control of hostile nonhuman beings. I know I don't have to convince you that they exist—our files indicate that you've encountered at least three of their over-lords and a much larger number of rank and file nonhumans and hybrid monstrosities, and that you've fathered a hybrid child. Is that correct, Mr. Martense?"

"Yes," Justin said.

"They controlled your mind and your feelings, Mr. Martense. They told you that you were receiving initiations and practicing spiritual exercises, but those were all ways to keep you from thinking clearly, so that you would obey the nonhumans and oppose us. Do you know what I'm talking about, Mr. Martense?"

"Yes," Justin said again.

That got him another grin. "Okay, good. We used a procedure to break their hold on you and keep them from getting control of your mind again. I know it's probably very unsettling right now but it really was for your own good, and you'll get used to it in a few days. I know other people who've had it done and they're fine."

Justin considered that. The gaping void where his own feelings had been left him unexpectedly sensitive to signs of the feelings of others, and he could sense something of what was moving through the man's mind. He wasn't telling the whole truth, Justin knew, but his words offered another clue. Owen had spoken of something like it—

The memory came through all at once: Owen sitting near him in a leather armchair, the golden sunlight of a Kingsport summer spilling through the windows at the room's far end.

Owen was talking about someone he'd known in college, who'd sided with the Radiance, who'd had something done to her brain that turned her into a hollow shell of herself.

I'm in the hands of the Radiance, Justin thought, and they've done something to my brain. The thought hovered in his mind, without meaning—but it would have meant a tremendous amount to him before the procedure. Memories cascaded through his mind, reminding him of what he would have felt about that, what he would have wanted to do.

"We need your help," the man went on. "Let me rephrase that. Humanity needs your help. The nonhumans are the enemies of humanity, the enemies of reason and progress. They enslaved humanity in the past, using our weaknesses against us. They're trying to do it again. There are three things they need to do in order to make that possible, and they've already accomplished two of them. We need your help to stop them from doing the third."

"Go on," Justin said. Half his attention, maybe less, was on the man's words. The rest pored over memories from before the procedure. He would have had strong negative feelings, he realized, about being a captive of the Radiance, and even stronger and harsher feelings about helping them in any way. They had damaged his brain to keep him from feeling those emotions. What did that imply?

"You know a man named Owen Merrill. We need to find him. He's a traitor to humanity, a high-ranking cultist serving the nonhumans, and he's associated with a much more important servant of theirs, a human-looking hybrid named Jenny Chaudronnier. He's been sent by his masters to do the third thing I've mentioned. We know what it is."

Memories of futile searching stirred a vague curiosity in Justin's mind. "Tell me."

The man sent a quick questioning glance off to Justin's left, where the other voice had been. Whatever silent response he got seemed to settle the matter. "Okay. There's a place buried deep underneath Brooklyn, down in the bedrock, a cavern that contains archaic machines, sealed away behind defenses we can't breach. They were put there by another intelligent species a long time before humanity evolved, for reasons we don't have time to get into now. Merrill's trying to reach the machines and activate them. We have to stop him."

Justin considered the man, and knew that he was lying: there was ample time for a full explanation. He filed away the knowledge, listened.

The man leaned forward. "We're pretty sure you know where Merrill is. You've been out of sight for days while your associates wandered around Red Hook distracting us. Our best guess is that you've been underground, down in the same tunnels Merrill is exploring, and that you've associated with cultists and hybrid monstrosities there. Is that correct?"

Justin surveyed his memories. "Yes, it is."

"Good. Mr. Martense, we need you to lead us to Owen Merrill. Will you do that?"

Justin regarded the man. The stillness they'd made in his mind left him acutely aware of the clamor in theirs. The man leaning over him was full of a hard-edged excitement that stirred memories of hunting deer in the hills near Chorazin. The woman further off looked on with clinical interest just faintly touched with contempt. They wanted Owen dead, that was certain, and if they found out about Belinda and Trintje they would want them dead as well.

That meant nothing, but Justin knew it would have meant a great deal before the procedure. Abruptly he decided on a course of action. "Yes," he said. "I'll help you."

* * *

They left him in the room for what he guessed was over an hour. He was never alone. The old woman with the precise voice sat in a chair a few yards away from him, and a younger woman sat near the door at a computer workstation, her fingers tapping on the keyboard any time he moved or spoke. Neither of them spoke to him, though, and that gave him the mental space he needed to explore what had been done to him and decide what to do.

The Radiance, he thought. The enemies of the Great Old Ones, the heirs of the men who'd desecrated seven temples older than humanity, who'd stolen tremendous powers by that act and used those ruthlessly to establish their secret mastery over the world. He remembered with photographic clarity his brief encounter with one of their negation teams in Chorazin, recalled also stories he'd been told by people he'd trusted, tales of desperate escapes and bitter struggles against an implacable foe. Those were abstractions to him, but they hadn't been abstract before the Radiance had damaged his brain. He assessed the memories, weighed them against what the man had said to him, considered how to follow up on the decision he'd made.

With an effort, he recalled the words he'd heard just before they'd anesthetized him. Still experimental, not enough time after, could have unexpected reactions: he noted the implications, compared them to his experiences. With his feelings replaced by a blank space, his thoughts moved with an unfamiliar speed, laid out the probable meanings before him.

First, the people he'd seen hadn't had the procedure done on them; he could read their emotions in their faces. That didn't fit with the claim that the procedure was purely a way of shielding him from whatever influence the Great Old Ones might exert, since Radiance personnel would have good reason to want to avoid any such influence.

Second, for all their talk about reason, the people around him were just as swayed by prejudices and emotional reactions as other humans. The pulse of loathing he'd sensed every time the young man had used the word "hybrid" showed that clearly enough. He measured his memories of Laura, Belinda,

Jenny, and his son Robin against that phrase, noted the mismatch, judged the young man's words accordingly.

Finally, they knew of a risk in the period just after the procedure. That suggested that something in his present condition made him unreliable as a tool of theirs. What?

The answer came back immediately: his memories. In the disorientation that the silencing of his feelings left in him, he noted a reflexive urge to turn to memories of former emotion as a source of guidance. And what did his remembered memories suggest he should do?

That response came back just as swiftly. He would have wanted to protect Rose, Arthur, and Belinda. He would have wanted to keep the Radiance away from them, and from Owen. And the Radiance personnel—

He would have wanted them dead. He pondered the thought in the gray featureless clarity of his mind, as though it was a matter of totting up figures. No, there was no doubt: he would have wanted every one of them dead, and if circumstances permitted, he would have wanted them to die shrieking in agony. He decided to see if he could make that happen.

Some time later the door came open and the man who'd spoken to him came in, leading an older man with a heavy-jowled face, grizzled hair in a military buzz cut, unremarkable civilian clothes. "Mr. Martense," said the younger man. "You said you'd help us. We'd like to find Owen Merrill right away if we can. Can you tell us how to do that?"

He'd already worked out most of the details by then, but realized he needed a piece of data. "When your people captured me, did anyone see them?"

The older man laughed a short hard laugh like a cough. "Yes. Someone aboard your sailboat opened fire on our team while our boat was still in range. Rules of engagement were not to return fire, so we lost one team member before the others could get belowdecks."

Rose, Justin thought, remembering the wickedly precise aim she'd learned as a girl in the Adirondacks, helping fill her family's larder with game. "It'll have to happen soon, then. Right away, if you have people ready."

"We've got two teams prepped," the older man said. "Where are they going?"

"They're coming with me," Justin said. "To a place in Red Hook. I can get your people into the underground tunnels there where Owen is, but I'll have to be with them. Partly there are passwords and signs, partly the guardians will recognize me." A difficulty in his plan surfaced, but an instant was enough to find a solution. "I'll tell them I escaped from you and need to talk to Owen right away. That should work."

The next moment was the one that counted, he knew that. He considered the two men, saw that the emotions that moved behind their eyes showed no sign of doubt. Something else stirred there, something he thought he recognized.

Fanaticism. He'd seen it in other faces often enough. They were sure they were right, sure no one could possibly have a valid reason to disagree with them, convinced that once Justin's emotions were silenced he would certainly rally to their side. In the gray emptiness of his mind he could see exactly how to test his guess, and if he was right—

"This is really important, isn't it?" he said aloud.

The younger man nodded. "Right now, it's more important than anything else in the world. We have to stop them from awakening the Third Sign."

"I'll do what I can," Justin replied.

The sudden grin that spread across the younger man's face gave Justin the answer he waited for. "Good. We'll be leaving for Red Hook in an hour or so."

The older man turned to look at his companion. "You'll be taking command personally?"

"That's the best option."

"Fair enough. I'll inform the dirigency." He turned and walked away.

Justin looked up at the younger man then. You are going to die soon, he thought, and so are all the team members that go with you.

The next thought followed at once, with perfect calmness: and so am I.

* * *

When he went down the stairs to the waiting car, he glanced around, saw nothing that he recognized. Somewhere in New York City? It seemed likely, but he couldn't tell and couldn't think of a reason why it mattered. He climbed into the back seat they offered him, waited while the others climbed in. Then doors slammed and the car pulled away from the curb.

Surface streets slid past, and then the car turned onto an expressway. The towers of Manhattan rose out of low-lying fog to Justin's right, dotted here and there with points of light. Closer, an urban landscape he guessed was Brooklyn's spread below the traffic, half visible through the murky air. Searching his memories, he recalled the frenetic life he'd sensed surging through New York City. That feeling had gone tumbling into the same void as all the others. He filed the knowledge, certain that it no longer mattered at all.

At length the car left the expressway and wove its way through streets that seemed half familiar to Justin. The shape of a church he knew he'd seen before appeared briefly, framed by the buildings edging a side street, and vanished in turn. Finally the car pulled over to the curb and stopped, and the young man with the scar turned to face Justin. "Ready?"

"Yes." He waited while someone else opened the door, climbed out.

He was standing on Gerritsen Street, he realized then, just west of Van Brunt Street. The streets of Red Hook seemed emptier than usual, but half a dozen cars pulling up at intervals along the street helped change that. Men and women in generic civilian clothes climbed out of them, extracted long metal shapes from the trunks, made off in various directions. Others loitered near their cars, began to follow Justin once he was far enough that they could make their pursuit look casual.

Fog off the Upper Bay coiled in the streets, turned the streetlight at the intersection of Gerritsen and Van Brunt into a vague orange blur. Further off, night wrapped New York City in a featureless murmur of noise and a dim glow of muted light. Somewhere nearby, he could hear music—an intricate drumbeat, a voice chanting tautly woven verses over the top—and caught the subtle details that told him it was blaring from a boom box on someone's shoulder.

Arthur and the others would be far away by now, Justin guessed. Rose would have been able to tell Arthur and Belinda what had happened, and that news would give them all ample reason to escape. None of that mattered to him, but his memories told him that it had mattered very much, would still matter if the Radiance hadn't damaged his brain. That was enough for the moment, enough for what he meant to do.

He walked up Gerritsen, passed Van Brunt, and kept going, along a dozen desolate blocks of machine shops and abandoned warehouses. Corlear Avenue wasn't far, just this side of the Gowanus Expressway. From there, Corlear ran north toward Cobble Hill, and passed a certain door that opened off an alley and a certain stair that slanted down into darkness.

Over the endless murmur of the city, he could hear the faint stealthy sounds of the men following him. Another piece of his plan fell into place. The backup force would take a different route—possibilities unfolded themselves in his mind—but so long as secrecy still mattered and they didn't dare use helicopters or explosives, they would have to go charging through the same door, down the same stair, into the same tunnels to meet the same fate.

Gerritsen Street wasn't quite empty. A few people straggled along it, most of them visibly drunk, and a few half-derelict cars and unlicensed taxis rattled down it, headlights blurring in the mist. By the time Justin got to the corner of Corlear Avenue, though, the passersby had thinned out, and Corlear itself ran straight and silent between abandoned buildings. He turned north onto it, heard the others following.

Streets to either side reached away into the vague unquiet night. Patches of fog-blurred light showed streetlights at long intervals; blocks away, too far off to matter, light and noise spilled from a corner bar here, a nightclub there. Sparse traffic hummed over the Gowanus Expressway off to one side, a dark presence against a darker sky. Justin watched the street signs, kept his pace steady as the alley he needed to reach came into sight.

A streetlamp close by cast orange light down onto the sidewalk, and the brooding glow that spread through the fog allowed him to see a short distance into the alley. The stair was unmistakable, descending a short distance to a door he could only half see, and going down from there into the tunnels Trintje Sleght had warned him about, the tunnels full of hungry things.

They would eat him soon, along with the members of the negation team. He would have wanted that. He knew that with perfect certainty.

He kept walking, listened to the night's sounds, heard the low hiss of whispering voices as the negation team coordinator sent his men to their places. Ahead of him, in the dim recesses of the alley, the rest of the Radiant force was already deployed: he could see human shapes crouched behind stairs and in alcoves, assault rifles in hand, waiting for the order to rush the door the moment it opened.

Something pale moved in a window looking down on the alley as he neared the stair. He noticed it without surprise: a child's face, gazing down at him briefly with a solemn intent look and then suddenly gone. The face stirred a chord of memory, but that meant nothing to Justin, and he kept walking.

His footfalls echoed down the alley, past looming shadows so deep the light from the streetlamp could not penetrate them.

He reached the head of the stair, and the shadows lunged.

The young man who followed Justin cried out in horror and pulled a pistol from his pocket. Justin turned to face him, ready for the release the bullet would bring. Before the man could level his gun, though, one of the shadows sprang at him from behind. A formless black shape struck him, knocking him to the ground and sending a spray of blood across the pavement. A moment later, blackness engulfed the man with a crunch that would have been sickening if Justin had been able to feel sick.

Justin turned, motivated by mild curiosity. All around him, chaos spun and flared. Automatic weapons spat three-round bursts, shattering the unquiet night. Voices shouted orders or cried out in terror, and massive black shapes surged with appalling speed, flinging themselves out of the darkness and gaping wide. The guns and voices fell silent in quick succession. One last cry of terror echoed in the stillness that followed, and that was all.

The black shapes considered Justin then. There were six of them in all, he realized, irregular dark masses maybe ten feet across, faintly iridescent in the dim glow from the streetlight. They regarded him with pale greenish eyes that shimmered with a pallid luminosity. A moment later the shapes slid back into the shadows and sank noiselessly out of sight. The negation teams were gone as though they had never existed at all.

A moment of utter silence passed. Then, close by, a door opened into darkness. "God *damn*," said Arthur's voice. "Justin?"

He turned. "Yeah. Where did you get the shoggoths?"

"We didn't," said Arthur. A moment later: "Are you okay?"

"No." He could see Arthur dimly in the faint light, and saw the rifle he carried. "They did something to my brain." Meeting Arthur's horrified expression: "The same thing they did to that college friend of Owen's."

"Shelby Adams."

"Yeah." Then, before Arthur could say anything else: "Please shoot me. I know I wouldn't have wanted to live like this."

A frozen moment passed, and then Arthur took his arm, and said, "We'll settle that later. Come on."

He let himself be drawn up the stairs and through the door. Quick footfalls and the gleam of a flashlight announced Rose's arrival; she saw Justin, stopped in her tracks. "Oh my God."

Justin, seeing her, noted a vague curiosity. "How did you get here?"

"Another of those typed notes," said Arthur. Then, with a brittle laugh: "That and Mazurewicz's car. He didn't want to lend it to me, but we settled that."

"Did you kill him?" Justin asked.

Both of them gave him long silent looks. "No," said Arthur, "though I would have. Money did the trick."

"We should get out of here," Rose said then.

"Yeah." Arthur took hold of Justin's arm. "Come on. The car's two blocks away, and we're going to have to get moving. If the Radiance has any brains at all, they've got a backup team on its way."

Justin let himself be guided into the darkness. It doesn't matter, he told himself. I can die a little later if that's more convenient.

* * *

The car lurched to a halt on an unfamiliar street. Justin got out in response to Arthur's gesture, stood on the sidewalk as the car drove away. "He'll be back in a few minutes," Rose said. "Come on." She took his arm, led him onto a dock he didn't recognize.

"Where is this?" he asked.

"A public pier," said Rose. "We came here as soon as Arthur got back."

"Good," said Justin, noting the evasive strategy they'd adopted. He let himself be guided along the pier. The black waters of the Upper Bay spread out before him, inviting. His usefulness had ended, that was clear, and all it would take was a few steps—

"Please don't," said Rose.

"Why not?"

He could see the bleak helpless look on her face, the search for a pretext. "They're going to want to study you. To figure out what those—those people did to you."

Pretext or not, it sent a cascade of thoughts moving through Justin's mind, pointing to possibilities he hadn't considered. "Okay."

"As soon as Arthur gets back, we're going to get out of here and cross over to the Staten Island side," Rose said. "Please, Justin. Come with me."

Their footfalls drummed on the dock. A turn, a few more moments hurrying between the dim shapes of other boats, and then the *Keziah Mason* loomed up ahead. Justin clambered aboard, let Rose guide him down through the companionway hatch, get him settled by the table, and head back topside.

Justin waited. The emptiness in him had swallowed any reason to do anything else. After a while, he heard a splash and then voices, followed by a sudden horrified outcry, more voices, and then another splash. None of it meant anything. It had meant something once, he knew, but he could not remember what, or why.

Hard and rhythmic, the sound of running feet reached him then. Arthur's voice followed, low and forceful. Rose answered him. Muffled noises told of the sails going up, and the *Keziah Mason* slid away from the dock. The engine stayed silent. Justin guessed that the running lights would go on only after the shores of Red Hook were well astern.

The hatch opened, and footfalls sounded in the companionway behind him. "Can I get you anything, Justin?" Rose asked.

He turned to face her, considered the question. "No."

Rose gave him a dismayed look, and went back up through the companionway hatch.

Time passed, and lights glittered in changing patterns outside the portholes. Justin sensed the slowing of the boat, a turn to port, footfalls on the deck. All movement stopped except for the slow rhythm of the waves. Then a different set of sounds reached him through the open companionway: quiet splashings, followed by low voices and then by a soft rustle of cloth.

The cabin light clicked on, dazzling him. A voice said, "Justin?"

Memory told him that it was Belinda, told him also that he would have wanted to greet her. He stood up and turned, saw the sudden change in her expression, heard the sharp intake of her breath. That communicated something, he knew, but the memory would not come clear.

Behind her, another woman climbed down through the companionway: naked except for ornaments of gold, her skin an unexpected color between olive and very pale blue-green. Her fingers were webbed, and her feet, also webbed, splayed like a frog's.

"Justin, this is Mha'alh'yi," Belinda said, indicating the other woman. "She's a Deep One sorceress. She's going to try to figure out what they did to you."

He nodded, more because he could tell that she expected it than for any other reason. The Deep One regarded him for a minute, then said something to Belinda in a language that sounded like bubbling water. She turned to Justin then, and in accented English said, "Sit down. Relax."

Justin did as he was told, sitting again, willing his muscles to lose some of their tension.

"Good," she said then. "My eyes. Look into them."

He met her gaze as she sat down across from him, noted without curiosity the sea-green color of her eyes, the gold flecks that sparkled in them. A moment later he realized he could not look away from them. A moment after that, his thoughts dissolved like mist.

Time passed unmeasured, and then he was blinking as his thoughts cleared. At first he thought that only a few moments had passed, but the change in the faint background noises and the dim gray light from the portholes told him otherwise: dawn, he guessed, or close to it.

"It is well," said Mha'alh'yi, still facing him. He glanced at her, saw sweat beaded on her brow, hollowness around her eyes. She'd spent hours of hard work on him, he knew then.

"Can you do anything?" This from Rose, in the galley. "To help him, I mean."

"Maybe. They have destroyed certain—" She struggled for a word, said something in the bubbling-water language.

"Cells," said Belinda.

"Yes. Certain cells in the brain. The parts that feel, they are still there, they were shielded somehow, and other cells might make a channel to flow—" Her hands gestured, like water surging around an obstacle. "There is a chance it will work."

Justin measured that against his memories. "Do it. Please."

Mha'alh'yi considered him. "There will be pain."

He wondered briefly why that should concern him, and then recalled how he'd responded to pain in times past. It was becoming harder to remember such things, harder to hold onto the awareness of what had been taken from him. The fact would have terrified him, he knew, if he could feel anything at all. "That doesn't matter," he said.

In response, the sorceress closed her eyes and placed her hands on Justin's head.

Minutes passed, and an odd sensation rippled through Justin's mind, like air rising from hot pavement. It shifted as though from place to place, first distorting his vision, then his hearing, then his thoughts, and finally the gray emptiness where his feelings had been.

"Ah." The word was scarcely a whisper. "There."

An instant later agony exploded white-hot behind Justin's eyes, kicked him in the midriff, shot down each of his limbs. He doubled up convulsively and clutched at his head, and a low cry forced its way through his teeth as he slid forward. Then it got worse. The only thing that kept him from slamming his head repeatedly against the nearest hard surface, just to make it stop, was the softness that pressed suddenly against him, the curved shapes that wrapped around him and reminded him that the world held something besides incandescent pain.

Moments or millennia passed, and the agony began to ebb. Only when it was mostly gone did he realize that it had never been physical pain at all. Terror and rage, hatred and wrenching grief, everything he would have felt from the moment the Radiance had damaged his brain to the moment that Mha'alh'yi healed him, all of it burst into his awareness at once, and in its wake—

He could feel again. Gasping and shuddering, he reached for the softness that curved around him, clung to it in desperate gratitude.

A tangled shape of sound drifted past him, and after a moment he realized it was a voice, and not quite human. The words took shape in his mind after another moment: "It is well. I think he is healed." Mha'alh'yi, he thought then. That was whose voice it was: Mha'alh'yi the Deep One sorceress. Another piece of the universe drifted slowly back into place.

Other voices, further off, talked of something, but Justin couldn't make sense of their words. Yet another voice, quiet, sounded much closer, and that was the voice that mattered, he was sure of it. Minutes passed before he was sure that the voice came from the softness that embraced him. More slipped by before he realized that what it was saying was his name.

He had eyes. That thought emerged suddenly, and made him force them open. Clear focus took time, but eventually the blur bending over him became Belinda's face, the softness that pressed against him her body, her tentacles the curves that encircled him. The emotion that surged up in him as he looked into her face was unexpected only in its intensity.

But another perception rose in him then like an incoming tide, heavy and shapeless. Mha'alh'yi gave voice to it, saying, "He will need to sleep." She was right, he knew that, and tried to speak, but the words went tumbling away into darkness, and so did he.

CHAPTER 8

THE NIGHT OCEAN

He surfaced slowly from dark dreams, felt warmth pressing against him long before he guessed at its source. A salt odor not quite that of the harbor tinged each breath. Time passed before he opened his eyes, and when he did, the first thing he saw was a head of curling brown hair resting on his shoulder. He was lying on his back, naked, in the forward double berth aboard the *Keziah Mason*, and Belinda was nestled up close against him. He had a sheet over him and she had her muumuu on, but those thin layers of cotton were all that separated them, and he was exquisitely aware of every curve of her body.

He considered that, felt her slow soft breathing, felt also a tremor move through her tentacles, echoing some dream of hers. A dozen different reasons why she might be there rose in his mind, contended with one another, and the feelings knotted into those reasons contended as well. Maybe it was a reaction to what the Radiance had done to him, maybe it was a side effect of Mha'alh'yi's counterspell, but his emotions felt raw and sharp-edged, more insistent than he remembered. Finally, lacking any other way to settle his confusion, he said, "Belinda?"

She raised her head abruptly, blinking. "Oh, I'm sorry. I didn't expect to fall asleep." Then: "I hope you don't mind.

Mha'alh'yi said that somebody should stay with you for a few hours, and this seemed like the best way to do it."

"I don't mind at all," he said. "What happened to my clothes?"

Her nose wrinkled. "They were a pretty fair mess once Mha'alh'yi finished. We had to wash you before we put you to bed."

"I bet." He watched her face, saw the slight flush behind the olive-green complexion and guessed what sent it there. "You held me the whole time, didn't you?"

"Well, yes," she said, looking away, a little embarrassed, a little—what?

"Belinda," he said again. She met his gaze then, and her look told him everything he needed to know. He reached for her, drew her face downward. She let out a little shuddering sigh, pressed her lips against his, opened them.

He'd thought to kiss her once and then tell her about his feelings, but the moment had its own momentum and brushed aside his plans with contemptuous ease. Her tongue, long and pointed like her tentacles, curled around his. Her tentacles and his hands pushed the muumuu up out of the way and the sheet down. She drew her lips away from his just long enough to pull the garment off and fling it somewhere else. One of his hands found her wetness, one of her tentacles coiled around his manhood, and then she raised her hips, straddled him, twined tentacles around his hips and legs. She cried out as he slid into her; after that, the tidal rhythms of their blood took over and everything else went far away.

Afterward, she nestled against his shoulder again. "I hope I didn't rush things too much."

Justin gave her a startled look. "I thought I was the one who rushed things."

She glanced up at him, smiled, said nothing.

"Belinda, you've been really good to me," he went on. "Not just now, ever since we met. I've been thinking for a while now

about whether we can spend some time together and see if …"
He let the sentence trail away, seeing her smile crumple. "What is it?"

She gave him a look he couldn't read. "Jenny."

He let his head sink back onto the pillow. "That's over and done with," he said. "I drew a line under it and walked away four years ago."

"I didn't know that," Belinda replied. "The thing is, she's here."

"Jenny?" His head jerked back up off the pillow. "Here on board?"

"No, she came south on a big cabin cruiser her family has. It's docked right next to us. Rose and Arthur are there now, and so is Mha'alh'yi." She glanced at him again. "She got here a few days ago, I think, and when I went to talk to the Deep Ones and see if one of their sorceresses could help you, they let her know what had happened. She came aboard the *Keziah Mason* after we got you tucked into bed, and we talked a little before I went to make sure you were okay. She was horrified that we were here at all."

He let out a frustrated sigh, lowered his head again. "I bet." Then, as much to distract himself as for any better reason: "Was she the one who sent the shoggoths?"

"I don't think so," said Belinda. "She looked surprised when Arthur told her about them."

"I hope the shoggoths are okay," Justin said after a moment.

"Oh, they'll be fine. A bullet wound isn't much more than a bruise for a shoggoth. It takes high explosives or flamethrowers to kill them."

"Good," he said, and let the conversation lapse. A silence came and went, and he found himself wishing just for a moment that he didn't have to fit his life around shoggoths and the spawn of the Great Old Ones. The soft curves of Belinda's tentacles reminded him a moment later of the consolations that entanglement brought with it, and he raised his head again, stretched a little, and kissed the top of her head.

She nestled down against him with a little sigh, and things might have gone from there if his stomach hadn't chosen that moment to growl loudly in protest.

"You must be really hungry," Belinda said then, laughing. "How long has it been since you had anything to eat?"

"Since yesterday breakfast," Justin admitted.

"Father Dagon." She sat up, and Justin found himself gazing abstractedly at the subtle curves of her bare body, the elegance of her tentacles. "Let's get you something, then. I bet Rose left a late lunch, if you'd like that."

"You know," said Justin, "I think I would."

* * *

He took the time to shower and dress before they ate, knowing that they might have visitors at any moment. Belinda borrowed the shower stall as soon as he was done with it and then put on her other muumuu with the same thought in mind. True to form, Rose had left a plate of sandwiches in the fridge with a note reading *For Belinda and Justin*. Outside, a light haze spread over the marina, making the summer heat even more stifling than it had been.

They set the plate and bottles of cider on the table, and Justin watched the way she ate, holding her sandwich poised between two curved tentacle tips. Every motion she made, every expression that danced across her features, dazzled him. It was a familiar reaction; he'd spent the first years after meeting Jenny at Chorazin in a state not too far from it, and labored to recapture the same state with the two women he'd been with more recently. He tried to clear his thoughts, failed, sank gratefully into the warm daze that came from contemplating her.

That only lasted a little while, though, before it was overpowered by other thoughts. Sitting there in the familiar cabin, with daylight spilling on the table between them and the dim nameless sounds of Staten Island and the Upper Bay as background,

Justin found his mind circling back incessantly over the days he'd spent in Red Hook, his failed attempts to find Owen, the ease with which the Radiance had captured him and the state from which Mha'alh'yi's sorceries had rescued him. It helped to know that the Radiance hadn't yet captured or killed Owen; it helped, too, that his plan had succeeded—but how had the shoggoths known just where to lie in wait? All things considered, he thought bleakly, Owen probably should have sent for someone else. A glance up from his sandwich to Belinda reminded him of the one thing worth keeping that had come out of the whole business, and he smiled despite his mood.

The two of them had just finished lunch when the companionway hatch opened a few tentative inches. The voice that followed, instantly familiar to Justin, was just as tentative. "May I come in?"

"Sure," said Justin, and braced himself.

She climbed through the hatch, closed it behind her, turned toward them. She'd aged just a little since the last time he'd seen her. The mop of unruly mouse-colored hair was edged with scattered strands of silver, the thin pale face slightly more angular, but none of the changes had done anything to unravel the tangle of frustrated feelings she roused in him.

"Hi, Jenny," said Belinda.

"Hi, Belinda. Justin, I'm glad you're okay."

"Thanks."

"You're welcome. Would it be intolerably rude of me to ask to take a look at your brain?"

Justin choked with laughter despite himself: "As long as you leave it where it belongs."

That earned him a smile that stirred too many memories. "I promise."

She came over to where he was sitting, raised both hands. He expected her to place them on his scalp as Mha'alh'yi had, but instead she held the palms a few inches away and closed her eyes. The sensation he felt inside his head was just as different: in place of the shimmer like heat rising from summer pavement, he sensed a quick flickering movement of light winding its way without hesitation to its goal.

"That's really curious," Jenny said then, opening her eyes. "The way the Radiance did that. I wonder why." She shook her head. "I'm glad Mha'alh'yi was able to work around it." She found a seat that folded down from a nearby bulkhead, settled on it. "Do you mind if I ask the two of you some questions? I've talked to Rose and Arthur, of course, but I think you two know more about what's going on here than they do, and I'm still baffled."

"Sure," said Justin, trying to suppress a feeling of unease.

"Maybe you could each just tell me how you ended up coming here and what happened once you got here," said Jenny.

Justin nodded uncomfortably, glanced at Belinda, caught the flicker of worry in her eyes, and said, "Okay." As briefly as he could, he described the letter he'd gotten in Lefferts Corners, the messages he'd sent and received, the journey down the Hudson, and his futile attempts to find Owen thereafter. He mentioned the search for the underwater tunnel but repeated the same story they'd told to Rose and Arthur, and left out Trintje Sleght. His memories from the time he'd spent in the hands of the Radiance needed less trimming, and to judge from her reaction, at least one of the details drove any other questions out of her mind.

"The Third Sign," she said. "You're sure that's the phrase the man used."

Justin nodded. "I'm sure of it." Then, looking away: "I don't know what it means."

"Neither do I, yet." Jenny turned to Belinda. "And you?"

"Me? My story's a lot simpler." Belinda leaned forward, propped her chin on her tentacles. "You remember the way I kept jumping around like a cat on a hot sidewalk once Laura told us that something might have happened to Owen? As soon as Justin's message arrived, and I knew that someone was trying to find him, I couldn't stay in Kingsport. I swam down here as quickly as I could, found Justin, searched for the tunnel, spent a lot of time waiting, and then went to find Mha'alh'yi once Arthur and Rose brought Justin back. That's all."

Jenny took that in, nodded after a moment. "Thank you." She drew in a breath. "I know neither of you are going to like this, but you both need to go somewhere else, somewhere safer. It's much more important than either of you realize."

"Not a chance," Justin said flatly. "Not until I find out what's happened to Owen."

"Justin, please. There's nothing you can do for him."

Her words matched his own unwelcome reflections so precisely that he turned away, hard. "In other words, I'm useless."

"That's not what I meant," said Jenny.

Justin's gaze snapped back toward her. "That's practically what you said."

"Justin, please." Her gaze met his, unhappy but unyielding. "I've already talked to Rose and Arthur. They've agreed to take the *Keziah Mason* out to sea first thing tomorrow, and go on with the voyage the three of you planned. Please go with them."

Dismay settled in him, cold and heavy. If Arthur had already agreed to Jenny's plan, he knew, nothing he could say would change his mind—and without the *Keziah Mason* as safe haven and Rose and Arthur to handle the parts of the search that had to be done in daylight, the chance that he could do anything for Owen was as small as Jenny claimed. He glanced at Belinda, saw the bleak huddled mood expressed in every curve of her tentacles, and knew that she wouldn't refuse Jenny's request. He let out a ragged breath and said, "Okay."

"You'll go?" Jenny asked.

"I said okay," Justin snapped. Anger at her and anger at himself twisted into a bitter knot, and all at once he couldn't stand the thought of sitting there a moment longer. Lacking other options, he hauled himself off the bench seat and went to the door to the forward cabin, said over his shoulder: "I'll go."

The door opened, closed behind him. He slumped onto the berth, shoulders hunched, staring at nothing he could name.

* * *

Minutes passed, and then the door opened quietly. "Justin," said Belinda, "she's gone. I can leave you alone if you want."

He glanced up at her, managed a smile. "No. I'd like your company."

"I'm glad," she said. She closed the door and settled next to him, and a pair of tentacles slipped around his waist, comforting. "I know you're upset," she said after a moment.

"Yeah. I just wish she hadn't been so up front about telling me to run along and play."

She drew in a sudden sharp breath as though to say something, and then apparently thought better of it.

"The thing is, she's right," he went on. The words didn't come easily, but they came nonetheless. "I really don't have any business being here in the first place. I don't know a thing about sorcery, I'm not a vet with combat experience like Owen or Arthur, I don't have any of Rose's skills, and she's got lots of them—" He forced a smile. "I don't even have tentacles. I have no idea why Owen sent for me. I'm just an ordinary guy whose family got tangled up in a mess they never understood, and I was dumb enough to fall in love with the wrong person and spend seven years poking my nose into things I have no business trying to deal with. It probably shouldn't hurt to have my nose rubbed in that." He shrugged again. "But it does—and it hurts even more that Owen asked me for help and I haven't been able to do a thing for him."

A tentacle slid along his arm, curled around his back. He glanced up, saw the expression on Belinda's face, let her draw him into her embrace. It occurred to him just how awkward limbs with joints were. Lacking tentacles, he reached for her with his arms, let himself settle against her not-quite-human curves. "You're being really sweet," he said.

"Thank you." She considered him, then leaned forward and kissed him.

"You know," Justin said after the kiss, "I could get used to this."

That got him a sudden unguarded look, full of tangled emotions he could only half read. She covered it with a laugh, said, "I bet you say that to lots of women."

"Not so much," he said.

That got the unguarded look again, and then she closed her eyes, and her tentacles tightened around him. She was afraid, he sensed—but of what? He could not tell. He drew her closer, felt her tense, and then the tension broke and she huddled against him.

"I've upset you," Justin said then.

"No." She opened her eyes, put on a smile. "It's got nothing to do with you."

"Do you want to talk about it?"

Belinda said nothing for a long moment. "I suppose so." She shifted and sat up; he did the same, sat watching her. "You talked about being ordinary. I know I don't look it—" She gestured at herself. "—but so am I. My mom's a Great Old One, my body—well, it is what it is. But I'm just First Circle in the Esoteric Order of Dagon and I'm never going to be more than that, because you have to have certain talents to go higher and I don't. And because I got a bad case of stupid when I was younger, most of the Innsmouth folk don't want anything to do with me. So I live in Y'ha-nthlei and try to be helpful when I can, which isn't that often. I thought I could help find Owen, and I promised Laura I'd do something, but ..." Her voice trickled away.

"I get that," said Justin. "I hope things are okay between you and Laura otherwise."

That called up a sudden smile. "Yes, and thank Mother Hydra for that. I don't know what I'd have done if Laura had turned her back on me, but she and Owen have been really good to me. They didn't have to be." Memories Justin couldn't read clouded her smile for a moment, passed off again. "That's a lot of why I'm here. I wanted to help Owen as a thank-you gift."

"I get that," said Justin. "God in heaven, I get that." He slid his hand up to her shoulder, drew her toward him, and she gave him a grateful look and pressed herself against him. After a little while, she glanced up at him and said, "You're being really sweet."

"Thank you," he said, and bent to kiss the top of her head.

She turned her face up, redirected the kiss to her lips. "You know," she said when the kiss was done, "I could get used to this."

* * *

Later, they went back out into the cabin. Later still, as night closed in, Rose and Arthur came back from the cabin cruiser. Whether Jenny had told them anything about what had been said, Justin didn't try to guess, but only Rose tried to start up a conversation, and she soon ran out of things to say. The four of them ate dinner in something close to silence. Only when the meal was over and Justin had done his part getting the dishes washed did he turn to Arthur and ask, "So what's the plan for tomorow?"

"Out to sea first thing." Arthur fixed his gaze on the table. "Jenny's put a spell on the *Keziah Mason* so the other side can't find or track her by what they do instead of sorcery, but they might be able to do it with shoe leather. Once we're well out into the Atlantic we can decide where to go."

"Do you know where you'll go now, Belinda?" Rose asked.

"I'm not sure." She huddled into the seat. "Probably back to Kingsport first. I need to tell Laura I couldn't do anything to help after all."

Rose gave her a dismayed look, said nothing.

When the silence had gotten unbearable, Arthur got up. "I imagine you two need some time to yourselves." Then, meeting Justin's gaze. "I'm sorry, Justin. I really am."

Justin nodded in response, acknowledging, and Arthur nodded as well and went to the forward cabin. Rose followed him a moment later, glanced back over her shoulder at Justin and Belinda, a wretched mood written on her face.

Once the door closed, Belinda turned to him. "Do you want to go outside? I think I'd like some fresh air."

"Please," said Justin, and followed her out into the gathering darkness. Outside, a breeze off the Atlantic lifted the heat of the day. The cabin cruiser loomed close by. None of the windows facing the *Keziah Mason* were lit, which was some comfort.

They sat in silence in the cockpit for a long time. The harbor rolled in its slow rhythm, rocked by the ocean further away. Off in the distance, on the far side of the Upper Bay, a few lights gleamed in Manhattan's vast dark towers; the low slatternly jumble of the Red Hook shoreline turned mostly blind eyes to the harbor, and Brooklyn rose up east from there toward Park Slope and north toward Cobble Hill and Brooklyn Heights.

Owen's in there somewhere, he thought. The words of the cryptic letter and the equally cryptic typed notes circled in his mind, mocking his failure.

Forward, pale gleams on the unsteady water vanished. Justin looked that way, realized that the light in the forward cabin had been switched off. We should do the same thing, he told himself: go below, try to get some sleep. The thought twisted in him, hard.

"I can't do it," he said, knowing the words were futile, that he had no choice but to accept the fact that he'd failed his friend. "I can't just up and leave him."

Silence answered him, but it was a different silence, suddenly intent. He glanced up, saw Belinda regarding him with a look he couldn't read at all. She drew in an unsteady breath, put a tentacle tip to her lips to warn him to silence, and then mouthed the words, "We don't have to."

He stared, then took two of her arm-tentacles in his hands. She nodded, encouraging, and then gestured with a third tentacle: down, then in a wavering motion that clearly meant swimming, then up to her shoulder to mime, one after the other, Trintje's three spidery limbs.

He nodded, the motion almost frantic. "Plastic bag," she mouthed, then indicated his clothing with a quick tentacular motion. A tentacle tip pointed to herself and then to the water. He nodded again, but then stopped her with a gesture, slid his arms around her and kissed her. She beamed up at him, then slipped away, wriggled out of the muumuu, and lowered herself over the stern so smoothly that she sank into the water without a sound.

He watched her go, then stripped to the skin as quietly as he could, got a trash bag from one of the seat lockers, tucked clothes and shoes and Belinda's muumuu inside and forced as much air out as he could. Once he'd tied the bag shut, he went to the ladder and slid into the night ocean slowly, making as little noise as possible. Once he was in the water he took hold of the bag, drew in a breath and went underwater, twisting around and kicking hard to go deep.

He could see nothing in the blackness, but as his descent slowed a familiar tentacle closed around one of his upper arms and squeezed a greeting. The mouthpiece of the artificial gill pressed against his lips a moment later. "Good?" she buzzed once she'd fastened it in place.

Justin nodded, hoping she could see the motion.

"You can't see anything, can you? Don't worry about it. Let me have that—" A tentacle took possession of the bag, which kept trying to drag him back to the surface. "Now relax. It's a long swim but I'll get us there."

One of her tentacles took hold of his right arm and pulled, and presently he was sliding effortlessly through the black water. He could feel turbulence all along his right side as her tentacles sculled, but that and her steady grip were all that reminded him that he was not rushing alone through a vast and silent void.

Time passed: an hour, he guessed, or more than that. Finally the movement slowed and stopped, and he floated in the night ocean waiting. A light appeared from one of the Deep One lamps Belinda kept on her swimming belt. Without the diving mask, everything around him was blurred, but he could see the masses of stone that sealed most of the tunnel.

"Here," Belinda buzzed, and handed him the other lamp. "Can you see okay? Good."

He motioned toward the gap between the stones, and she smiled—he could just catch the expression in the light that strayed from the lamp beam. Together, they swam over to the tunnel entrance, threaded the gap between stones and brick-work, reached the tunnel beyond.

"Before we go on," Belinda buzzed then, "I wanted to say thank you. I was trying to be brave enough to stay here and keep looking for Owen, and not getting anywhere. Then you said what you did and it was easy."

Justin reached out a hand, patted her shoulder, and she smiled and slid a tentacle along the side of his face, then turned and swam up the tunnel. Justin followed. The mile or so of tunnel slid past, and they reached the hidden pool beneath Parker Place. It was a familiar process by then to wait while Belinda unhooked the artificial gill, and then swim to the surface. He broke through into the noisome air, waited for Belinda to join him, and then swam over to the stair.

He had just hauled himself up above the water when three points of green light gleamed down at him from the darkness ahead. "Hi, Erlik," he said aloud. "Can you tell your mistress that we need her help? Please?"

The three points of light vanished, and a faint scuttling noise faded to silence. Justin glanced at Belinda, and then opened the plastic bag and skinned into his clothing while Belinda donned her muumuu. That done, they picked their way up the rest of the stair.

He settled on the pier. She sat next to him and wrapped a pair of tentacles around him; he slid his arm around her waist, let his tangled thoughts dissolve in the simple reality of her presence. Maybe it was the rebound from what the Radiance had done to him, but that it didn't matter. Once the business in Red Hook was over and he went somewhere else, whatever he was going to do with his life, if she was willing, Belinda would be part of it.

Once it was over—

If they were both still alive then.

He tried to push the thought away, but it refused to go anywhere.

A splashing noise somewhere off in the darkness broke into his thoughts. He looked up, saw dim phosphorescence in the distance. A glance at Belinda told him that she'd seen it too. He drew in a breath and braced himself.

The phosphorescence drew itself together into a dim shape, pulled itself up onto the pier. Before it scuttled a dark presence Justin couldn't see clearly at first, until it turned three gleaming green eyes toward him. He tried to think of something to say as the phosphorescent shape drew closer, but before he managed it, Belinda said in a clear voice, "Miss Sleght?"

The shape stopped, and then a tittering laugh echoed off distant arches. "Oh, that's good," said Trintje. "Very polite." Then, hard and intent: "Why are you here?"

It occurred to Justin suddenly that he had no idea what to say in response. Before he could find something that would serve, another voice spoke in the darkness: deep, with a trace of an accent Justin didn't recognize. "They're here because I sent for them," it said.

Belinda turned suddenly toward the voice. Even in the dim light from the Deep One lantern, Justin could see the astonishment and awe in her face. She stood up, and after a moment he did the same. That was when he heard the long swinging rhythm of the footfalls approaching them, and recognized the dim towering shape that loomed out of the darkness: Nyarlathotep, the Crawling Chaos, the soul and mighty messenger of the Great Old Ones.

* * *

"Owen Merrill is alive," said Nyarlathotep. "The tunnels under Cobble Hill are entirely safe if you know the language of shoggoths, and he does." The dark unhuman eyes turned toward Justin. "Yes, he sent the shoggoths who devoured the negation team and freed you. Yes, my masters and I are well aware of what happened to you."

The Crawling Chaos sat at ease, legs folded. Erlik had finished licking his hands, and settled in his lap, emitting a wet-sounding purr. Over to one side, Justin and Belinda sat close together, his arm around her waist, two of her tentacles around his. To the other, Trintje squatted, listening with a mocking smile on her face, and Dr. Muñoz stood close to her—he'd come to the pier a few minutes after Trintje's arrival, following Erlik out of the same stair as before. In the middle of the rough circle they formed, one of Belinda's lamps provided what light there was.

"I'm glad to hear that," Justin managed to say. "About Owen, I mean."

"Do you know why Owen is here?" Nyarlathotep asked him.

Justin and Belinda both shook their heads, but Trintje replied with her tittering laugh. "These two? They're innocent as lambs. They've scarcely heard Robert Suydam's name. They don't know a thing about what he tried to do."

"That's true," said Justin, with a little uncomfortable laugh. "And I didn't know that you sent for me, Old One. I thought Owen did that."

"He wrote the letter at my request," said Nyarlathotep, imperturbable. "My masters wish a certain task to be accomplished, and that task requires two people whose voor is joined in a certain manner. Shub-Ne'hurrath chose the two of you for the task, and saw to it that the joining took place. The question now is simply whether you're willing to make the attempt."

"That sounds like Mom," said Belinda. Then, visibly gathering up her courage: "Tell me what to do and I'll do it if I can."

Justin could hear the dread and the resolve contending in her voice, and that gave him the push he needed to get past his own uncertainties. "That goes for me too," he said.

The Crawling Chaos nodded, acknowledging.

"Perhaps, Old One," Muñoz said then, "it would be helpful for me to explain the matter."

"I meant you to do so," said Nyarlathotep.

Muñoz came forward, sat on the bricks next to Trintje. "All this has to do with a discovery I made twenty years ago. Long ago, before and during the First World War, many Kurds from Syria came here to escape the fighting in their homeland. With them came members of a secret society whose Arabic name you might know—the Ikhwan al-Azif."

"I think so," said Justin. "Doesn't von Junzt mention it?"

Muñoz beamed. "Indeed he does. That was one of the clues that led me to the discovery I mentioned." He leaned forward. "The Ikhwan al-Azif, the secret society founded by none other than Abu al-Asrad Ja'far ibn Husayn al-Hadrami, the author of the *Necronomicon*, whose name poor von Junzt garbled so badly. They brought with them certain fragments of lore Abu al-Asrad learned, fragments that are known nowhere else, and they did not come here by accident. They were seeking a place where a thing of great importance could be done.

"It so happened that a little more than fifty years ago, I treated the last surviving member of the Brooklyn *diwan* of the Ikhwan al-Azif in his final illness. He had no one else to care for him, for the Syrians up on Atlantic Avenue are by and large good Muslims, you understand, and consider the Ikhwan al-Azif to be the worst sort of apostates. He recognized me as a fellow worshiper of the Great Old Ones. Before he died, he gave me certain papers, and told me where to find certain other things. Since then, why, I have followed up the clues I received. I learned what it was that Robert and Cornelia Suydam learned from the Ikhwan al-Azif, what they were trying to do and why it matters as much as it does—and it matters a very great deal.

"You both know of the moon paths, the old straight tracks set out by the serpent folk of lost Valusia long before the Atlantic Ocean was born? And you know they are channels for the bright and dark voor, the twofold forces of life? Good. Far underground here in Brooklyn is another thing the serpent folk left, a relic of their technology that relates to the moon paths. You have noticed the, shall we say, frantic vitality of New York City? And the way all life seems to drain out of the regions close by? Those are both works of the relic in question.

"This is what I learned from the papers of the Ikhwan al-Azif. There are three seals that must be opened, three signs that must appear, before the words of the prophet Hali can be fulfilled, and the third of them is here, beneath Red Hook: the relic I mentioned."

"So we're supposed to awaken the relic?" Justin asked.

"No," said Nyarlathotep. "It has been awake since the Permian era. The task given to the two of you is to shut it down forever."

A silence filled the tunnel. "What do we have to do?" Belinda asked then.

Trintje's tittering laugh echoed off cold stone. "Little enough," she said. "One of you has to go to Greenwich Village and get a silver key there, then go down a stair to a place nobody's been in long ages, and use the key. The other has to do certain things to make that possible. Simple, eh?" She laughed again, and the sound took on a mordant tone. "It's not simple. The key hasn't been there since 1702, yet it can be gotten there and nowhere else. As for the stair, no living thing can descend it, and don't even think about what waits at its foot. Erlik!"

The cat-creature glanced up at her from Nyarlathotep's lap.

"Leave your wallowing, child, and come here."

Erlik aimed an unfriendly glare at her, but unfolded his eight legs, climbed out of the lap of the Crawling Chaos, and padded over to her. "Look at him," Trintje said. "He was an ordinary cat who stuck his nose a little too far down a certain stairway—not the one I mentioned, merely the one that leads to it. By the time he got back to the top of the stair he looked like this."

The creature gave her another glare, and busied himself washing behind one ear.

"What did that?" Justin asked after a moment.

"Voor," said Muñoz. "Too much of it, more than any living thing can abide. It causes cells to divide, things to sprout and grow. Erlik was very fortunate that none of the things that grew from him made it impossible for him to live. Had he stayed a few more moments, beyond a doubt, it would have been all up with him."

"Okay," Justin said. "So how can one of us go there?"

"Nothing living can do it," Trintje said. "Nor a machine— that's been tried, too, and those who tried it didn't like the result, oh, not at all." Her laugh had an edge to it that made Justin shudder. "The powers that guard the place took control of the machines and sent them back to kill their masters. The last time, the batteries blew up, but not until each of the machines had pressed itself against a human face." Her spider limbs gestured her amusement. "So that's not an option either. But a dead man animated by sorcery, that's another matter entirely."

Justin stared at her for a moment. "You're saying one of us has to die."

It was Nyarlathotep who answered. "That's correct. One of you dies, and the other does what's needful to animate the corpse and bring it back to life afterwards. The joining of voor that unites the two of you makes that possible, just as it would have done for Robert and Cornelia Suydam. If all goes well and you succeed, the death in question will be temporary. If you fail, though, both of you will be dead, and that will be that."

"And Robert Suydam—"

"He and Cornelia both failed, each in their own way," said the Crawling Chaos. "Her failure doomed him, his failure doomed their attempt. You need not repeat their failure."

Justin considered the Great Old One for a time. I should be afraid, he thought. I should be pale and shaking at the thought of doing this, but I'm not. Maybe it was some lingering effect of what the Radiance had done to him, maybe it was the sting of the contempt Jenny so obviously felt toward him or the bitter taste of his own repeated failure, but all at once it was easy for him to say aloud, "I'm willing to try."

CHAPTER 9

THE ISLE OF THE MANHATTANS

"Y ou're sure," said Belinda.

They sat on the side of a bed in a spare room Dr. Muñoz had lent them, a pleasant little space with white plaster walls and a window letting in the fading light of evening. The unending mutter and hum of New York City sounded outside, muted by the glass. From beneath the door, clattering noises spoke of Muñoz busy in the kitchen close by.

"Of course not," Justin replied. "But I'm going to do it anyway."

He sounded more confident than he felt. The two of them had spent the small hours of the morning with Trintje, Muñoz, and Nyarlathotep, going over the details of what had to be done once the next day came and went, then climbed what seemed like countless stairs to Muñoz's apartment. A breakfast of rolls and chocolate followed, and then as many hours of sleep as they could manage. Dinner would come shortly, and then—

His mind veered away from the final step in the sequence. Belinda made a fine distraction: bare and smiling, with a splash of sunlight glowing on her skin and her tentacles all aswirl across the bedding. "Once all this is over," he said, "and I can go to a Starry Wisdom church again, I'm going to make a thank-you offering to your mother."

Belinda blushed. "I've already thanked Mom in my prayers. I know this is one of the things she does, but I'm really glad this happened between us." Then: "I hope you don't mind that she made it happen for her own reasons."

Justin shrugged. "I'm not much of an initiate, but I get that the Great Old Ones do everything they do for their own reasons. I'm sure she had some plan of her own in mind when she gave me Robin, but he still means the world to me, and I'm still grateful for that—and if she's decided to send something else sweet my way, you know, I think I'll deal."

She drew in an uneven breath as though to say something, but just then a discreet tap sounded at the door—Muñoz, come to call them to dinner—and whatever it was went unsaid.

Afterward, Justin had no recollection at all of what Muñoz served them that evening. All his attention was on the tasks ahead of him: the journey to Greenwich Village, the finding of the silver key, the trip back to Red Hook, and then a series of enchantments and acts that might bring the Weird of Hali one step closer to its fulfillment and might simply leave him stone cold dead in some forgotten place far below the streets of Brooklyn.

Finally the last daylight guttered out over the Jersey shore. "I have taken the liberty of finding you a few things," Muñoz told him then. "A light jacket to keep the night chill at bay, a bus pass for the journey, and—" He handed Justin a folded sheet of paper. "Instructions to guide you. I shall take you to the bus stop. When you return, come here as quickly as you can, and we will go below." He turned to Belinda. "Miss Marsh, if you will wait in the parlor for me, I shall take you down into the tunnels as soon as I return. Miss Sleght will need your help with the preparations for the ceremony."

A quick tentacular hug and a kiss later, Belinda was on her way to the parlor. Justin put on the jacket, pocketed the other items, thanked Muñoz and followed him down the stair to the entry. "Miss Sleght has done certain things to keep you safe," the doctor said as they reached the ground floor, "and I know a few things as well. Still, there are no certainties in this."

The night outside was stifling, full of heat and nameless noises. Muñoz turned toward Gerritsen Street and set out at a brisk pace, and Justin followed. "There is one more thing," Muñoz said as they walked. "It is just possible you will have to avoid someone else once you reach Greenwich Village. I believe you have studied a little of New York City's lore, have you not? You may have heard of a certain Matthew Hyde."

"The books I read said that he lived and died back in the eighteenth century," Justin said, aiming a puzzled look at the doctor.

"Why, yes, he did. You may encounter him there."

Justin stopped in his tracks, had to hurry to catch up to Muñoz.

"The key came to Agatha Sleght in 1644 with the English sea captain Humphrey Carter," said the doctor, "and it left again in 1702 with his nephew Edmund, who took it to the Massachusetts Bay colony. It is there, or rather then, that you must go to get it." He glanced at Justin. "You are hardly the first to make that journey, you know, and Erlik will guide you."

They reached the corner of Gerritsen and Van Brunt, stopped at a battered bus stop sign close by. "And there it is," Muñoz said, craning to see down Van Brunt; Justin looked the same way, and saw the distinctive lights of a MTA bus pulling away from a stop two blocks away.

"One more thing," said Muñoz. "Take this." He handed Justin a little pouch tied shut with a cord: leather, Justin thought, but not any kind of leather he recognized. Something clinked inside. "Give that to Agatha Sleght. Miss Sleght wishes her to have it." Justin agreed, and Muñoz shook his hand and said, "Go in the name of the Great Old Ones."

The bus pulled up, and Justin climbed aboard.

* * *

It took two buses to get to Greenwich Village. The first left him at a corner on Flatbush Avenue, where he waited with half a dozen other passengers, then climbed aboard a crowded bus when it finally came. The crowds were important, Muñoz had explained, for they made it harder for the Radiance to trace what they were doing, but the press of people and the constant noise that surrounded him left Justin's nerves on edge.

The second bus let him off at Washington Square, took on a few more passengers, and rattled away into the night. Justin glanced at the paper he'd been given and headed what he thought was west, caught his mistake when the wrong street name appeared, turned around and went the other way. Greenwich Village still buzzed with an autumnal life, though its glory days as the heart of a dozen countercultures had long since faded into memory, and the wave of gentrification that had followed was receding as the economic crisis tightened its grip. Even so, little cafés and nightspots spilled noise and customers out on the sidewalks, and lights burned in windows over the streets. Justin's heart pounded as he wove his way through the crowds, but no one seemed to notice him at all.

The route the note laid out for him was baffling, a zigzag path through narrow streets that led away from the noise and light between tall brick buildings and century-old trees. He wasn't sure he'd followed the right track until he turned off Perry Street into a little black court half full of dumpsters, and spotted three green points of light on a crumbling concrete stoop.

"Hi, Erlik," he said aloud, and the cat-creature made a low wet mewling sound and scuttled ahead of him, stopping at a narrow gap between buildings. Peering into the gap, Justin saw what looked uncomfortably like infinite blackness. The creature glanced at him, its green eyes gleaming, and then it scurried into the gap. Justin braced himself and followed.

The way turned out easier to follow than he'd feared, for lights shone down from windows here and there. Once, from an open window, he heard voices, and then the opening bars of an old Simon and Garfunkel piece. He smiled, remembering how Aunt Josephine had treasured that album, and then walked under the window and heard very distinctly the faint hiss of a vinyl record on a stereo. He gave the window a startled look, kept going.

The passage ended at a blank brick wall, and Erlik sprang up three steps to a door to one side and pawed at it, glancing at Justin to make sure he got the point. The door turned out to be unlocked, and on the far side a dark silent corridor stretched away, lined with worm-eaten doors. Justin followed Erlik down the corridor and out the door on the far side, into a narrow courtyard between the backs of crowded tenement buildings. An elderly man in torn and filthy clothes of old-fashioned cut lay half sprawled on the steps to the back door of one of the tenements. He blinked and stared as Erlik scuttled down into the courtyard, swore aloud, then reached for the bottle next to him. As Justin followed the cat-creature to the end of the courtyard, another snatch of music came from an open window: a rich full tenor voice singing something from an Italian opera, mixed with pops and crackles that made the performance sound unnervingly like a wax cylinder recording.

At the end of the courtyard was a half-ruined brick wall. Erlik leapt up onto it and then sprang into the darkness beyond, and Justin scrambled after him. On the far side was a narrow street lit unexpectedly by gaslamps, and then a sharp turn into an alley led to another narrow street where the streetlights were oil lamps with lozenge-shaped glass panels surrounding them. The faint sound of a piano came from the building to Justin's right; the melody wasn't one he knew, but it made him think of old hymn tunes from before the Civil War.

Another alley led to a low, arched passage of stone that Justin had to traverse on hands and knees. When he finally pulled himself to his feet in an alley on the far side of that long and twisting passage, he found to his astonishment that the streetlights had candles burning in them and cast only the faintest glow down onto the cobblestones below. Small-paned windows let out the mellow glow of more candles within, and from one came the sound of men's voices slurred with alcohol, singing in a very rough approximation of the same key:

> "Anacreon had a red nose, so they say,
> But what's a red nose when you're happy and gay?
> Gad split me! I'd rather be red while I'm here,
> Than white as a lily—and dead half a year!"

Erlik mewed at him and led onwards, through an archway and a courtyard so dark Justin had to find his way by feel, to a wall pierced by a door it took minutes for him to find. When he finally stepped through the door into a faintly lit alley, winded and shaking, it took him a moment to notice the streetlights: tin lanterns with conical tops and holes punched in the sides, in front of every seventh house.

The alley ahead slanted steeply uphill toward a building Justin could almost make out against the sky, but Erlik mewed at him again and scuttled through a gap between two low wooden houses to the left, and he followed. Beyond the houses were scattered outbuildings, then gardens burgeoning with summer crops, and beyond that—

An untouched meadow stretched out around him. Further off, trees rose up tall and verdant. He glanced around, amazed, to find New York City gone. Even the houses he'd passed between a moment earlier had vanished. To the west the Hudson glimmered and the Jersey shore rose dark and silent, and to the north and east trees rose tall. Off to the south, low shapes hinted at a little town, and a few dim lights closer by suggested outlying houses. Fireflies hovered in the still air and frogs chorused from a nearby marsh.

He raised his eyes to astonishing brilliance. Growing up in Lefferts Corners had taught him just how bright the stars could be far from the big cities and their countless lamps, but the sky above him blazed with a glory he had never seen before. The great arc of the Milky Way sprawled across the sky, and against that backdrop so many stars crowded one another that Justin could not pick out the constellations he knew. It occurred to him then that he'd never before seen the sky the way that his ancestors had seen it, unmarred by the glare of electric lights.

He drew in a ragged breath, stared upwards. Though the frogs kept up their chorus and the hoot of an owl came murmuring out of distant trees, an immense silence seemed to hover above the meadow. Beneath the tremendous indifference of the stars, it was easy for Justin to remember again just how little his quest meant to anyone but the momentary lives caught up in it and the handful of eternal beings who'd chosen to concern themselves briefly with it.

Erlik made another wet mewling noise, scuttled a short distance to one side, then stopped and glanced back to be sure Justin would follow. "Yeah, I'm coming," Justin said aloud, and went the way the cat-creature was going.

The same hill the alley had climbed rose before him—or was it an artificial mound? Steep sides and flattened top reminded Justin suddenly of Elk Hill in Chorazin, where he'd faced his family's terrible destiny. The building he'd seen earlier atop the hill had vanished utterly, but a dim point of flickering light shone somewhere ahead of him, under the crest of the hill but not too far down from it. Erlik hurried on toward the light, glancing back now and then at Justin, who picked his way up the slope, dodging tangled shrubs.

The light came from a little square window, he saw presently, and the window was set in the side of a shack huddled beneath the crest of the hill. He had nearly reached the shack before he realized the window wasn't glass, but hide scraped so thin that light glimmered unsteadily through it. The dim glow from the stars told him nothing of the shack, but Erlik went up to what Justin guessed had to be a door and pawed at it, mewling.

Low noises came from within the shack, and then a woman's voice: "Bide a moment, puss." The door opened a little, letting out flickering red firelight. "Ah," said the voice. "And another with ye, too." The door opened wider. "Come in, whoever ye be."

Justin came forward out of the darkness. Facing him, half lit by the dim flickering glow, stood a bright-eyed old woman in a shapeless brown dress. She waved him into the shack, closed the door. Inside there was only one chair, a frail little thing with a wicker seat, and even if Justin had been minded to deprive the old woman of a place to sit, he was sure it wouldn't bear his weight. He sat on the floor by the hearth, which was made of rounded stones mortared with baked clay, and waited. Flames flickered from a little fire in the hearth, and smoke tinged the air. The firelight revealed almost nothing of the shack's interior.

The old woman picked her way back to the chair and sat. Erlik came scuttling after her, settled down at her feet and folded all his paws underneath him.

"You're Agatha Sleght, aren't you?" Justin asked then.

"I am. And ye?"

"Justin Martense."

"I believe it," she said. "Young Adriaen Martense has paid more than one call here, and ye have his eyes and much of his look."

Justin managed to keep his reaction off his face. He recognized the name, for Adriaen Martense had been the younger brother of Gerrit Martense, the Nieuw Amsterdam merchant who'd settled on Tempest Mountain near Lefferts Corners and brought the Martense name and destiny into the Catskills. He drew in a breath, reached into a pocket, brought out the little pouch of strange leather. "Trintje wanted me to give you this."

She took it. "Aye, I fancied she sent ye. 'Tis well with her?"

"Very much so."

The old woman smiled, glanced inside the pouch. "So good of her." Then, closing the pouch again: "Ye have need of the key."

"Yes, please."

She got up, vanished into the shadows of the shack's far end. Somewhere outside in the night, an owl hooted, and the distant chorus of the frogs reminded him just how far he'd come from the little black court off Perry Street.

* * *

The old woman came back presently with a shape that glittered in the firelight. "Take it," Agatha said, handing the shape to him. "There's writings that go with it, but ye have no need of those, not for the work ye mean to do."

Justin considered the key. It was almost as long as his hand, an ornate shape of tarnished silver covered with cryptical arabesques.

"Now attend," the old woman said. "Until ye come to the place ye know of, only the one who casts the spell with ye may touch the key. Once the thing's done, why, it will return here—that much magic I still have, old as I am—but until then it must not leave ye and it must not pass to any other's hand but hers. It must stay safe with ye, and then safe with me, until young Edmund Carter takes it where it's rightly to go."

"Okay," Justin said, and realized an instant later from her expression that she didn't know the word. "I'll make sure it stays safe."

"'Tis well. When ye go hence, another might well follow ye, the one that'll come to dwell here when I die, the one that'll deal so hardly with the Manhattans and take in hand ceremonies he'll have no right to deal in."

A name surged up out of memory. "Matthew Hyde."

"The very one. Above all he must not touch the key, not for a moment. Pale his face is and cold his hands; by that ye shall know him. Flee him, no matter what befalls ye."

"I'll do that," said Justin, taking this in.

"'Tis well. Go now. Puss here will guide ye." She reached down and stroked Erlik's head, and the cat-creature responded with a wet purr.

Justin got to his feet. "Thank you." He slipped the key into the inside pocket of his jacket. Trying to remember the pleasantries of centuries past: "Thank you, Mistress Sleght."

She smiled in response. "Bear my love with ye to Trintje. Now get ye gone."

Erlik sprang up and darted to the door, glanced back at him and mewed. Justin managed some approximation of an old-fashioned bow, went to the door, and followed the many-legged cat out into the starlit night.

Fireflies hovered and danced as he picked his way down the slope through the green stillness of a Manhattan Island four centuries gone. A dozen paces past the foot of the hill, a few scattered outbuildings came into sight. He followed Erlik through them, and came to the narrow alley with the tin lanterns in front of every seventh house. Erlik mewed again, and scuttled more quickly than before, leading him back to the unlighted courtyard where Justin had to find his way in total darkness. The archway beyond that opened onto a half-familiar street where the streetlamps had guttering candles in them, and Justin was sure he heard the same chorus of half-drunken voices singing another verse to the same tune as before:

"Young Harry, propp'd up just as straight as he's able
Will soon lose his wig and slip under the table,
But fill up your goblets and pass 'em around—
Better under the table than under the ground!"

As he reached the end of the street and crouched down into the low arched passage he could only traverse on hands and knees, the voices faded into silence, and he heard something less familiar and more menacing: the sound of measured foot-falls behind him.

He scrambled after Erlik through the passage, climbed out into an alley and followed it to a street lit by oil lamps, where the piano's notes still sounded. As that faded into silence, he listened intently. For a few moments he heard nothing, but then the same steady footfalls sounded again, somewhere not far behind him. He glanced back nervously and followed the cat into a street lit by gaslamps, and then over the top of a half-ruined brick wall.

The Italian opera was still playing in the courtyard on the other side of the wall, though the splendid tenor voice was cut off abruptly, and a moment of silence passed before the crackles and pops of another wax cylinder announced the next several minutes of the solo. The man in old-fashioned clothing was still sprawled on the steps, and he spotted Erlik again, let out an even more colorful burst of profanity than before, and reached for his bottle.

Justin had nearly reached the door on the courtyard's far side, and the tenor voice was rising toward a high note, when a hand closed on one of his arms. "Stay, Sir," said a soft and hollow voice. "I would speak with you—"

Justin turned. A man had come up behind him, wrapped in an old-fashioned cloak and wearing a broad-brimmed hat. For an instant he thought it was Nyarlathotep, but the man was shorter than Justin, and a stray beam of light from a nearby window fell on a face as pallid as a corpse's, showed the man's cadaverously slender build. The thing that clinched it, though, was the hand that clutched Justin's arm. Even through the jacket it felt as cold as dry ice.

Justin twisted away from the frigid grip and ran. A dark arch-way loomed up ahead. He darted through it, plunged through the blackness of the narrow alley beyond. As he ran he heard inchoate noises, then silence, and then the sound of waves sweeping up and crashing onto a rugged shore. The rush and splash of the waves could hide pursuing footfalls, Justin knew, and so he veered toward the first alley that he saw, plunged through it and reached the street beyond.

There he stopped, staring up at the skyline of a city beyond his imaginings.

Vast black pyramids soared up to the pallid stars, glittering with bright windows, ringed with broad stone terraces, linked by aerial galleries, while dirigibles glowed splendidly above. It was a night of festival, Justin gathered, for crowds dressed in garments of orange and red danced their joy to the thunder of kettle-drums, the crisp rattle of crotals, and the intricate harmonies of horns that wove together in the rhythms of a strange counterpoint. It was—

It was New York, Justin knew at a glance, whatever its name was in that distant time. An unwilling smile forced itself onto his face. Uncomfortable though the city made him, it mattered somehow that that the silent ruin he'd felt creeping through its streets would turn out to be just one more passing phase.

The thought occupied only a moment. He had more pressing concerns: first, to get away from the cadaverous man, if the sudden dash through the dark alley hadn't shaken him; then, to find his way back somehow to the New York City he knew—

Something tugged at his trouser leg. He looked down to find Erlik there, mewing at him unheard. Once the cat-creature was sure he'd been seen, he darted away toward an angle between strangely shaped buildings. Justin ran the same way, for he'd caught a glimpse of movement back the way he'd come, saw what might have been a pale face in the dimness there.

The angle turned into a gap that zigzagged away into darkness. Justin plunged through it, following the faint scutting sound of Erlik's movements, and all at once came out from between narrow walls into half-tropic greenery. Great writhing roots and trunks clung to tumbled ruins around him, and the rush and wash of the ocean was close by, though a dense fog filling the hot motionless air kept him from seeing the surf. He scrambled over masses of brick, hauled himself up onto an outthrust root, slid down the debris slope on the far side, and then followed Erlik into a narrow space between two half-fallen buildings. He'd gone no further than a few yards into the gap when the buildings rose up tall and unbroken into the night; another half dozen paces, and a window high above gleamed with light; a sudden twist to the left, and he was darting through a little black courtyard half full of dumpsters. A moment later he was on Perry Street, with the tall brick buildings and old trees of Greenwich Village around him and the first pale light of the approaching dawn spreading into the eastern sky.

Behind him he heard footfalls slow, stop, and then start up again, retreating into silence.

* * *

The bus at Washington Square came promptly enough, but once he got off at a corner on Flatbush Avenue and stood waiting there in the dim light of earliest morning, time seemed to stretch out into eternities. He was acutely aware of the key in the inside pocket of his jacket, the pedestrians beginning to flood the streets, the cars clattering past, the buses that sighed and rattled their way toward destinations that weren't his. Finally his bus arrived. After most of an hour following a roundabout route along cracked and potholed streets, passing abandoned brick warehouses and homes covered with vinyl siding that had seen many better days, the bus finally wheezed to a stop and let him off on the corner of Gerritsen and Van Brunt.

He'd worried all the way from Perry Street that someone would come after him as soon as he left the bus—maybe the Radiance, maybe Matthew Hyde, maybe something else who'd caught his scent as he scrambled through alleys that crossed more than space—but the streets were empty. Once the bus pulled away and rounded a corner, Red Hook could have been one vast necropolis peopled only by the dead. Even so, Justin hurried through the unquiet dawn up Gerritsen Street, turned onto Parker Place and jabbed the intercom button. He waited in tense anticipation until the loudspeaker crackled and Dr. Muñoz's voice said, "Hello?"

"It's Justin—" he began.

The door buzzed instantly, letting him in. As it clicked shut behind him, he heard footsteps hurrying down the stairs.

The physician appeared a moment later. "Mr. Martense!" he said. "You have it? Excellent. Come, come, there is no time to spare. The other side has had drones all over this area since not long past midnight."

Justin followed him down a long corridor, and most of the way back to a narrow door that looked like a closet. Muñoz unlocked it, revealing an unlit stairway leading down. "Here," the doctor said, handing Justin a flashlight. "Go quickly now."

Justin clicked on the light and started down the stairs, saw the glow of another light behind him, heard Muñoz lock the door and hurry after him. The stairwell walls were brick at first, but maybe ten feet down the brick gave way to gray stone mortared together in what Justin guessed was a Colonial style. Another ten feet or so, and the stair opened onto a cellar of the same gray stonework, with vaulted ceilings supported by great stone piers, and broad flagstones covering the floor. He stopped, uncertain, until the doctor joined him and motioned with the beam of his flashlight at an angle across the cellar.

"We may be safe," the doctor said as they went on. "They might have missed you—"

A sudden dull sound came down the stairway behind them. It took Justin only an instant to recognize it: the sound of a hard object striking a heavy door.

"Quickly!" Muñoz said, grabbed Justin's arm, and broke into a run. "They have followed you, as I feared. We must hurry."

They reached the far corner of the cellar moments later, but by then two more blows had thudded against the door above, and the last of these sent splintering sounds echoing through the cellar's stillness. At the corner a gap led into a narrow passage, and a short distance down the passage a great iron door gaped open. In response to Muñoz's quick gestures, Justin hurried through the gap and then, once the old man had joined him, helped push the door shut and turn the great lever that barred it.

"That will hold them," said Muñoz, "maybe for a little while, maybe longer. Quickly!"

The passage veered to the right and then plunged down another stair. They were halfway down when low indistinct sounds came echoing from above, and had just reached the stair's foot and started down the passage beyond it when a sudden *whump!* out of the darkness behind them knocked Justin to the floor. He scrambled to his feet and helped Muñoz up. The two of them sprinted down the passage, and heard boots drumming on the stairs as they reached the end of it.

"This way!" Muñoz panted, gesturing to a narrow side passage. A dozen feet, and it opened onto a wider corridor with roughly fashioned stone walls and a low ceiling that looked as though it had been blackened by centuries of soot.

They sprinted down the corridor. At the far end, Justin's flashlight beam showed nothing but darkness, but he caught the stale stagnant smell of the flooded tunnels beneath Red Hook and guessed where they were. The sounds of pursuit hammered behind them, gaining ground; Justin glanced back reflexively over his shoulder—

And saw an eye, pallid green and faintly luminous, blink open in the blackness of the ceiling and close again.

It took Justin an instant to understand what he had seen, and by then he and Muñoz had passed two black pilasters he didn't recall seeing when he'd been that way before, and veered at a sharp angle onto the pier beneath Parker Place.

"Enough," said Muñoz, catching his breath. "We are safe."

As Justin turned toward him, uncertain, a sudden loud wet noise sounded behind them. The sound of running boots ended as though someone had thrown a switch.

Muñoz turned and pointed his flashlight beam back at the mouth of the corridor. Iridescent black, a shapeless mass half filled the opening, opened pallid luminous eyes to regard the two humans. The pilasters to either side of the entrance had sprouted eyes, too, and flowed down to join the feast. Dim movements further in told Justin that the entire ceiling of the corridor from end to end must have been temporarily lined with shoggoths.

"We have certain arrangements with the shoggoths," said Muñoz then, with a thin smile. "They protect us, and we provide them with food."

Justin tried to think of something to say in response. Before he could do so, another sound—a shrill whistle that rose and fell in complex patterns over two octaves—rang from the darkness further up the underground canal. One of the shoggoths piped an intricate response, returned to its meal. Then, from the same direction as the whistle, came the low steady sound of footfalls, walking toward the shoggoths and their two observers.

There was something familiar about the rhythm of the footfalls, and for a moment Justin wondered if it was Matthew Hyde, then if it was Nyarlathotep. The pace was too firm for the one, though, and not long enough for the other. Where had he heard those steps before?

Then he remembered in a blaze of sudden delight, and turned his flashlight beam that way. Sure enough, it lit up a broad-shouldered figure with sand-colored hair and a ragged beard, approaching out of the darkness.

"Owen!" Justin dropped his flashlight, ran to greet his friend. "You're okay?"

"Yeah, I'm fine." His grip was so familiar it ached. "Hi, Justin." Then, turning to the doctor, who came up at a more sedate pace: "You're Dr. Muñoz? Owen Merrill. Pleased to meet you." They shook hands. "We need to get out of here—there are two more negation teams on their way, and the tide's coming in fast. Nyarlathotep told me to bring the two of you to the old stone chamber, but I don't know where that is."

"I know it well," Muñoz said. "Please come with me, both of you."

CHAPTER 10

THE SILVER KEY

The old stone chamber deserved its name, Justin decided. Great blocks of black stone fitted tightly together formed its walls and vaulted ceiling. The odd proportions of the stonework left him wondering if it had been made by something far more ancient than humanity. Two little oil lamps sat on the floor, spreading a dim yellow light over all.

Justin had other things to think about as soon as he followed Muñoz into the room, though. He heard a wordless cry in Belinda's voice, the quick whispering sounds of tentacles on cold stone, and then she flung herself into his arms and wrapped arm-tentacles around him, burying her face in his shoulder. He kissed her hair, she glanced up at him, and then she looked past him and her eyes went round. "Father Dagon," she said, "Owen! You're okay?"

"More or less," Owen said. "Hi, Belinda."

Trintje's voice sounded from the darkness. "We've little time," she said. "Come."

Belinda detached herself, and they crossed the room. Trintje sat against the far wall, a phosphorescent shape against near-darkness. Erlik sprawled on the floor near her, licking his belly. Two leatherbound books with hasps and hinges of dark metal sat on the floor close by. "Sit," she said, gesturing at the floor. "You have it?" When Justin nodded: "No troubles?"

147

"I had a run-in with Matthew Hyde," said Justin.

"Did you? No surprises there." Her lopsided mouth twisted in a bleak smile. "He's been after the key for many years, and no wonder. He ran from death into the spaces between time, and found out too late that escaping death needn't get you any more life. So there he is and there he'll stay, unless the key releases him." Her laugh echoed off the stone. "And it won't."

She leaned forward then, intent. "You're still resolved to go on?"

"Yeah," said Justin. "I don't see any point in turning back now." He could feel Belinda and Owen both watching him, and tried to thrust that fact out of his mind.

Her gaze, cool and amused, met his. "That's because you don't know what awaits you. Well, be it so." She turned to Muñoz. "You know what needs doing next."

"Of course," said the physician.

Spider-limbs motioned at Belinda. "Take her to the den, and make the preparation." The two of them left, and Trintje turned to Owen. "You know how to speak with shoggoths."

"Yeah," said Owen. "That's the only reason I'm still alive right now."

"I don't doubt that at all." She regarded him. "Have them take you and your friend to some safe place." The spider-limbs indicated Justin. "I'll send for you when it's time."

Outside a narrow brick-lined passage veered off into the darkness. Through gaps in the floor, gurgling and splashing sounds spoke of the incoming tide. Once Owen had whistled to the shoggoths, he and Justin picked their way around the gaps, squeezed through tight places where someone or something had broken through a wall to the space on the other side, and climbed a short stair to an old steam tunnel with rusting iron pipes along one side. In the darkness around them, low sliding noises spoke of heavy shapeless things moving not far away.

"Where'd you learn to speak shoggoth?" Justin asked as they walked.

"In Dunwich. There's a colony of them under Sentinel Hill, and the Dunwich folk have been trading with them since the Great Old Ones know when."

"What do you trade with shoggoths?" Justin asked, surprised.

"Food, mostly. They eat pretty much anything organic, and the ones by Dunwich have plenty of brown coal to feed on, but that's kind of boring. They have odd tastes—imagine dining on coal seasoned with molasses and farmhouse cheese."

"No thanks," Justin said, laughing.

"Shows that you're not a shoggoth," said Owen, with a grin. "They like cheese enough that they'll trade iron ore for it. That's what the Dunwich forge uses for raw material, so a lot of people in Dunwich speak shoggoth. I figured it would be smart to learn. Then for a while we had one a lot smaller than these staying with us, so I got a fair amount of fluency—though not as much as the kids." In response to Justin's startled look: "It's a long story. I'll tell you about it sometime when we've got an hour and a couple of beers each."

The steam tunnel ended at a little square room where the pipes bent and rose straight up through the vaulted brick ceiling. To one side, a gap had been forced in the brickwork; Owen squeezed through it, and Justin followed. Beyond it was a ragged open space, and beyond that a darkness Justin's flashlight could not penetrate. Owen whistled an intricate pattern of notes, and the darkness opened three pale green eyes and whistled back.

"Up we go," Owen said. Justin was about to ask him how and where when something black and shapeless closed around him and lifted him straight up. "Reach up," Owen called to him from below. "When you feel the sides of the gap, pull yourself up through it."

Justin raised his arms, felt concrete and then a ragged gap. A moment later he got his arms through it, let the flashlight roll away, and hauled himself through the opening as the pseudo-pod that held him released its grip. Once he'd gotten his legs through he scrambled away and picked up the flashlight, and a moment later Owen climbed up through the same opening: a hole in a poured concrete floor, Justin saw. It looked uncomfortably as though something had gnawed its way through from below.

* * *

A little oil lamp flared and sputtered on the floor. By its uncertain light, Justin saw concrete-block walls, moldering crates marked with old civil-defense labels, an odd pattern of lines and curves drawn with chalk on one wall.

"Yeah, this was my hiding place," said Owen, sitting on the other side of the lamp. "An old fallout shelter somebody dug out under their basement back in the 1950s. The house was demolished and the property got turned into a parking lot, so there's no way up to the surface, but the shoggoths found this a long time ago, and used to hide here from the Radiance."

"They brought you here," Justin said.

"Yeah." Owen stared at nothing in particular. "I was lucky. I spent the first week or so after I got here playing cat and mouse with a couple of negation teams, and they nearly caught me three times. The third time they'd have gotten me for sure if I hadn't found the shoggoths."

"They caught me easily enough," Justin said bitterly. "I'm out of my league here."

Owen considered him, nodded. "This whole project has turned out to be far more risky than I thought it would be. When I tried to meet you, they nearly caught me again."

"The lecture at the library?"

"Yeah. I meant to be there. Did you talk to Ruth Frankweiler?"

Justin gave him a startled glance. "No. Is she on our side?"

"Seventh degree in the Starry Wisdom. She's got things in her files I don't think anyone else has." Owen shrugged. "When that fell through, I tried to make other arrangements, but before I could do that they caught you."

"Okay," Justin stared at the hole in the floor for a while. "This relic Belinda and I are supposed to shut down. Do you have any idea why it's so important?"

Owen considered him for a moment. "I know part of it has to do with the moon paths. The relic and the moon paths were made at the same time by the serpent folk of Valusia, back before the Atlantic Ocean opened up, and the two of them are linked. The energies of the moon paths are bound up in the relic, and they have to be released. I don't know why, but apparently that might have something to do with the Weird of Hali."

Justin nodded in response, and silence closed around them.

"Can I ask a personal question?" Owen said after a while, and when Justin gestured for him to go on: "When did you and Belinda become an item?"

"Day before yesterday. We met when she came down to look for you, we got along really well, and after Mha'alh'yi fixed what the Radiance did to me, things kind of happened. Apparently the Black Goat made them happen."

"I bet," Owen said. "Any idea where things are headed between you?"

"Not yet. I'm still trying to process the fact that it happened in the first place."

"Fair enough," said Owen. "If it doesn't work out, though, please be kind to her. She's had a very rough time with men."

"She said she's done some things she regrets," Justin ventured.

"Did she tell you any of the details?"

"No." Justin glanced at him. "I get the sense it was a big deal."

"Yeah," said Owen. They sat for a while in silence. "When this business is over, if you spend any time around Innsmouth folk, you're going to hear some ugly stories. If you want, I can fill you in on what actually happened."

"Please," said Justin.

"The first thing you need to know about her is that she's lived her whole life in Laura's shadow," Owen went on. "Don't get me wrong, they're really close, but everything Belinda wanted, Laura got. Belinda managed decent grades in school, Laura was the class valedictorian. Belinda's not going past first circle in the Esoteric Order of Dagon, Laura's going to be the next Grand Priestess of the Arkham lodge. And—" He stopped.

"Kids?" Justin said, remembering the way she'd talked about Asenath and Robin.

"Yeah. Belinda loves kids, she's really good with them, but she can't have any of her own. You wouldn't expect that from a daughter of the Black Goat, would you? But there's a lot of infertility in the Innsmouth families, and that's just it. When Laura's family came to Dunwich, and Laura and I got married, Belinda came with them, and threw herself at every man who was willing. She wanted to prove the witches wrong and have a baby before Laura did, and she didn't care that some of the men she bedded were already married."

"That's a problem with the Innsmouth folk?"

"A big problem," said Owen.

"I thought the Esoteric Order of Dagon was a fertility religion."

"That doesn't mean it's a sexuality religion. There's a difference." Justin took that in, and Owen went on after a moment. "Laura and I finally had to sit her down and explain to her what a mess she was making of things. There were guys who might have married her if she hadn't become the center of a scandal, and they could have gotten children at the Black Goat's altar, but you know how people in small towns are."

"God, yes," Justin said.

Owen nodded. "So she went to live with her aunt Fh'ylh'lya in Y'ha-nthlei. She still lives there most of the time."

"She thinks the world of you and Laura," said Justin.

"I'm glad to hear that." He was quiet for a time. "It took us a long time to convince her to visit us, or to come on land at all. A lot of her other relatives still haven't spoken to her. Her dad was really angry with her. It wasn't until after he passed on that Annabelle started coming with us to Kingsport for the summer."

"Ouch," said Justin, catching the implication.

"Yeah." He gestured, dismissing it. "Belinda's a very sweet person who made some dumb choices when she was a teenager, when she was stressed and miserable and scared. That was a long time ago, but some people won't let it rest."

"Thank you," Justin said at last. "For telling me about that."

"You're welcome. You'll hear about it soon enough." He shook his head in disgust. "Even though it shouldn't matter at all."

A line from the poem he'd read in Muñoz' office surfaced in Justin's mind. "The things that matter stay when all else passes," he said.

Owen's face lit up. "I didn't think you knew Justin Geoffrey's poetry."

"I read that in a book in Dr. Muñoz' study," said Justin. "Justin Geoffrey—he's one of Jenny's favorite poets, isn't he?"

"And mine," said Owen.

A complex whistle came up through the hole in the floor. Owen answered, then turned to Justin. "They're ready."

Justin drew in an uneven breath. "Then let's go."

* * *

Belinda, Trintje, and Dr. Muñoz were waiting for them in a brick-walled room with a low ceiling—an opium den in some earlier period, Justin guessed, recalling a stray bit of history he'd picked up at the Brooklyn Public Library. Moldering remains of low divans ran along the walls, and half a dozen thin clay pipes with tiny bowls lay, broken but recognizable, here and there on the flagstones. Three of the little oil lamps provided a flickering uncertain light.

Belinda looked unnaturally pale, and crouched on the floor in a huddle of tentacles. Trintje squatted close by. Muñoz stood back over to one side, his face unreadable.

"Are you ready?" Trintje asked, and then laughed her tittering laugh. "Of course you aren't. Sit down and attend, if you really want to go through with this."

Justin sat down next to Belinda, who forced a smile. Owen went to stand near Muñoz.

"In a little while we're going to leave the two of you here," said Trintje, "and you'll do a little ritual." She laughed again. To Justin: "You'll summon the Alala." To Belinda: "You'll speak the words that command it. If you panic, why, then it'll kill you, too, and then it's all up with you both." To them both: "Once the Alala does its work, we'll carry a corpse to a different place for a different ritual. Then we'll go on to the next part of the working. Understood?"

Justin nodded, said nothing.

"Good," Trintje said. She turned to Muñoz and said, "The ritual." He nodded and smiled, extracted a yellowed envelope from inside his jacket and handed it to her.

"Don't open it," Trintje said, giving it to Justin. "Not until the rest of us have left the room, not unless you want to end up with more corpses than we need. Once we've left, open it, read it together, and do exactly what it says."

The two of them nodded, and Trintje considered them both, stood up, and motioned to the others. "Out of here," she said to them. "We don't have enough time as it is."

The doctor went out through the door. Owen followed, then turned to face Justin and Belinda. "I don't think there's anything I can say. Just—thank you, both of you. If this works—"

"Out with you," Trintje said, and prodded him with one of her spider-limbs. He gave her a wry look, let himself be herded out the door.

"Ready?" Justin asked Belinda then. "You look kind of pale."

She made a little low laugh in response. "They had to take a lot of my blood. Am I ready? No, but I'll do it anyway." Before he could open the envelope: "Are you frightened?"

"Of course."

"Good. I was hoping it wasn't just me." A tentacle pointed at the envelope. "Go ahead."

Justin turned the envelope over, found words typed on the back:

If found please return unread to Mr. Robert Suydam
36 Parker Place #11, Brooklyn, N.Y.

Inside were two folded sheets of yellowed paper, one with *Frater Mysticus* typed on the back and the other with *Soror Mystica*. Justin knew just enough Latin to give Belinda the latter and keep the other himself. They glanced at each other, then unfolded the sheets of paper.

His had a long column of strange words typed on it in capital letters, and below it the instruction *Pronounce these names distinctly and do not fail to recite them all*. That seemed straightforward enough, and Justin glanced at Belinda again, waited for her nod, then drew in a deep breath and spoke the name ZAWEZETH.

A sudden chill spread through the air, and Belinda's lips began to move, whispering an incantation. Justin spoke the next name, RIMAY; the next, XEHTRIANO, and then the next, YSEHYGORGOSETH.

Something listened and answered. Justin could sense it, though he heard nothing but the echoes of his own voice and the low steady whispering of Belinda's. Something moved toward them out of the darkness, and he felt with uncanny clarity the death it carried with it.

He forced his attention back to the list of names, made himself keep reciting them. One after another, the names echoed off the low ceiling, and each one took a greater effort to speak aloud. Toward the end it felt to Justin as though the air had turned thick and gelid, resisting every movement of his mouth and jaw, and each word had to be forced out through a mass that fought back against his efforts. His voice rose, harsh and shrill, as he reached the last three names and shouted, "ZUY! ZURUROTHOTH! ZHYWETHOMORMO!"

As the last syllable of the last name echoed into whispering silence, the Alala came.

Justin had wondered from Trintje's words whether the Alala was a spirit or an impersonal energy. In the first shuddering rush of its arrival, he thought it might be both, but as it seized him he realized instead that it was a process, one of the great transformative flows that surges through the kingdom of Voor and holds the cosmos in its embrace. Dazzled with the wonder of it, he tried to open his mouth to tell Belinda, but there was no breath left in his lungs for him to speak with, and an immense silence gathered in his chest where his heartbeat should have been. He tried to reach out toward her, but his whole body went limp, and something he could barely perceive laid him down flat on the cold flagstones of the floor.

Then the world dissolved into billowing white emptiness, and the cold heavy mass of his body went tumbling away from him—or was he tumbling away from it? He could not tell. The void beckoned to him, and with something like relief, he let himself fall forward into it.

* * *

He drifted for a time through formless white vapors, heard as though from a vast distance a high thin keening like the music of flutes, an intricate patterned rhythm like the pounding of drums. Being dead seemed more peaceful than he'd expected.

He waited, and finally another sound made itself heard, a sound that came shrill and grating out of the shadows, shattering the peace that surrounded him and drowning out the distant flutes and drums. He twisted around in the vapors, tried to move further from the noise, but some intangible force had him in its grip and drew him down. Around him, the vapors took on a reddish cast and began to swirl in vortices, and the shrill unbearable sound became a voice chanting words he did not understand: "In the name of Thaphron, and in the name of Latgoz, and by all the powers of Dzannin, come forth, I adjure ye! Come forth!"

Justin's eyes blinked open. He was lying on his back, naked, with cold stone pressing up against him. Over him, Trintje Sleght loomed phosphorescent against blackness, her one hand extended with fingers spread, the spidery limbs that rose from her other shoulder arched and bent at strange angles. Closer, felt rather than seen, Belinda crouched by his head, tentacles coiled around his shoulders. He tried to draw in a breath, to say something to Belinda—

And felt his lungs, collapsed and lifeless in his hollowed chest.

He was dead. He could feel that with appalling certainty in every fiber of his cold and silent body. Stark terror surged in him, and he sat up in a sudden spasmodic motion, ready to struggle to his feet and flee if he could.

"No," said Belinda, pulling him back down. "No, Justin, don't."

All he could think of was the death that clung to him. Panic surged in him.

Her tentacles tightened their grip. "Remember what we're trying to do," she said, her voice low and desperate. "Please try to remember."

Her words didn't dispell the terror but it gave him something he could use to anchor himself. Presently he remembered, and let himself be guided back down to the stone floor.

"Good," said Trintje. "Maybe you'll do." With a sardonic look from her bright eye: "Maybe." She squatted next to him. "Open your mouth if you can."

He managed the motion, though it felt unpleasantly as though his jaw had simply fallen open. Trintje nodded curtly, and Belinda picked up a glass bottle and poured a thin stream of liquid into his mouth. Justin could feel it trickling down his throat.

"Shut your mouth," said Trintje; he made an effort, and his jaw snapped shut. "Good," she said then, and turned to Belinda. "You remember what comes next? Good. Do it."

Belinda took the bottle in one tentacle, used it to anoint the tip of another. Trintje brought over one of the leatherbound books and held it open, revealing a page of strange glyphs. One by one, the tentacle drew the glyphs on Justin's bare skin. Finally Trintje closed the book.

"Justin," said Belinda then, "that fluid was made out of my blood, so you have some of my life, my voor, in and around you. Don't try to move. Let me move you."

His body sat up then, clumsily, without any effort on Justin's part. "Good," said Belinda. "Now come with me."

His body lurched to its feet, helped by Belinda's tentacles. She put an arm-tentacle around his waist and another around his shoulders, and the two of them started walking toward a dim uncanny glow in the middle distance. Justin could feel another's life moving the cold stiff muscles of his body, but he could feel also whose life it was, and let himself slump against Belinda's voor the way he'd slumped against her body in the aftermath of Mha'alh'yi's spell.

The dim glow drew together at last into a faint shimmering haze, and at the center of the haze was a shape he remembered after a moment: a carved golden pedestal on an onyx base, sitting on the edge of a black pool that rippled as though something moved deep within it.

"The Throne of Eibon," Trintje said, somewhere behind him. "There's a treasure such as you've never seen and will never see again. Eibon the sorcerer fashioned it in Hyperborea when your ancestors and mine weren't quite human yet. It's seen plenty of things you wouldn't want even to think about." She laughed, sending echoes scurrying.

"I'm going to put you on the Throne," said Belinda, "and make you say some words. Trintje says those will give you an artificial life that will get you past the spells. Then all you have to do is go down the stair and use the key."

He wanted to say "Okay." He wanted to say other things, too, but his mouth would not respond. Instead, he stood motionless as she uncoiled her tentacles from him, then walked over to the pedestal, hauled himself up onto it and sat.

He could feel her will gather in him, take control of his lungs and his mouth. A sudden jarring movement drew air into his chest, and then he said aloud in a clumsy choking voice: "DIES MIES JESCHET BOENE DOESEF DOUVEM ENITEMAUS."

Sharp as an electric current, something shot through him then, setting off spasms in every muscle. It was not the life he knew, but it jolted his body back into something like animation, set blood moving sluggishly through his arteries and breath hissing mechanically through his throat.

"You can get up now," Belinda said.

He got to his feet. A little past Belinda, he could see Trintje watching him. "That's two tests the two of you have passed," she said. "Are you ready to attempt the third?"

"I think so," Justin said. His voice sounded clumsy in his ears, but he could speak again.

"Good. The stair's there." She pointed into the darkness. "Take a light, take the Key. Go to the foot of the stair, take the tunnel through the water to the longer stair, and then down.

That's all." She laughed, went to the edge of the pool, dove in, vanished from sight.

"Belinda—" Justin said.

She smiled at him. "You need to go," she said. "We'll talk more after you've used the key." He nodded, uncertain, and she gave him the flashlight she held, then lifted up the silver key—she'd found a cord for it—and hung it around his neck. Her lips brushed his, and then she went to the pool and followed Trintje out of sight.

* * *

Justin watched her go, then made himself turn away. The movements of his body felt unnatural, but his muscles obeyed his will and his senses seemed abnormally acute. He could hear the rhythmic lapping of wavelets against the brick walls of the pool with uncanny clarity, and the thin beam of the flashlight illuminated far more of the space around him than it should have. Dim vibrations moved through the stone paving beneath his feet, spoke of traffic on the streets above and, just possibly, stranger things somewhere far below.

Beyond the pedestal the tunnel ended in a wall of smooth featureless stone. In the middle of the wall was an opening into blackness. He walked over to the gap, shone the flashlight into it, saw a stairway slanting down into unknown depths. The size and proportions of the steps made him doubt that they had been made for human beings.

As he started down the stairway he could feel forces whispering and pressing against him. Down the stair, he reminded himself. Then to the tunnel through the water, and then down another stair. It seemed simple enough, and he reminded himself that he'd already gotten further than Robert Suydam. The old scholar had failed the second test, Justin knew, and his bride Cornelia had failed the first and doomed them both. How many others had passed those dangers, and then failed the third test? Justin had no way to tell, and knew it. He kept going, and after a time his flashlight beam caught on pale and misshapen things on a step below.

They had been human bones originally, Justin guessed—a skull, a pelvis, a few scraps of long bones—but none of them had kept its original form. The skull had opened up in the middle of the face to make room for two long fanged jaws reaching off at random angles, the pelvis had sockets for far too many limbs, and the long bones forked in disquieting ways. Justin gave them a dismayed look and kept on walking. If the teachings Muñoz had learned were wrong, he knew, the same thing might start happening to him within moments.

Another jumble of bones too far gone in decay to interpret lay a dozen steps or so further down, and yet another, little more than fragments, a half dozen steps below that. A few more, and Justin reached the foot of the stair.

A lightless space stretched beyond it, and it was littered with bones, not all of them originally human. The beam of his flashlight strayed over something that must once have been a rat, until it elongated to a python's length, sprouting jaws and limbs and tails at random all along. He tried not to pay attention to any more of the remains than he had to, and managed fairly well until his flashlight beam caught on clothing that had not yet had time to molder.

There were three corpses so dressed, and all of them wore the gray and white urban camouflage the negation teams of the Radiance favored, though the garments were torn to shreds by what had happened to their wearers. Monstrous contortions and bifurcations had remade them into caricatures of humanity, with twisted half-faces and boneless limbs protruding from every member. If Justin's body had been alive, he would have felt sick with horror. Instead, his body walked mechanically onward, untroubled by the sight, and Justin made himself look away and wished his feelings could express themselves in plain healthy nausea.

He reached the last of the misshapen skeletons and kept going. Ahead, finally, a wall loomed up. He thought at first that it was more black seamless stone, and then that it was some kind of glass, but as he neared it he realized that it was flowing water, held in check by some unknown force. He reached out a hand to within an inch of it, felt the chill of the water, watched it ripple and surge. A little searching with the flashlight showed an opening off to one side, and he walked over to it and shone the beam into it.

The tunnel through the water was exactly that: a cylindrical space maybe ten feet across with its floor, walls, and ceiling made up of nothing but water, held in place by the same unknown force. Justin paused, then made himself go on. A first tentative step showed that the water or the force that held it was solid enough to walk on, and Justin hurried through the tunnel. Maybe fifty feet later he stepped off the water onto a floor of smooth black stone, and when he shone the flashlight around he saw no trace of bones.

Maybe, Justin thought then. Maybe this is going to work after all.

The flashlight beam showed what looked at first glance like a cavern hollowed out of polished black stone. A closer look left Justin wondering whether the stone was somehow living, for it curved and thrust in oddly biological shapes. An entrance, or perhaps an orifice, gaped on the far side, rising high like a corbeled arch. Justin crossed to it, peered through.

On the far side a corridor led between two great carved masses of black basalt. Justin stared up at the shapes, and only after a time realized they were meant to resemble reptilian figures, vaguely humanoid, with heads that reminded him of snakes, clawed hands and feet, and muscular tails. He stood there, awed, realizing that the minds and hands who had shaped those statues had dwelt in cities before the ancestors of human beings started bearing live young.

He walked between the statues, down a corridor so silent that his bare feet set whispering echoes into the darkness.

Finally another opening like a corbeled arch came into view. Beyond it, another stair slanted down into unbroken blackness. He paused, started down.

* * *

He lost track of the number of steps he descended long before he reached the bottom of the stair. The force that animated his body left no room for weariness, but he paused anyway, shone the flashlight through the corbeled doorway at the stair's foot into the space beyond. The beam glinted off dark metal. Gathering up his courage, he went forward.

The space on the far side was too irregular to be called a room and too obviously artificial to be called a cavern. A smooth floor of some translucent black stone, walls fashioned in great uneven facets like a crystal turned inside out, a ceiling lost in immeasurable darkness above: that was as much of an impression as he got, because almost all his attention was taken up by the machines, if that was what they were. Huge intricate masses of dark metal and polished black glass, they loomed high above him, and a faint wavering hiss and a flicker of lights within the glass told him that they still functioned after more than two hundred million years.

For a while he stood there staring at the machines and the space around them. It felt as though something was watching him out of the darkness, but he could see nothing but the vast devices and the shadows that surrounded them. Finally he began searching for anything that could pass for a control panel or a place where the key could be used. The level he was on yielded nothing, but early in his search he found a slender stair leading up. It was made of the same dark metal as the machines. Like the chamber high above, it had something unnervingly biological about it, as though the stair had grown in place and still had some slow subtle life in it.

When he shone the beam of his flashlight up into the darkness, he caught sight of balconies and walkways high above.

He considered searching each balcony as he climbed, but then remembered a scrap of lore from von Junzt: the serpent people had raised soaring towers in lost Valusia, and their loremasters had worked their spells from atop those towers. If there was something like a control panel, he guessed, it was at the very top.

He climbed stair after stair, until a flashlight pointed down no longer showed the floor below, and kept on climbing. Finally he reached the summit of the vast machines, and found twelve pinnacles there linked by a circular catwalk of living metal. He walked around it, checking each pinnacle carefully. The fifth of them had a flat featureless mass projecting out into the catwalk at an odd angle. As Justin approached it, a pale light spread across the surface.

Had it detected the key? Justin did not know. He stopped before the glowing surface, stared at it and wondered what to do.

A sequence of meaningless sounds whispered themselves in his mind then. "I don't understand," he said aloud. In response, a series of shimmering patterns flowed across the surface, and he heard in his mind another sequence of sounds a little more like spoken syllables.

"I don't know if you can speak English," Justin said, "but I've come from the city above here to use the silver key."

Key, the whisper in his mind repeated.

"If you can, please tell me what to do to release the energies."

Release, said the silent voice.

Then an image of the key appeared on the glowing surface before him. It seemed to pivot, and then traced out a figure of five curving lines. The image shifted, and he saw an image of himself tracing that figure in front of a certain flat portion of each of the twelve pinnacles.

Do, the voice said, and a pallid light showed from within the pinnacle to his left.

Justin took the key from around his neck, looped the cord around his wrist, and walked over to the glowing pinnacle. On the flat surface, the figure of five lines appeared, traced in brighter light; then a different figure of three lines, then another of eight lines. When the figure of five lines appeared again, Justin used the end of the key to trace it, following the lines of light.

The light in the pinnacle brightened. Then the whole soaring machine suddenly went dark. Justin gave it a long considering look, and went on.

The next pinnacle to the left lit up, and Justin repeated the process with the same results. One after another, he traced the figure of five lines over the flat space on each pinnacle. One after another, the huge incomprehensible machines went black and silent.

Finally he reached the pinnacle with the broad glowing surface again. *Do*, the silent voice whispered, and the screen showed him the figure of five lines. *Release. Release.*

Justin considered it for a moment, then traced over the figure with the tip of the key.

The instant he finished, the last of the machines went dark and silent. As they did so, the artificial life that the Throne of Eibon had given Justin vanished, as though a switch had been flipped. He crumpled to the floor of the catwalk, and darkness closed in.

Then his body spasmed, drew in a sudden shuddering breath. He lay there, unbelieving, while his lungs filled and emptied, then moved his left fingers to his right wrist. A pulse stirred there, at first sluggish, and then strong.

CHAPTER 11

THE FUNGI FROM YUGGOTH

He sat up slowly, dazed and shaking. The beam of the flashlight gave him his bearings. It had dropped and rolled when he'd fallen, and lay at an angle against the pinnacle. He picked it up, and only then noticed that the key was gone. A baffled moment passed before he recalled Agatha Sleght's words, and nodded slowly to himself. The silver key had returned to her, and would go to Salem with young Edmund Carter now that its work was done. He thought then of Matthew Hyde, doomed to wander the back alleys of Greenwich Village forever, and while part of him wanted to grin, another part felt a sudden stab of pity for the man, guessed at the tangled web of fears and desires that had drawn him into a trap he would never escape.

Shaking his head, he went to the stairway and started down it. The vast dark machines, their aeonian labors finished, loomed up around him, and he thought about the whispering voice in his mind that had guided him. The only words of English it knew were ones Justin had spoken, that seemed plain enough, but why had it said "release" twice? Were the machines somehow conscious, and after all those millions of years, were they ready to die? It made sense to him, just then, that he would probably never know.

He descended stair after stair, passed balcony after balcony. A faint rushing noise came echoing up from below, though a long time passed before he noticed it, and more time slipped by before he recognized it. By then he'd descended far enough to point his flashlight over the edge of a balcony and see, in place of the floor far below, black roiling waters rising up toward him.

Cold horror gripped him then. He thought at once of the walls of water held in place by strange forces. If those forces had vanished when the machines shut down, he realized, the water in the underground canals would pour down the stair— and the canals opened onto the Upper Bay and the Atlantic Ocean beyond. He was trapped just as completely as Matthew Hyde, he realized. He could fill his lungs with air and try to swim for it, but even if the downward torrent slackened, his chances of reaching air again before he drowned were too small to worry about.

He sat down on the balcony, turned off the flashlight to save the batteries, and a darkness more complete than any he'd ever known closed around him. He'd succeeded where Robert Suydam and the Great Old Ones alone knew how many others had failed, and done something that would bring the fulfillment of the Weird of Hali a little closer; that mattered to him, but it didn't change the fact that he would be dead soon and this time there would be no way back. The water was getting close to the balcony where he sat, he could tell that from the sound, and he tried to decide whether there would be any point in climbing to a higher balcony.

A half-familiar splash sounded above the roiling of the water. A moment later, he heard a voice he recognized at once: "Justin?"

He scrambled to his feet, turned on the flashlight, and called out, "Belinda!" The flashlight beam showed something lighter than the water off between two of the silent machines.

He hurried that way, and was rewarded by the sight of her head and shoulders rising above the surface of the water maybe five feet below the level of the balcony.

"Are you okay?" she called up to him.

"Yeah. I've got a pulse again."

"Father Dagon," she said, in a low shaken voice. A moment passed, then: "I've got the artificial gill with me. Once the water started to flow in from the harbor, I knew you'd be in real trouble, and I got Trintje to tell me the route here. It's safe now—well, more or less."

"Thank you," he said, meaning it. "I hope the trip down wasn't too rough."

She laughed, but behind the laugh he could hear the dangers she'd faced. "It was kind of a wild ride. We'll have to wait until the flow's slackened a little before we try to go back up—and once we do that it's straight out to the Upper Bay and across to the marina."

"I'm good with that," said Justin. "Any reason I shouldn't join you?"

"None in the world."

"Good." He clambered over the balcony railing, jumped out as far as he could, plunged feet first into the water. He could see nothing, but once his descent slowed, two tentacles pressed the artificial gill against his lips and fastened the ties behind his neck. As he drew in a breath of salt-scented air, all Belinda's tentacles wrapped tight around him; he put his arms around her, stroked her head and neck and shoulder, felt the shuddering dread she'd held so tightly in check the whole time.

Her leg-tentacles sculled, drawing them downward. After a time she loosed three of her arm-tentacles from him, leaving one to coil around his right arm and shoulder, and turned on one of the golden lamps from her swimming belt. By its light she drew him down to the bottom of the vast faceted chamber, slid over to one side of the doorway through which water still streamed with prodigious force. Once they settled into a relatively still pocket of water, he put an arm around her waist, and she beamed at him and slipped two tentacles around him.

Time passed and the torrent slackened. Finally Belinda extended a tentacle into the flow, gauging it, and said, "Okay, we should be able to go up. We'll need to stop a couple of times on the way so the air doesn't bubble in your blood." He nodded, she handed him one of the Deep One flashlights, and once he'd strapped it to his head they swam to the doorway.

The flow down the stairway had turned sluggish, but it still pressed against Justin as he swam. He didn't care. Somewhere up beyond the stairs and the statues, the brick canals and the waters of the Upper Bay, the *Keziah Mason* waited for him—and for Belinda.

* * *

Even though they stopped twice on the stair, he was winded by the time they passed the paired statues of the serpent folk. They found another place out of the main current to rest. "Don't worry about it," she buzzed, guessing his thoughts. "How you manage to swim that well without even webbed toes, I don't know."

He wished he could say something, and she caught that, too. "I really should teach you how to talk underwater." He nodded enthusiastically, and she beamed and leaned over to kiss the side of his face—the artificial gill put anything more romantic out of reach. Minutes passed. Then, considering him: "Do you think you're ready to go further?"

He nodded, and they swam out into the current again. The tunnel through the water had vanished, as he'd expected, and the channel where the water had flowed between banks of invisible force was open to them. Belinda led the way into the channel and then off to the left, into the current, which was some relief; the thought of swimming through water tainted by the distorted corpses Justin had seen on the way down had been troubling him.

They swam for most of a mile before the tunnel came to an end in a chaos of tumbled stone black with ancient ooze. "Up we go," Belinda buzzed then. The beams of their lamps showed a ragged opening in the ceiling overhead, and they rose up through it, to emerge maybe twenty feet higher in a brick-lined tunnel Justin recognized at once.

"One more tight place," Belinda said, "and then—" Her buzzing voice trickled away. Justin glanced at her, saw where her lamp was pointed, and understood.

The great stone blocks closing off the end of the tunnel were still there, and so was the gap on one side, but the beam of Belinda's lamp got only a short distance in before it stopped against debris. Justin swam closer, explored the opening with his own lamp. The gap wasn't wholly blocked, for water still streamed sluggishly through it, but it would have been hard for Erlik to get through the spaces that remained, and impossible for him or Belinda. He pushed at the nearest pieces of debris, found them solidly wedged in place by the force of the water.

"This is bad," said Belinda. "We'll have to go back and try to find Trintje. She told me that there are other ways out into the bay, but she didn't say where." Justin nodded, and they swam back along the familiar route.

They surfaced once he'd given her back the artificial gill. The air above the underground pool still tasted stale and fetid, but the salt scent of seawater was stronger than it had been. Justin tried to guess how strong a torrent had rushed through the pool when the waters of the Upper Bay plunged down to flood the ancient chambers the serpent folk had built, then wondered uneasily whether Trintje might have been caught in it and hurt or killed.

The darkness offered no answers. They swam over to the steps, climbed up toward the surface of the brick pier.

He'd gotten most of the way up when a flashlight beam swept out of shadows further up the canal, searching. He ducked as fast as he could, guessed he hadn't been fast enough. A moment later, though, a familiar voice came out of the darkness: Arthur's. "Justin? Is that you?"

Grinning, Justin stood up and went the rest of the way onto the pier. "Yeah," he said. "Hi, Arthur. Belinda's with me."

"Good to hear," Arthur called back. From the way his voice echoed, he was maybe a hundred feet further up the canal.

All at once a dozen more flashlights clicked on, streaming out of the darkness on the side away from the water. "Freeze," said a harsh masculine voice. After an instant, Justin recognized it: the older man who'd spoken to him in the Radiance headquarters on Frost Street. "Put your hands up, all of you, or we'll open fire."

* * *

For once, the words that surfaced in Justin's mind were the right ones: "You're too late. The third sign's happened."

"Maybe so," said the voice, unimpressed. "But that's not going to save you."

Justin drew himself up, tried to brace himself for the torrent of bullets. As he did so, somewhere off near the end of the pier, another voice sounded: Owen's. "Maybe not," he said. "But you're not just facing them."

A wet noise followed. The Radiant commander snapped an order, and flashlight beams swept from side to side, searching. They gleamed on wet black shapeless masses dotted with pallid green eyes, flowing up out of the canal onto the pier and the walkway to either side. There were more of them than Justin had seen before, and still others slid up after them.

The negation team commander barked another order. Just visible in the flashlights' gleam, half a dozen men with bulbous tanks on their backs and oddly shaped weapons in their hands ran forward and knelt, facing the water. "We've got flamethrowers," the commander called out. "If those monsters of yours move another inch toward us we'll open fire."

A complex trilling whistle came out of the darkness in response, not quite where Owen's voice had been before. One of the shoggoths answered in low resolute harmonies.

"I know," Owen's voice said then, "and so do they. Some of them are ready to sacrifice their lives so the others can get to you—and if they manage it, you better hope you get smothered and crushed by a burning shoggoth, because the alternative's going to be a lot worse."

Justin stood there, knowing there was nothing he could do. In the faint light he could make out dim shapes where the negation team crouched, men with assault rifles, men with flamethrowers, the commander standing by himself in the middle of the group, and someone or something else a little further away that somehow didn't look even remotely human.

"That doesn't have to happen," said Owen. "Some of you might have heard about the business at Chorazin in upstate New York eleven years ago. We got the drop on a negation team there, and we let them go. You've got the same option. We've already won this round, and there's nothing you can do about that. If you don't want to throw your lives away, just leave the way you got here and nobody's going to stop you."

Silence hung in the noisome air. The commander turned to the other shape, the one that didn't look human, and said, "Sir—"

"That is not acceptable," said the other, in a droning buzz. "You are to negate them."

The commander did not move or speak. The negation team members crouched, weapons at the ready, but the gunfire and flame Justin expected never came.

The droning voice spoke again, louder. "Negate them!"

Nothing happened. A long moment passed, and then a familiar voice—Jenny's—came out of the darkness along the end of the canal that led to the bay. "I'm afraid he's indisposed," she said, "and so are the rest of them. Halpin Chalmers said the spell I used is one your people don't know how to break. I've wondered for years whether he was right."

Justin glanced over his shoulder, astonished. He could see nothing at first, but the quiet sound of Jenny's footfalls whispered in the silence. Presently she crossed one of the flashlight beams, gave Belinda a quick bright smile and Justin a troubled one, and stood facing the dim unhuman shape on the far side of the negation team.

"You are Jennifer Chaudronnier," the droning voice said.

Jenny allowed a little edged laugh. "As though you have to ask."

"You are foolish to oppose us," said the creature, moving out from behind the motionless figures of the negation team.

Jenny said nothing in response. The alien shape passed through one of the flashlight beams, and Justin had to suppress a shudder. The eleven years since Chorazin had left him few qualms about dealing with creatures that looked little or nothing like human beings. Nor was there anything impossibly hideous about the creature that stood there: perhaps five feet tall, pale reddish in color, shaped somewhat like a crab walking upright, with ten jointed limbs protruding from its carapace and a wrinkled ovoid head that bristled with short antennae. What sent a feeling like cold metal sliding down Justin's spine was what that shape implied, for he recalled enough of von Junzt to recognize one of the Mi-Go, the intelligent fungi from the cold world of Yuggoth at the solar system's fringes. His muscles tensed as he watched it approach.

"And that folly will be punished," said the Mi-Go. One of its forelimbs snapped up, gripping a strangely shaped device that could only be a weapon.

Justin scarcely had time to notice the movement before instinct took over. He lunged forward toward the creature, trying to get between its weapon and Jenny—but at that same instant, the Mi-Go's weapon flew out of its grip and went tumbling away into darkness. A sharp report echoed off the brick vaults of the tunnel. A moment passed before Justin realized the noise had been a gunshot.

"Nice try, Mister Crab," Rose's voice said in the darkness. The lever action of her .243 went click-*thunk*, chambering another round. "Try it again if you think I just got lucky."

Justin backed away, facing the creature. It clutched a wounded limb in two others. "For that," it said in a shrill voice, "you will suffer as no being has ever suffered." The droning buzz of its voice rose higher still in a pattern of harsh discords. In response, the air turned cold, and something half-seen began to writhe in it, reaching outward toward Justin and Rose.

"No you don't, you son of a bitch," said Jenny. "*Xosoy, Ulathos, Omegros, Sarsewu, Xiixor, Xarosaij, Zaloros! In nomine secretissime septiplice Sadoguae tibi interdico!*" Violet light blazed suddenly from her upraised right hand.

* * *

An instant later the crack of Rose's rifle echoed off the tunnel walls again, followed an instant later by the deeper bark of Arthur's. Neither bullet hit the Mi-Go, and one of them ricocheted off the brick paving uncomfortably close to Justin's feet.

"Hold your fire," Owen shouted. "It's deflecting your bullets."

Justin hazarded a quick glance around. Belinda was crouched near him, tentacles tensed, watching Jenny. Back toward the end of the pier, Owen stood near the shoggoths; he had his fingers twined together in some initiate's spell. The shoggoths themselves waited, poised to attack. Dim shapes further up the tunnel showed him where Arthur and Rose stood. The negation team stood frozen in place, and Jenny and the Mi-Go were nearly as motionless, but the air in the tunnel shuddered with voor.

Justin knew little enough about sorcery, but he could sense the outward pressure of protective spells around each of them, warding off hostile sorceries and more physical assaults as well. Blackness pierced by the rays of flashlights framed the scene. Was it just his imagination, Justin wondered then, or was the blackness somehow becoming thicker, the flashlight beams less penetrating?

Something else moved then, at the head of the stair that led down to the water. Justin glanced that way, startled, and saw three points of green light in the shadows. An instant later Erlik padded up onto the pier, folded his eight legs under himself, and regarded the scene with ears tipped forward and what looked unnervingly like an expression of interest.

Behind him, a naked phosphorescent shape clambered up the stair, gave Justin a glance of cool amusement, then considered Jenny and the Mi-Go and scratched her chin with her one hand.

She nodded to herself, then, and pointed a long pallid finger at the Mi-Go. Her voice rang shrill in the trembling air: "*Kalath ak Kadath astu Kamathaoth!* I invoke the Doom of Nithon!"

The Mi-Go's harsh buzzing voice rose to a sudden shriek, and it staggered backwards as though something had struck it. The tension in the air shattered. Jenny made a quick gesture in the air with her right hand, tracing something that hovered there briefly in pale luminous lines, and then turned toward Trintje with a look of astonishment. Trintje paid her no attention. Her finger did not waver, and her mismatched eyes narrowed in concentration. Next to her, his interest at an end, Erlik began licking one of his legs.

Justin, glancing back at the Mi-Go, found that it had toppled to the pavement. A flashlight held by a motionless figure shone on it. For a moment Justin wondered if something was affecting his vision, for the thing's carapace seemed blurred. A moment passed before he realized that carapace, limbs, and head had all begun to sprout long reddish spines.

Belinda rose from her crouch, came over to Justin and buried her face in his shoulder, wrapping her arm-tentacles around him. He embraced her, tried to think of something to say. Owen whistled to the shoggoths, paused to hear the answer, and then started up the pier toward the others. Rose and Arthur, rifles in hand, appeared in a flashlight beam, approaching as well.

Another glance at the Mi-Go showed its carapace buckling and tearing, and green fluid leaking out through the gaps. That was when Justin realized that the carapace had sprouted the same long spines on the inside as on the outside.

Finally Trintje lowered her hand, when the Mi-Go had become a torn mass of unhuman flesh in the middle of a pool of greenish fluid. Her high tittering laugh stirred the noisome air. "Didn't know that one, did you?" she said to Jenny. "Sorceresses these days don't learn the half of what they ought, I'll wager." She laughed again.

In the silence that followed, footfalls sounded in the near distance. Justin recognized the long swinging stride at once.

"You need to leave, all of you," Nylarlathotep's voice called out in the darkness. "The fungi from Yuggoth fear one thing more than the spell that's just been worked here, and that is the knowledge you now have. They have weapons they'll use in retaliation." He came into sight, crossing the furthest of the flashlight beams. "You have just over seventeen minutes before their orbital craft are in position to strike."

"What's the best way out of here?" Owen asked as Nyarlathotep neared them.

The Crawling Chaos turned to Trintje, who nodded at once and said, "The church? Oh, yes, Erlik knows the way there. If something's going to come down from the skies, though, that might not be far enough."

"It will serve for the moment," said Nyarlathotep. He whistled to the shoggoths, who responded and then slid into the water. To the others: "Go."

"I need to find the Throne of Eibon first," Jenny said. "That's worth any risk right now."

"Oh, it's drowned deep," Trintje said. "I took it down to its hiding place once your friend there did what was needful. If you can't breathe water I don't advise looking for it."

Belinda gave Justin a quick squeeze, turned toward them. "Jenny, I've got an artificial gill with me, and I know where the throne is. I helped Trintje bring it up and take it back down. Come on. We can swim there in a few minutes."

"I'll take the two of you there," said Trintje. "The rest of you, you'd best get going. Get out of Red Hook if you can. Erlik! Show them the way to the church."

Belinda gave Justin an encouraging smile, and then hurried down the stair to the water. Justin watched her go and forced himself into motion. Erlik unfolded himself, gave Justin what looked uncomfortably like a sardonic look, and padded away toward the end of the tunnel where Rose and Arthur waited.

Justin turned toward Nyarlathotep; the Great Old One met his gaze coolly and then nodded in acknowledgment; Justin nodded too, grinned, and hurried after the cat-creature. Nyarlathotep regarded them for a moment longer, then turned and strode away into the darkness. His footfalls faded out into the unquiet air.

Owen met Justin a short distance up the tunnel, and slapped him on one shoulder, saying, "You did it. I know, it sounds stupid to say that, but—"

"I get that," said Justin. "I've got no idea why I'm still breathing."

"Pure stubbornness," Owen said without missing a beat.

Justin's laugh didn't need to be forced. "The Martenses are good at that." Erlik mewled at them. Owen grabbed a flashlight from the motionless hand of one of the negation team members, and the two of them hurried after the cat-creature.

It was about the time they reached Arthur and Rose that it occurred to Justin that unlike everyone else there, he was stark naked. He reddened, said, "I don't suppose any of you thought to bring some clothes for me."

"Well, of course," said Rose. Her shoulderbag disgorged a tee shirt, a pair of sweat pants, and slip-on boat shoes. "Get into those and then let's get out of here," she went on. "I don't like what that odd creature said about something coming from the skies."

* * *

As they hurried after Erlik, Justin turned to Arthur and Rose and said, "What I want to know is how on earth you got down here and found me."

"We had help," said Arthur. "First thing this morning we found another typed note. That told us where you'd gone, and Rose suggested that we should go talk to the doctor."

"I figured he might at least be able to let us into the tunnels," Rose said, "and it turned out—oh, there you are, Dr. Muñoz."

A flashlight clicked on in the darkness ahead, and a short figure in a linen suit detached himself from the shadows. He had a sturdy leather valise in one hand. "You are all well? Excellent—but I was told that there is some danger."

"We could all be dead in minutes," said Owen, and Muñoz nodded briskly and motioned for the journey to continue.

"I thought it was worth seeing if Dr. Muñoz knew the Outer Sign of Recognition," Rose went on as they turned and followed Erlik down a long narrow corridor. "And he did. So we told him everything, and he brought us down here through a stair in the basement of the building."

"And I," Muñoz said, "was happy to be of help. Besides which, yes, I know the tunnels down here quite well. Miss Sleght has helped me hide in them more than once, when someone showed an unwelcome interest in the year I was born." They left the canal, hurried down a cramped tunnel lined in brick.

That got a sudden sharp glance from Owen. "So you're *that* Dr. Muñoz," he said. "Did you know a man named H. P. Lovecraft?"

Muñoz gave him a startled look, and then beamed. "Why, yes, I knew Howard. An odd young man but very polite. We lived in the same rooming house for a while, when I was very sick—I imagine you know some of the details."

"Only what he put in his story," said Owen.

The physician laughed. "Ah, the story. He was always writing, and he talked often about his stories. I never expected to feature in one of them. But he was there when certain things happened. Of course he could not resist dragging in some nonsense out of Arthur Machen, I think it was—I assure you I did not dissolve into a pool of slime! Fortunately I sent a telegram weeks beforehand to a young friend of mine, and he reached me in time to claim my body. It was a few years before he was able to help me, but as you see, I am quite recovered now."

"I may have known your young friend," Owen said. "Charles Dexter Ward?"

They reached the end of the corridor and hurried through a door, and the beams of their flashlights fell unexpectedly on pews, a stone altar ornamented with the Elder Sign, a forest of organ pipes soaring into the shadows of tall Gothic arches. "So you are *that* Mr. Merrill," said Muñoz. "Yes, I heard from Charles a few years back, in a certain very odd manner." He turned to face them. "We are beneath the old church: a community center, these days. Fortunately I have good friends on the board of trustees, and—" He held up something that jingled. "Keys. Do you think this is far enough to be safe?"

"Miss Sleght told us to get out of Red Hook," Arthur said at once. "Is this the community center over by the Gowanus Canal?"

Muñoz nodded. "The very one."

"Then we're fine. We've got a boat moored on the canal and it's got plenty of room."

"Excellent." The doctor scooped up Erlik in one arm. "Come with me."

A few moments later they were hurrying up a stairway. Justin kept pace with the others, but his thoughts were back in the tunnel where he'd left Belinda—and Jenny.

It would be easier, he thought sourly, if I could stop caring about her. A useless wish, he knew: however little she thought of him, he couldn't return the favor. The sudden impulse that had sent him leaping forward to try to save her life reminded him of that, and the knowledge that she might die soon closed around his heart like a vise. And if she and Belinda both—

He tried to shove the thought away. It hovered in the darkness, mocking him.

Keys rattled as Muñoz unlocked the door at the top of the stair, led the way down a narrow corridor, unlocked another door. A moment later they were outside, beneath the pale distant stars of a summer night half drowned by the orange glare of sodium lamps. The half-familiar mass of the old church loomed up behind them. Abandoned brick warehouses, their windows sealed with graffiti-tagged metal sheets, rose across the street.

"Okay," Arthur said. "I know where we are. Come on." He hurried across the silent street. Justin and the others followed.

* * *

Another three blocks brought them to a gap between two half-collapsed buildings, where a chainlink fence overgrown with climbing weeds tried and failed to block access to the lot beyond. Arthur led the way through a gap in the fence, and then down a ragged slope past rust-streaked shipping containers. There at the bottom of the slope, the waters of the Gowanus Canal slid past, glimmering with reflected lights. Against them rose the mast of the *Keziah Mason*, tied up neatly at what was left of a decaying dock.

"Watch your footing," Arthur warned, and then ignored his own advice, leaping over rotting boards at not much short of a dead run. The others hurried after him. By the time Justin clambered aboard, Arthur had the companionway hatch unlocked. "Owen, Dr. Muñoz," said Arthur, "if you'll head below."

They went. "Rose, take the wheel," Arthur went on. "Justin—"

"Which line first?" Justin said.

"Forward."

Justin hurried up the dock, got the forward line free, sprang back onto the bow of the *Keziah Mason*. The tide was ebbing, and the bow pivoted neatly away from the rundown pier. The diesel engine growled to life belowdecks. A little work with the wheel and the aft line, and the sailboat finished swinging about and slid down the Gowanus Canal. Justin stood just aft of the bow to keep watch, called back a terse word or two when necessary, tried to make the labor of piloting the sailboat down a narrow canal keep his mind off the tunnels he'd fled or the two women he'd left there.

Minutes passed, and then the sides of the canal opened outward; they had reached Gowanus Bay. A lively breeze came sweeping out of the northeast, and Justin and Arthur scrambled to the mainmast and then forward, hauled up the sails.

They'd just finished, and Rose was shutting off the diesel, when a sudden streak of light shot down from the heavens and buried itself among the buildings of Red Hook. An instant later a blossom of flame unfolded itself over what Justin guessed was Parker Place. A great rattling boom like summer thunder burst over the sailboat a moment later, and then faded into silence, or as close to silence as any part of New York City ever experienced.

In the moments that followed, as the first sirens began to wail, Rose held the wheel steady, and the *Keziah Mason* sped across the Upper Bay in total darkness, running lights off in flagrant violation of Coast Guard rules. Only when Staten Island loomed up close did Rose switch on the lights, and only when the Kill van Kull gaped ahead did the diesel rumble into action again. Under power, the sailboat slid past a dozen rundown wharves to the marina where the big Chaudronnier cabin cruiser waited, a pair of its windows lit from within.

Justin did his part getting the *Keziah Mason* tied up next to the cabin cruiser, gave Arthur a thumbs up once the sailboat rode comfortably beside the dock. When Arthur and Rose went below, though, he stayed in the cockpit, waiting.

Time passed and the stars circled slowly in the blackness above. Faint noises across the Upper Bay hinted at wailing sirens, faded away at last. After an interval Justin didn't even try to calculate, the companionway hatch opened, and Arthur came on deck with a cup of coffee. He handed it to Justin without a word. Justin nodded his thanks, Arthur nodded in response, and went below again, leaving Justin to the solitude and silence he needed so badly.

He sipped coffee for a time, finished the cup. Then, in the cold stillness that followed, a low plashing noise sounded behind Justin, somewhere by the cabin cruiser.

He turned. Something troubled the waters near the cabin cruiser's stern. A moment later, a pale slight shape hauled itself up the ladder onto the deck. By the time Justin realized what he'd seen, he heard another splash, and a familiar face surfaced by the *Keziah Mason*'s stern.

"Oh thank God," Justin said aloud. "Belinda?"

"Hi, Justin," she said.

He reached for her, felt tentacles grip his forearms, then helped her aboard and flung his arms around her, burying his face in her shoulder. Her tentacles closed tight around him.

After a long moment, he raised his face. "Is Jenny—"

"She's fine. I just got her aboard her boat."

"Thank you. Trintje?"

"She's fine too," said Belinda. "She's got places to hide all over the Upper Bay. I made sure she got to one of them before Jenny and I came here."

"And the Throne of Eibon?"

"Jenny did something with it, I don't know what, but she says it's safe." With an eloquent tentacular shrug: "That's all I know."

Justin let out a long ragged breath, tried to convince himself that his fears really had been laid to rest. "It's okay." With a little choked laugh: "I'm just an ordinary guy, remember."

"No you aren't," she said. "Not to me."

His face reddened. Lacking anything to say, he pressed his lips to hers. The kiss kept them busy for some time thereafter.

"I know this is silly," Belinda said then, "but I'm sorry about one thing. The muumuu Arthur got me—I had to leave it behind, along with Jenny's clothes. We had to swim fast to get out of there in time." In a dispirited tone: "You'll probably have to get me a blanket."

"Nope," Justin said, grinning. "You lost one muumuu in a good cause, but the other—" He extracted himself gently from her embrace, opened one of the seat lockers, and brought out the muumuu with seahorses and seaweed printed on it. "Here you are."

Belinda let out a little delighted cry, took it, and wriggled into it. "I'm going to wear this until it falls off me in shreds," she said. "We should probably go talk to the others."

"I get that," said Justin. "Owen's going to want to know."

"So is Dr. Muñoz." In response to his startled look, she said, "You'll see."

CHAPTER 12

THE TOAD GOD'S DAUGHTER

Belowdecks Arthur and Muñoz were sitting at the table, coffee cups before them, and Owen sat nearby on a seat folded out from one of the bulkheads. He surged to his feet the moment he saw Belinda in the companionway. "Is Jenny—"

"Safe and sound aboard her boat," said Belinda. With a grin: "I'm fine too."

Muñoz stood as well. "If I may ask—"

"Trintje's safe," she said at once. "She asked me to tell you that she's in the tunnels below Governor's Island right now."

"Thank you," he said. A discreet hand pressed against the edge of the table and a slight stiffening of his face were the only changes in his outward appearance, but Justin sensed a profound relief surge through the man. Relief, and something more? He could not tell.

"She also wanted me to make sure Erlik is okay," Belinda went on.

"That," said Rose's voice from the galley, "I can guarantee." She came out with a plate heaped with sandwiches and set it on the table, returned to the galley as Owen and the doctor sat down again. "Finished already?" she said to something there. "Let's get you some more." The refrigerator door opened, liquid splashed, and the door closed again.

She reappeared a moment later with a stack of small plates. "He's going to clean us out of half and half at this rate," she said, smiling. "Not that I grudge him."

"You are kind to Erlik," Muñoz said then, with a little bow. "And to the rest of us."

He turned to Justin and Belinda then. "Mr. Martense," he said, "Miss Marsh, thank you, both of you. What you have done—" His voice choked. Then, mastering himself: "It is a blessing beyond words that I have lived to see this day."

Justin stammered his way through something more or less gracious; Belinda simply blushed and managed a fluid curtsey.

"It is a little thing," Muñoz said then, "but I have something I wish to give you in return. You recall, I trust, what I said about the three seals and the words of Hali. This is how I learned those things." He reached down, pulled something square and flat from inside the valise, held it out to the two of them. Justin took it, held it so Belinda could see it too.

A black metal frame maybe six inches across held two panes of glass pressed together. Between them was a fragment torn from a sheet of something thin and brown—parchment, Justin guessed—with faded writing covering it.

"This came to the Ikhwan al-Azif by strange ways," said Muñoz, "and many people died to keep it safe from the enemies of the Great Old Ones. After the temples were desecrated, one who took part wrote a letter telling what he had seen and heard. This is what remains of a copy of a copy of that letter, and tradition says that it preserves a part of the final words of Hali himself."

Everyone else in the cabin was staring at him by the time he'd finished. Justin looked from the cryptic letters before him to Muñoz's face, stumbled through words of thanks, and then said, "The only thing is, I don't know how to read this."

"Of course not," said the doctor. "But you will bring it to those who can. The third seal is open and the work of the Ikhwan al-Azif, the work I took up in their place, is done. It is time for this to pass to other hands. I have something to give to Miss Chaudronnier, too, a gift from an old friend of mine, but that will happen when time permits."

Other voices spoke then, but Justin was too tired to follow them. He took his share of the sandwiches, thanked Rose, and sat down on another of the folding seats. Belinda settled down on the cabin floor next to him, and when he tried to get up and offer the seat to her, a tentacle pulled him gently but firmly back down. He put a hand on her shoulder; she smiled up at him; he managed a smile of his own, had to bring his attention back more than once to the sandwich in his hand. Now that he was back aboard the *Keziah Mason*, he could let himself feel the immensity of what had happened in the hours just passed, felt also the leaden ache in his muscles and the aftermath of the dread and desperation he'd felt.

He blinked awake suddenly from a doze. "You should finish that sandwich," Belinda said, smiling, "and then I think we both need somewhere more comfortable to sleep. You're not the only one who's had a long day."

"Well, of course," said Rose, who was sitting nearby. "You two take the forward berth. I'm going to go next door and see if Jenny's boat has room for our guests."

Justin ate the last few bites of his sandwich and got to his feet. Belinda rose unsteadily beside him. Voices surrounded them, saying things that probably made sense, but Justin found he was too tired to interpret them. He and Belinda went past the galley to the door of the forward cabin, ducked through it. Belinda closed it behind them. The frame with the precious document went into a locker, and then Justin fumbled his way out of his clothes as Belinda shed her muumuu. They managed to get onto the berth and pull the covers up. He felt her tentacles slip around him, then settled against her and sank into oblivion.

* * *

He woke slowly, and some minutes passed before he realized he was alone. Gray dim light spilled in through the portholes, and swells off the ocean rocked the berth beneath him. He lay there for a while as the clouds of sleep cleared away from his thoughts with glacial slowness.

The door opened then, and Belinda came in. She sat on the side of the berth next to him and said, "How are you doing?"

"Okay, I think. What time is it?"

"Just past two in the afternoon." He gave her a startled glance, and she looked embarrassed. "I wouldn't have let you sleep so long, but I think you needed it."

"You're probably right," he admitted.

Something had shifted between them. He knew that the moment he saw her, though it took some minutes before he realized what it was. Whatever subtle pressure the Black Goat had exerted to bring them together—that was gone, now that the task she'd assigned them was done. They could walk away from each other if that was what they wanted, he could sense that clearly enough. He considered the possibility, and thought: not a chance. "Where are we now?"

That earned him a smile. "Jamaica Bay. We left Staten Island this morning, as soon as Dr. Muñoz got back—he went to Governor's Island and took Erlik with him. Everyone else is over on Jenny's boat. I begged off—I wanted to make sure you were okay, and I had to swim down to the Deep Ones to find out some things—and so I've had a really nice quiet morning."

"You like quiet mornings?" Justin asked. "I think we're really going to get along."

She looked away. Then, changing the subject: "Rose made sure there's enough breakfast left to feed a hungry shoggoth. If you're ready for that—"

"Not quite," said Justin. "There are a few things I want to do first." He reached for her, and she laughed and let him draw her down into a kiss.

Half an hour or so later they were sitting at the dining table. Belinda hadn't exaggerated much; between the biscuits, the ham and egg pie, the poached apples, and a thermos of hot coffee, Justin felt comfortably gorged by the time he finished. "There," he said. "I don't know how I kept going through all that on no food." Then, with his little choked laugh: "I suppose you don't eat much when you're dead."

She looked away. "When you died, that was—really hard to deal with."

"I'm sorry," Justin said at once, contrite. "I wish you didn't have to go through all that."

"I had the easy part," she reminded him.

"I'm not so sure about that." He considered her for a moment, went on. "If you don't mind, I'd like to talk a little about—well, what happens now."

He could see Belinda brace herself. "You're going back to Lefferts Corners, I imagine."

"No." To her startled gaze: "When the letter from Owen arrived I'd just finished selling my farm to a couple of cousins. Now that the porphyria's active—" He shrugged. "I'd make a hell of a poor farmer, not being able to go outside when the sun's up. So Rose and Arthur and I planned to go for a sailing trip while I figured out what I'm going to do with the rest of my life."

She pondered that. "What do people in your family usually do?"

"Depends. My Aunt Josephine became everybody's favorite aunt and raised me and most of my cousins. My great-uncle Orrin Typer got a job as a night shift janitor and lived to be more than a hundred. My third cousin Bobby van Kauran blew his brains out with a shotgun because he couldn't stand staying indoors all day." He shrugged. "I never saw the point of that, but I had no idea what to do. I didn't expect to get caught up in anything like this." He reached out and took two of her tentacles in his hands. "And I certainly didn't expect to fall in love."

She met his gaze, but her lower lip was trembling. "You really mean that, don't you?" When he nodded: "I—I spent most of this morning trying to find the courage to say goodbye. I was so sure you'd go back to Lefferts Corners, and I'd go back to Y'ha-nthlei—and I didn't expect to fall in love either." Her gaze fell, and she drew in an unsteady breath. "Justin, I want to—to see if we can make this work—but there are things I don't think you know about me."

Guessing what she meant, Justin said, "Owen told me a little about what happened after you and your folks went to Dunwich."

She glanced up at him again, but the smile didn't come back. "Did he tell you that I tried to seduce him?" He shook his head, and she burst out: "It was the stupidest thing I've ever done, and that's saying something. I was so jealous of Laura, and—" She stopped, started again. "He went and got Laura, and we talked." Brown eyes stared at nothing Justin could see. "If they'd told me to get out of their house and never come back, I wouldn't have blamed them for a minute, but they didn't. They were so much kinder to me than I deserved." She squeezed her eyes shut, opened them again. "I'm glad Owen told you. I don't think I could have done it."

"If you think you're the only person who ever did something dumb when you were young," Justin said, "I should tell you some stories." With a sudden sharp laugh: "Starting with falling in love with Jenny. I still can't believe I made such a fool of myself over that."

"You still care about her, don't you?"

He gave Belinda a dismayed look. "Not the way I care about you," he said. Her gaze met his, questioning, and he made himself go on. "Is it that obvious?"

"The way you went for the Mi-Go when it tried to shoot her," said Belinda, "it was kind of hard to miss." Her arm-tentacles coiled around his forearms then. "Justin, I don't mind at all. Jenny's one of my dearest friends. When I finally let

Laura talk me into coming to visit her and Owen in Kingsport, Jenny was unbelievably kind to me—well, honestly, everyone was, but we ended up becoming really close."

Justin nodded after a moment. "I hope she doesn't mind that we're an item. I know she doesn't think much of me."

Belinda gave him a long solemn look. "You two need to talk."

"I don't think there's anything we can say to each other," Justin told her.

"No, seriously. You two need to talk sometime soon."

He was about to argue, but second thoughts arrived in time. Maybe she's right, Justin thought. Maybe it's time for me to apologize, and then walk away once and for all.

* * *

When the two of them climbed through the companionway hatch into the *Keziah Mason*'s cockpit, Justin blinked in surprise. He'd expected to find the boats tied up at a marina, but they lay side by side at anchor in a little sheltered cove ringed with trees. Off in the distance, sails gleamed against the gray sky as a few New Yorkers kept up the old habit of sailing Jamaica Bay in small craft, and beyond it the dim skyscrapers of Manhattan rose pale against afternoon haze. Justin regarded those. He could sense a difference in them. Partly it was that the old frenetic life had begun to depart, flowing out through the moon paths into a broader landscape, but there was more than that. It felt as though the age of which New York City was a part and an emblem had finally broken loose from its moorings in time and was sliding inescapably into the past.

The cabin cruiser was a big model from the 1950s or 1960s, its stern lined up with the *Keziah Mason*'s, its bow stretching out some twenty feet further. He recalled seeing it in the covered dock the Chaudronniers owned in the Kingsport marina, and recognized the name on the fantail: *Susran*, after the greatest of the cities of drowned Poseidonis. Jenny's family came from there, he remembered—one more reminder of the gap that separated them.

It was an easy leap from the *Keziah Mason* to the *Susran*, and when he turned to help Belinda across he found she had already made the same leap. Her smile as she took his hand set his heart pounding. Flustered, he climbed the steps to the deck and headed for the wheelhouse.

Inside, a stocky black-haired man in a polo shirt and jeans looked up from a nautical chart and grinned. "Hey, Mr. Martense! Good to see you again. Welcome aboard."

"Hi, Kenny," Justin said. "Thank you. How's Henrietta?"

"Fine. You'll see for yourself in a bit—she came along." He glanced past Justin, saw Belinda and grinned again. "Oh, hi, Ms. Marsh. Henrietta says thank you for the fish."

"You're welcome," said Belinda. "I'll pass that on to the Deep Ones."

"Please do," said Kenny. "Everybody's in the aft saloon, by the way." They thanked him, went belowdecks and followed the companionway aft toward the sound of voices.

The aft saloon turned out to be a big open room that reached from one side of the *Susran* to the other. Couches ringed it, upholstered in dark leather, and everyone Justin had expected to see sat there: Owen, Jenny, Dr. Muñoz, Arthur, and Rose. Greetings met Justin and Belinda as they came through the door, and the two of them found seats next to Dr. Muñoz.

"You'll want to see this," Arthur said, passing over a newspaper. It was that day's *New York Times*, and the lead headline screamed *BLAST LEVELS THREE BLOCKS IN RED HOOK*.

Justin read it, glanced up at Owen. "I hope your shoggoth friends got out in time."

It was Belinda who answered: "They're fine. I asked the Deep Ones about that before we left Staten Island, and got the answer after we got here. They all got out safely. I think they're up by the old naval shipyard right now."

"That's good to hear," said Justin. "They saved my life at least twice. I'd like to thank them for that sometime, if there's a way to do it."

"I'll talk to the shoggoths in Arkham," said Owen. "We've got quite a little colony there, and they have connections with other shoggoth colonies up and down the eastern seaboard. I bet they can get a message down here—and if they can't, the Starry Wisdom church here can get word to them."

"Thank you," said Justin. He tried to turn his attention to the paper, but his mind strayed off to the shoggoths, the tunnels beneath Red Hook, the vast machines there. "Does anyone know what the things were that I shut down?"

"The old tomes don't say," said Jenny. "Something the serpent folk built more than two hundred fifty million years ago, something that reshaped the currents of voor all over the eastern third of North America. That's literally all we know."

Justin took this in. "They must have been able to repair themselves."

Muñoz nodded and smiled. "Exactly. *The Book of Hidden Things* says that the machines were alive, and could regenerate themselves and the structures around them. I do not know if that is true, but—" He shrugged eloquently.

"Yes." Memory reminded Justin of the subtle life that trickled through the stairs and balconies he'd seen. "Yes, it is—or it was."

"They could do that," said Owen. "The serpent folk, I mean. We've got sciences that they never learned, but the reverse is true, too: they knew how to do things we can't. They're still around, and I hope that someday we can find out what it was that you shut down."

Justin nodded slowly. In the silence that followed, he turned to the newspaper and read the first few paragraphs of the lead article. "This sounds really bad," he said after a moment.

"I think everyone on our side got away safely," Owen added. "I called Ruth Frankweiler in Farmington this morning before we left Staten Island, and she'd already heard from the lodges in Yonkers and New Rochelle, and some others." He grinned. "Including the shoggoths."

"So it was just the negation team," said Justin.

"No, they got out too," said Jenny. "I released the spell as soon as everyone was out of range, and used the Fourth Sign of Terror to send them running." She looked away. "I know they probably deserved to die, but—" She shrugged, fell silent.

The face of the young man who'd died in the alley off Corlear Avenue hovered in Justin's thoughts. "No," he said. "If the Mi-Go hadn't been there I'm pretty sure they'd have backed down." He turned to Owen then. "Just like at Chorazin."

Owen nodded. "We can't win by killing them all. That's the way the Great Old Ones and the elder races think, and they've tried that ever since the temples were desecrated—" He shrugged. "Without much result. I figure it's time to try something else."

"I get that," Justin said. He turned to the article, made a little choked laugh when he saw speculations about natural gas leaks and abandoned fuel tanks. He handed the paper to Belinda, and said: "I can't be the only person who saw something drop out of the sky."

"No," Owen agreed. "But the media aren't talking about it—at least not yet."

"The other side can just cover that up, can't they?" Justin asked.

"To some extent." Owen's gesture showed his uncertainty. "They don't control the government or the media completely, you know. They've got people in both, but so do we, and so they usually go out of their way to avoid anything that might get into the news."

"So this business is as surprising as I thought," Arthur said to him.

"Yeah, and that wasn't even the biggest surprise. Until now we didn't know the Radiance and the Mi-Go had anything to do with each other."

The room went silent. "That's important, isn't it?" Justin asked.

Owen gestured his uncertainty. "I wish I knew. The Radiance has allies who aren't human—Nyarhathotep mentioned that, so did von Junzt, and some Radiance people I tangled with in Providence talked about allies in a way that might mean the Mi-Go. If the Radiance and the fungi from Yuggoth are in this together, though, we're in even worse trouble than I thought."

"I guessed there might be some connection between them," Jenny admitted. "Enough to learn some protective spells—though nothing like the one Trintje knew. I'm going to want to learn that from her if she'll teach it."

"I think you will have no trouble there," said Muñoz. "Though I think I can promise you she will want to learn something of yours in exchange." Jenny considered that, and nodded.

"So what's the plan now?" Justin asked after a moment.

"We need to get out of here," said Jenny. "We're not out of danger yet. As soon as the sun goes down, the *Susran* will be heading back toward Kingsport. I don't know where you're planning on going, but you should get out to sea fast."

Arthur nodded to her, then turned to Justin. "I figure we can decide where we're going once we get out into the Atlantic, if you're okay with that."

"Sure," Justin said. He glanced at Belinda, wondered whether she would be willing to sail aboard the *Keziah Mason*, or whether they would meet somewhere else—and where? The obvious place was Kingsport, but the thought of staying under Jenny's roof after everything that had happened left a bitter taste in his mouth.

He was still caught up in those thoughts when Belinda gave Justin a kiss on the cheek and stood up, saying, "Jenny, can we talk in private?"

Jenny gave her a puzzled glance, but said, "Of course." The two of them left the saloon.

* * *

Justin watched them go, and then turned to the others. "Do any of you have any idea what that spell was about?" he asked. "The Doom of—" He stopped, tried to recall the word.

"Nithon," said Owen. "It's one of the planets out past Yuggoth in the Ghooric zone. That's as much as I know about it."

"I can perhaps add a little more," said Muñoz, smiling. "According to the *Testament of Carnamagos*, the fungi from Yuggoth traveled out to Nithon long ago. It is a beautiful world, so Carnamagos said, with great fields of flowers that turn to face the distant sun, but it is not well for beings of most other worlds to go there, for spores from the flowers sprout in the bodies of anyone so unwise, with the results we saw." He motioned with splayed fingers, imitating the spines. "Humans are fortunate—we do not make good hosts for the spores. The fungi from Yuggoth are not so lucky. The spores proved infectious and returned to Yuggoth with surviving explorers, and the whole of Yuggoth might have been depopulated had the fungi not found spells that would keep the spores inert."

"So her spell disrupted that," Owen said.

"Or hindered it from working, just for a little while." Muñoz gestured his uncertainty. "I will have to ask Miss Sleght when we next meet. It may be a while—I know it will be best if I let people think I perished in the blast—but I have ample time, and so does she."

Something stirred behind his smile, complex and reminiscent. Watching him, Justin wondered what exactly he and Trintje had going between them. Well, what of it? he thought. If they're an item, it's not much stranger than me and Belinda.

"But I should ask how you are doing, Mr. Martense," Muñoz said then.

Justin could hear the unspoken question behind his words. "Okay, I think," he said. "If you've got the time at some point, I'd be grateful for a checkup." He forced a grin. "I haven't been dead before, and I think that's kind of a specialty of yours, isn't it?"

"It is indeed," the doctor said, "and I would be delighted to be of service. Miss Chaudronnier has very graciously invited me to stay with her in her home in Kingsport for the time being. Perhaps you will visit there?"

Justin drew in a breath and wondered how he could explain to Muñoz why that was the last thing on Earth he wanted to do. At that moment, though, the door to the saloon opened again and Belinda came through it. "Justin," she said, "can you come here for a few minutes?"

"Sure," he said, and pulled himself to his feet. Muñoz said something polite and smiled, and Justin responded in kind, but nearly all his attention was on Belinda. She had a smile fixed on her face, but behind it moved something brittle and hard he hadn't seen in her before.

The door shut behind them. "What is it?" he asked, but he knew she wouldn't answer. One of her arm-tentacles wrapped around his arm, guided him down the companionway to a door on the starboard side. Another opened the door, revealing a pleasant little cabin with more leather-upholstered seats, and Jenny.

"Belinda," Jenny said in an agitated voice. "Please—"

"No," Belinda snapped. "You're both full of reasons why you can't talk to each other, and I've had enough. Okay? You've got a choice. Either the two of you sort things out now, or I'm going to sit you both down and repeat everything that each of you told me about the other."

Justin gave her a horrified look. "Belinda—"

"One or the other," she said. "Take your pick." Then, with tears starting in her eyes: "You're two of the sweetest people

I know, and I won't have you turn your backs on each other because you're both too proud to sit down and talk."

Justin opened his mouth to say something, closed it again, knowing she was right. He turned to Jenny, who glanced up at him, and then looked away. "I suppose we can talk," she said.

"Good," said Belinda. "I'll be in the hallway outside." The door clicked shut behind her.

* * *

Justin went to a seat facing Jenny's, settled on it, tried to think of something to say. The thought of baring eleven years of his private wretchedness, and to Jenny of all people, appalled him. Still, the hurt and anger in Belinda's face warned him that his refusal could sour their relationship in ways he wasn't sure he could mend.

While he was still struggling with his thoughts, Jenny spoke. "When I asked you and Belinda to leave, it wasn't for the reason you thought."

The words flicked his emotions on the raw. "Why not?" he said. "You were right."

That got him a bleak miserable look. "After what happened, how can you say that?"

"Because it's true." He struggled to find words that would reach across the gap between them. "You know that as well as I do. You're Dr. Chaudronnier the toad god's daughter, and I'm a dumb farm kid from the Catskills and that's it."

She looked at him in silence for long enough that he couldn't bear it, and looked away. "I wanted you and Belinda to leave," she said then, "because I guessed what Nyarlathotep had in mind and I didn't think either of you had a chance. Yes, I thought that you were just a farm kid from the Catskills. Not dumb—you're anything but stupid—but unprepared. And then you and Belinda succeeded where Robert and Cornelia

Suydam and all those others failed, and I got to see just what an arrogant and patronizing fool I'd been."

His gaze snapped back to her. "No," he said. "You're not a fool. It's sheer dumb luck that I'm not rotting somewhere under Red Hook right now."

Jenny flinched as though she'd been struck. "I'm sorry," Justin said then. "But it's true. If it wasn't for you and Belinda and Mha'alh'yi and Owen and Arthur and Rose and Léon Muñoz and Trintje Sleght and a lot of other people, there's no way I'd be here right now." A memory surfaced. "Do you remember how back when I was spending summers in Kingsport, you and Laura and Owen would be talking about sorcery, and I'd come into the room and you'd all change the subject? I used to feel like the maiden aunt who couldn't be told about the family scandals." With a little harsh laugh: "Now I think you were all trying to do me a favor."

She looked away, and a moment passed. "Was that why you stopped coming?"

"I wish," he said. The whole bitter tangle of his feelings surged up in him. "No, I finally got around to noticing that I'd spent seven years being Owen's annoying friend who wouldn't take a hint and just go away and leave you alone."

A silence filled the cabin. "I didn't want you to go away," Jenny said then. "When you did, I thought that since I couldn't be what you wanted, you didn't want anything to do with me."

Justin stared at her in dismay for a time, then clenched his eyes shut, saying, "Oh my God." All at once he could see his own actions from an angle he'd never anticipated. For four years he'd taken it for granted that Jenny had been glad to see the last of him. If that wasn't the case— "It wasn't that," he forced out.

"I'm sorry." Her voice was ragged. "I shouldn't have been so blunt."

He made himself open his eyes. "Yes, you should have. I'd rather know."

"You're braver than I am," said Jenny. She was half turned away from him, and her hunched shoulders spoke of a wretchedness that equaled his.

"I'm sorry," Justin said. "I really did think you just wanted me to leave you alone."

"Not at all," said Jenny, as though she didn't expect him to believe it. "I appreciated our—our friendship, if that's what it was. I tried to tell you that a few times early on, and every time you thought I was encouraging—the other thing." She shrugged. "The romance thing."

"Yeah," he said after a moment, tasting the bitterness of the memory. "Yeah, I did."

Another silence came and sat in the cabin beside them. "I don't suppose," she said then, "that there's any point in trying to start over from the beginning."

He looked up at her then, startled; it was much more than he'd expected. "I'm willing to try if you are."

"Thank you." She drew in an unsteady breath, then went on. "Justin—can I invite you and Belinda to come up to Kingsport? Please? I think maybe it might help."

Eleven years of bitter emotion stood between him and the answer he knew he needed to give her. He made himself go on anyway. "I'll have to see what Belinda thinks," he said, "but if she's good with it, yeah." Then: "And thank you."

A little of the tension left her shoulders. "You're welcome." After a pause: "Do you think we could have her join us now?"

He nodded, hauled himself off the seat and went to the door.

Belinda was in the companionway as she'd promised, sitting on the floor, huddled and miserable. She looked up, startled, as Justin opened the door. In that moment he could imagine all too clearly the expression that must have been on her face as she waited for Owen to come back with Laura for the conversation that sent her to Y'ha-nthlei, could imagine just as easily the expression she'd worn in childhood as she grappled with the bitter realization that the older sister she loved and admired would achieve all the things she wanted and could never have.

He reached for her, tried to smile. "It's okay."

Tentacles clutched at him. "Did you—" she managed to say, and then her voice broke.

"We talked." He helped her up. "Come on."

As he closed the door behind them, Belinda shut her eyes and said in a shaking voice, "I just hope the two of you don't hate me now."

"Belinda," Jenny said, gently chiding. "Of course not."

By way of answer, Belinda burst into tears. Justin got her settled down on the nearest seat and held her. Jenny extracted a pair of handkerchiefs from her purse and brought them over. Justin took them, gave her a wry glance, and handed one back to her; she met his gaze, nodded, and dabbed at her own face while Justin helped Belinda to mop hers. He ended up doing most of the mopping, for her tentacles had a hard time handling the cloth; by the time her face was dry, he'd begun to sense some of the roots of her insecurities.

Just then a low musical note sounded over to one side of the cabin, and Jenny went that way and lifted a phone handset. "Yes?" she said, and listened for a time. "Okay. They shouldn't be able to find us, though." More time passed. "You're right, of course," she said then. "Let the others know, send a message to the Deep Ones, and get under way as soon as you're ready."

She put down the handset. "That was Kenny," she said. "There are a pair of helicopters doing a search pattern over the Lower Bay. If they know their business they'll be here in an hour or so. They can't see us, but they might be able to find us anyway if we stay put."

"Is there anything I can do?" Justin asked.

"Not yet," said Jenny. "You know your way around boats, though. It would be best if we stayed well out to sea until we're off Kingsport, and that means sailing all night. Arthur told me about the porphyria, but do you think you can handle taking some night watches?"

"Any time," said Justin, grinning.

* * *

Exactly how it happened, Justin was never entirely sure afterwards, but somehow he and Belinda ended up aboard the *Susran* and Owen, Dr. Muñoz, Rose, and Arthur ended up on the *Keziah Mason*. By nightfall the two boats were tied up temporarily at a pier in a Long Island bay, close by a little town whose name Justin never heard, and Owen, Rose, Arthur, and Jenny's maid Henrietta were hurrying back from a grocery run with bulging canvas sacks in their hands. Once they were aboard, the *Keziah Mason*'s engine sang its tenor note, the *Susran*'s responded in a robust baritone, and the two boats wove their way through a maze of islands and slipped out into the blue vastness of the Atlantic Ocean.

By then Justin was in the *Susran*'s wheelhouse. He'd napped for a few hours in the forward cabin he and Belinda had been given, and once the sun hid below the western horizon he shed his broad-brimmed hat and black jacket and faced the night with his head held high. He'd spent more time on sailboats than on powerboats, but it took only a little of Kenny's coaching to get him comfortable with the *Susran*'s habits. By the time the last daylight had guttered in the west, Kenny grinned, gave him a couple of pieces of useful advice, and headed below.

Two hours, maybe more, slipped away, and so did the dim line of the Long Island shore astern. The *Keziah Mason* had headed out on a different course to take advantage of the winds, and the last white gleam of her sails had long since vanished. The horizon made a perfect circle around the *Susran*; great dark swells rolling in from the southeast rose and fell beneath the stars. There were powers in the ocean the Radiance couldn't overcome, or so he'd been taught in the Starry

Wisdom church in Lefferts Corners, and as he felt the Atlantic surge beneath him he believed it. No matter what allies the enemies of the old gods of Nature had, no matter what powers they called down from the cold emptiness of space, no matter how ruthless and desperate they became, there were realities that lay forever beyond their reach.

A line from the poem he'd read in Dr. Muñoz' study murmured itself in his mind: "The things that matter stay when all else passes." Someday, he knew, the stars would come round right at last; someday the cold glory of the Radiance would be extinguished once and for all; whether he would live to see it, not even the Great Old Ones could tell, but it made a difference that some of the things that mattered to him would still be there, when the long bitter day that dawned when the seven temples were desecrated gave way at last to the peace of night.

Whisper of the hatch and a shadow fringed with tentacles told him that he was no longer alone. "I couldn't sleep," said Belinda. "Do you mind if I sit with you?"

"Not at all." He expected her to perch on one of the bench seats on either side of the wheelhouse, but instead she settled on the floor next to him, nestled up against one of his legs, curled tentacles around it. He stroked her hair, and she raised her face and kissed his hand.

"Is it okay if I talk just a little?" she asked then, and when he said something agreeable: "I wanted to say thank you. You and Jenny could have just sat there and stared at each other, or gotten into a fight, or I don't know what else, and you didn't." She drew in a deep breath, went on. "You care about her. She cares about you. I care about both of you, and I think you need each other." Looking up at him: "Not the same way you and I do, but—but just as much. When you didn't come to Kingsport four years ago, she was really upset, and she stayed upset."

He glanced down at her then. "When did you start spending summers in Kingsport?"

"That year," she told him. "It took Laura that long to talk me into it." Then, smiling up at him: "I wish you'd come to Kingsport then. I bet we'd have fallen in love right away, and then you and Jenny could have sorted things out, and you'd both have been a lot less miserable for the last four years."

He would have said something in response, but habits he'd spent years developing made him look around the horizon, and the lights of a big ship—a freighter, he guessed—showed to port, far off but closing the gap between them. He gauged the freighter's angle and turned the wheel. Belinda glanced up at him, then rested her head against his leg and fell silent.

Some minutes passed before he was sure the *Susran* and the freighter weren't headed for each other, and then the freighter's wake reached the *Susran* and it took careful handling of the wheel to keep the cabin cruiser from rolling hard. By the time he could spare the attention to glance back Belinda's way, she had fallen asleep. She was still there, and still asleep, when the stars turned pale with the oncoming dawn and Kenny came up from below to take the helm.

CHAPTER 13

THE PLACE OUTSIDE THE PORTAL

Three days passed before the *Susran* put into Massachusetts Bay and the soaring gray spires of Kingsport Head stained with sunset light rose above the waves to the northwest. Few other craft came within sight during that time: half a dozen small freighters trudging wearily north or south along the coast, two sailboats, and one big three-masted schooner with the look of a working ship, riding the wind toward points south. Early the second evening, the setting sun glowed off a lone contrail high overhead, but that was the only one Justin saw. There were still passenger jets crossing the Atlantic, he knew, but not many of them, not any more. He recalled the crowded airports of his youth and shook his head, feeling the world shift around him.

Those brief presences helped frame the voyage; so did the unseen threats of the Radiance and the fungi from Yuggoth, whatever the relation between them might be, and the equally unknowable promise of the Weird of Hali; and so did the surging ocean that surrounded the *Susran* and the immensities of the sky above her. Within that frame, though, what mattered most to Justin was Belinda and Jenny.

He'd been certain since the moment Mha'alh'yi healed his brain that he loved Belinda and wanted her in his life. The voyage to Kingsport taught him a little of what that would mean, the adjustments and efforts it would require of him, the comforts and delights it would bring. Long quiet mornings in their cabin, evening conversations on deck, careful negotiations when this or that misunderstanding got between them, insistent passions, the first faint outlines of habits that would weave their lives together: he'd experienced something like those in earlier relationships and found it easy enough to adapt to them again.

With Belinda it was otherwise. She'd had one furtive affair with a young man in Innsmouth, he learned, and then the events that led to scandal in Dunwich. After that the cool stately rhythms of Deep One society made it easy for her to hold relationships at tentacle's length. He found himself leading her through the first passages of their life together in much the same way that she'd led him through the waters of the Upper Bay.

One thing got sorted out early on. The morning after the *Susran* left Long Island behind, as they lay in a tangle of limbs and tentacles atop rumpled bedding, the two of them talked about the days and weeks ahead, and somewhere in the middle of it the words "after we get married" surfaced. It was, Justin recalled later, the third time one of them used those words when they both stopped talking at once. Belinda hid a smile behind the tip of one tentacle and then said, "Wasn't there supposed to be a big romantic scene where you proposed to me?"

"I could do that if you want," he replied, "or we can just take it as given."

She kissed him, and then said, "Let's take it as given."

That was half of what filled the wide spaces that the sea and the sky left open. The other half was Jenny. The first day of the voyage he saw little of her, and the few times she came out of her cabin she seemed to huddle away from him. It took most of that day for him to guess at the tangle of worries and miseries that lay behind that, and then he went to work drawing her out. It isn't that she doesn't want anything to do with me, he reminded himself, it's that she's still afraid I don't want anything to do with her. With that in mind, he teased her gently, got her talking about mutual friends, strategized with Belinda about ways to put her at her ease.

It helped that he found an unexpected ally in Jenny's maid Henrietta. That first morning aboard the *Susran*, as he and Belinda had breakfast before he caught a few hours of sleep, Henrietta finished pouring coffee for them and said to Justin, "If you don't mind my saying so, I hope you and Miss Jenny can work things out. She's missed you these last four years."

Justin glanced up at her. "You've known her a long time, haven't you?"

"I was there the day she first came to Kingsport to meet the family." A reminiscent smile creased her round pleasant face. "A fragile little thing, I thought."

"If there's anything I should know, or anything I should do, could you tell me?"

Henrietta considered that, nodded, and then deftly changed the subject. A few moments later she'd left the room, but over the days that followed she dropped him useful hints from time to time, and though she never spoke of it, he guessed that her conversations with Jenny helped smooth over what awkward patches remained.

Even so, it took all three days before he finally managed the thing. The sun was down as the *Susran* neared Kingsport, so Justin went on deck with Belinda and Jenny. Orchard Island and Hog Island, the guardians of the channel, rose up to either side of the cabin cruiser, and the roofs of Kingsport came into view. Belinda eyed the waters ahead, and turned to the others. "I could use a good hard swim," she said. "Would either of you mind if I met you at the marina?"

"No, of course not," Jenny said. For his part, Justin took her in his arms and kissed her. She beamed, went to the railing, shed her muumuu, and leapt. Justin, who'd followed her to the railing, watched her plunge into the waves. A minute or so later her head popped up above the water some yards away, smiling back up at him, and then she vanished again.

"She really is an astonishing person," Jenny said then.

"I won't argue," said Justin, grinning.

Jenny went forward onto the bow, and after a moment he followed.

"Have the two of you decided what you're going to do?" she asked then.

"You mean besides getting married?"

That got him a sudden luminous smile. "Congratulations. I'm delighted to hear that."

"Thank you. Besides that, we're probably going to look for a place in Arkham."

"I hope that won't be difficult," she said. "With her tentacles and everything."

He shook his head. "The Starry Wisdom church has been buying up vacant houses there and letting parishioners buy or lease them. Belinda says Owen can put me in touch with the right people, and we can find a place that way."

"I think the Esoteric Order of Dagon is doing the same thing."

"I know. It'll be the Starry Wisdom, though, because Belinda won't have anything to do with the Esoteric Order of Dagon any more, not after what happened. She's talking about asking for initiation in the Starry Wisdom, so that the two of us can go to church together."

Jenny gave him a startled look. "I hope that won't upset Laura too much."

"I don't know," said Justin. "They'll have to work that out."

Moments passed and the scattered lights of Kingsport drew closer. "I'm glad you'll be in Arkham," Jenny said then. "I'll be living there myself soon."

"Not Kingsport?"

"No." Misery showed in her face then. "The way the seas are rising, Kingsport's going to have to be abandoned in a few years. Did you know that there's a prophecy about that?" Justin shook his head, and she went on. "You know that a lot of the families that settled there came from Poseidonis, right? The prophecy says that Kingsport's going to end the same way as the cities of Poseidonis, Pneor and Umb and Susran and Lephara—it'll be swallowed by the sea like they were." With a little helpless shrug: "I just wish I didn't have to see it."

"I get that," said Justin, meaning it.

"I know you do." She turned back to the sea. "Uncle Martin's already found a new home for the family. I don't know if you've heard of the Billington place—it's north of Arkham, a nice old mansion with a stone circle and a tower close by. I'll have rooms there, but it won't be the same, and I'll be renting rooms in Arkham to be closer to the university and the library."

She fell silent. Justin glanced at her, saw her shoulders hunch up.

"The house on Green Lane was the first place that ever felt like home to me," she said then, "and having to leave it forever really hurts."

It was a rare moment of self-revelation, and Justin gave her a startled look. The taut grief in her shoulders made him wish that he could comfort her. A moment passed, and then he thought: maybe this time I can. "Jenny?" When she glanced up at him, her eyes wet, he held out an arm, inviting, and she closed her eyes again and nodded.

He moved closer, put the arm around her shoulder. She tensed reflexively, then let herself relax against him, and after a moment her arm went around his waist.

He'd wondered, through all the years when their only physical contacts were rare and wholly casual, what it would be like to hold her. The pallid fantasies that survived those years had already lost themselves somewhere in the tunnels beneath Red Hook, and nothing even remotely like them came back as she settled against him. A little awkward, a little unfamiliar, the not-quite-embrace had no more romance in it than the hugs he'd given over the years to his aunt Josephine or his son. Even so, sensing the tension in her shoulders lose a little of its grip, her body settle a little more easily against his, felt like a triumph of sorts.

* * *

Night wrapped close around Kingsport as the *Susran* slid past the great dark shape of the tall ship *Miskatonic*, still at her place alongside the Harbor Street seawall, and nosed into the town marina. The Chaudronniers had a private dock there, and the *Keziah Mason* was tied up neatly near the outer end of it. The *Susran* went further in and finally came to rest. Justin jumped down onto the dock as soon as he could, caught the lines Kenny threw to him, got them secured: all the little details he'd learned sailing with Arthur and Rose. He was still busy with that when a splash ahead of the *Susran*'s bow told him that Belinda had surfaced.

She hauled herself up a nearby ladder, accepted a towel Jenny handed down to her, wriggled neatly into the muumuu that followed. "You took your time," Belinda said, laughing, and Justin laughed as well. He glanced up at Kenny, who was standing on deck, and caught the grin and the gesture that told him that his work was done. He went to the side of the *Susran* and helped Jenny down onto the dock, and the two of them joined Belinda and left through the locked gate at the shore end of the dock.

"Should I stay back?" Belinda asked as they reached the ramp that led to the street.

Jenny shook her head. "You don't need to. This end of Kingsport is abandoned now. Not even the Terrible Old Man lives here any more."

By the time they reached the street Justin realized that she wasn't exaggerating. The little shops and cottages that lined the narrow streets of the old waterfront turned lightless windows on the night, and the blurred light of the one streetlamp within view showed water damage everywhere and more than one roof fallen in. Justin remembered the way the same street had looked when he'd first come to Kingsport eleven years before, and winced.

They heard the car before they saw it: low rumble of the engine, crunch and mutter of tires on broken pavement. A little later, an elderly Cadillac Justin recognized at once rolled into the pool of light beneath the streetlamp, came toward them, and stopped. The engine sputtered to silence, and a short figure in an old-fashioned black suit extracted himself from the driver's seat: Michaelmas, the Chaudronniers' butler. "Miss Jenny," he said, with a precise bow. "Miss Marsh, Mr. Martense. Welcome home."

The leather seats of the Cadillac felt impossibly comforting as Michaelmas drove uphill. Black and silent buildings gave way to a few houses with lights in the windows, and then to the sprawling Georgian mansion on Green Lane. Lamplight glowed in the windows as the Cadillac pulled up to the carriage port; more light spilled out as the doors opened. Inside were familiar faces, voices, hugs and handshakes. Owen and Laura were there, so were their children Asenath and Barnabas, so were Arthur and Rose, so was Dr. Muñoz, so were a dozen of Jenny's relatives, and so was one other, a thin boy with colorless hair who stood back from the others, smiling.

Justin spotted the boy a moment after he'd received a solid hug from Laura. "Robin!"

"Hi, Dad." He came over. "I'm glad you're okay."

"Me too." Justin scooped the boy up in his arms. "How'd you get here so soon?"

"Mrs. Merrill talked to Mom and told her what happened, so I got sent back to the Merrills' house day before yesterday."

Justin set him back down. "Well, I'll have to thank your mother and Laura both. It's really good to see you, kiddo—and we've got a lot to talk about."

Arthur and Rose came over to Justin then, and Robin grinned up at him and went over to where Asenath was standing, with a creature that looked a little like a large rat perched on her shoulder: a kyrrmi, the witch's familiar of the old legends. She and Robin started talking intently, but Arthur's voice kept Justin from hearing what they said.

Moments later, old Annabelle Marsh came down the stair in nightgown and bathrobe. She went to Belinda at once, gave her a hug, talked to her for a little while, and then came over to Justin and said, "It's so good to see you, Justin. I understand you'll be part of the family soon. I'm very happy for both of you." He could hear echoes of old sadness in her voice, but the hug she gave him and the smile that followed it showed no hesitation.

As conversations began to tumble over one another, one of the servants came to Jenny's uncle Martin, the gray-haired patriarch of the family, and murmured something Justin couldn't make out. "If you'd all like to come with me into the lilac parlor," Martin said then, "there's a little food and drink set out."

"A little food and drink" turned out to be ample enough to feed Owen's shoggoth friends, had they come to visit: hearty sandwiches, soup, freshly baked biscuits, sliced fruit and cheeses, and amazingly crisp ginger snaps. Justin loaded a plate, settled on one of the sofas with Belinda next to him, and turned his attention to food and drink for a time.

A little later, one of the servants came to tell Justin which rooms he and Belinda had been given. Not long after that, bone-weary, Justin got to his feet. He went to Robin and arranged to meet for breakfast, then he and Belinda wished the others a good night and left the parlor. They were both blinking and yawning by the time they got to the rooms, and the big four-poster bed in the bedroom offered far more temptation than Justin had any thought of resisting.

When morning arrived, a dazed minute or two passed before Justin remembered why the bed wasn't rolling beneath him. He sat up and watched Belinda. She'd thrown off the covers as she slept, and dim morning light spilled across her curves, caught on the sinuous grace of her tentacles. Just then she seemed impossibly beautiful, a creature of some more exquisite world. He woke her with a kiss, and things took their course from there.

Afterward, Justin treated himself to a long hot shower, came out of the stall to find Belinda luxuriating in a cold bath. They teased each other about the difference while toweling off and getting dressed, and then he went to Robin's room while she rang for breakfast. He heard the soft drone of the dulcimer as he neared the door, playing "The Desrick on Yandro."

"So where did you get that?" Justin asked, after they'd hugged and said the usual things. He meant the dulcimer, which wasn't Robin's.

"It's Emily's," said Robin. Emily was Jenny's eldest niece, Justin knew, a tall brown-haired girl with a gift for music. "She lent it to me once I got here."

"Good to hear," Justin said. and once Robin had the instrument back in its case they left the room and headed for the suite at the end of the hall.

As he and Robin came into the sitting room and Belinda stood to welcome them, Justin tried to think of something to say to ease the beginning of what might turn into a difficult conversation. Before he could speak, though, Belinda stepped smoothly into the gap. "Good morning, Robin. Your father tells me you got to spend the summer with Mom. Did she take you to see the elder Pharos?"

That was all it took, and as breakfast appeared and promptly vanished, the two of them chatted about the black pit, the carven rim, the proto-shoggoths, the windowless solids with five dimensions, the nameless cylinder, the primal white jelly, the wings, the eyes in darkness, the moon-ladder, and other things about which Justin knew precisely nothing. Somewhere in the middle of it all the words "getting married" made their appearance, and Robin nodded as though it was the most obvious thing in the world.

Listening to their talk, Justin smiled and watched, polished off a robust meal, and sipped coffee. The two of them, he guessed, would be as much big sister and little brother as stepmother and stepson, but the look of delight on his son's face reassured him. It helped, too, that Robin responded enthusiastically to the thought of moving to Arkham, where he already had friends. Maybe, he thought. Maybe it really will work.

Later, when the last of breakfast was gone and the maid had taken away the plates, they all stood. "Belinda," Robin said, turning to her, "you know I don't always look like this, right?"

"Of course," she replied, smiling. "And if you think I'm going to be upset about a few tentacles, you really haven't been paying attention."

Robin laughed, and then relaxed visibly. His arms and legs splayed apart, what looked like clothing flowed outward, and the boy became a mass of ropy tentacles dotted with pale eyes. Belinda reached out to him, and Robin accepted the hug and returned it. Justin, a lump in his throat, put his arms around them both, felt their tentacles encircle him and draw him close.

* * *

Later that morning, Justin and Belinda spent most of two hours talking with Laura and Annabelle. That was by turns tense and subdued, for Belinda, chin up, told them of her intention to become a member of the Starry Wisdom church and leave the Esoteric Order of Dagon. "Of course I'll keep my initiation oaths," she said. "I'm not stupid! It's just—" Her voice wavered, and she drew in a breath and went on. "There are too many people in the Order I don't ever want to see again, and I'm pretty sure a lot of them feel the same way about me."

Laura bowed her head, conceding. "I hope you'll still come visit."

"Lolo," Belinda said in a reproachful tone, and Laura blushed; it was her childhood nickname. "Of course I'll visit. In fact, I plan on making a complete pest of myself. Justin and Robin and I are going to move to Arkham if we can find a place."

Laura's face lit up, but Annabelle started to cry, and though they were tears of relief—or so she insisted—too many bitter memories hovered in the air to let any more general sense of relief spread far or accomplish much. Justin was glad when he and Belinda climbed the stair to their own rooms. Then it was Belinda's turn to cry, but after the tears were done and she'd washed her face she stood straighter, as though a burden she'd carried for too long had slipped from her shoulders.

They had lunch together in the sitting room, just the two of them, talking quietly about the details of making a home together in Arkham. They'd reached that comfortable place where everything that matters has been said when Belinda happened to glance out the window, blinked, and stared open-mouthed at the scene below.

Justin gave her a puzzled look, then got up and stood beside her. Outside, the front lawn of the Chaudronnier mansion stretched away to a wrought iron fence and, beyond it, the narrow arc of Green Lane. Someone had come up the sidewalk to the gate in the fence and was starting up the walk to the front door: a tall figure in a long black coat and a black broad-brimmed hat, whose long swinging stride erased the distance to the door in moments.

Justin and Belinda looked at each other when the figure disappeared under the portico. "Do you think they'll call us down to talk to him?" Belinda asked.

He pondered that. "I hope not."

"Me too," she said.

The place outside the portal, he thought. He'd spent all those years chafing at being stuck in that place, but the tunnels under Red Hook had taught him a little of what it might mean to stand on the portal's other side, and he knew for certain that he didn't want to go back there. He put a hand on Belinda's shoulder, and the smile she gave him reminded him of everything the place outside the portal had to offer.

Later, after the two of them had a long conversation about Jenny, Justin got out the cards that had belonged to Sallie Eagle, shuffled, and dealt three cards as Belinda watched, intrigued. He turned the first one, saw the familiar image of billowing clouds. "The Clouds on the left," he said aloud. "That's a good sign. The bright side is toward the rest of the reading, so it means coming out of uncertainty." She nodded, pondered it.

"The Stork," he said, and when she gave him a sudden delighted look: "Yes, but not just that. It also means moving, finding a new place to live. In the center, that's about to happen."

He turned the third card. "The Lady," he said. "That's a person who's part of the question. On the right it means she's a presence in the future. I wonder—"

All at once he guessed what the card meant, but before he could say anything a crisp knock sounded on the door.

Justin gathered up the cards, folded their silk wrapper loosely about them, and tucked them into the drawer of the little round table. When he opened the door, he found Owen waiting there with a half-familiar shape in one hand. "Do the two of you have a minute?" Owen asked. "Nyarlathotep's been and gone, and I should fill you in."

By the time Owen had settled in an armchair, Justin recognized the thing he was carrying: the letter with a few lines of the Weird of Hali. "I forgot all about that," he said, embarrassed. "I hope Dr. Muñoz wasn't offended."

"Not at all," Owen said with a grin. "He figured the two of you had other things to think about. Arthur found it the night we left Long Island, and the next day he and Léon went to work on it." When Justin looked startled: "In their day you learned

Greek if you went to a good school. So Rose and I sailed the *Keziah Mason* for a few hours while they worked it out."

Belinda opened her mouth, closed it again.

"You want to know if it's really the Weird," said Owen. "We can't be sure, of course, but Jenny and I both think so, and the way Nyarlathotep reacted, I think he agrees." He handed the frame over. "The bit on the top is unreadable except for part of the last word, which looks like some form of *thalassos*, 'ocean.' The lines after that—well, I'll skip the Greek. In English they work out to something like this." He closed his eyes and recited:

"I send three signs. Your worst deeds will not turn them aside.

By the stone-crowned hill a door opens to awaken the sleeper,

The empty chamber again receives the jewel of the king of Egypt,

A key in a dead hand frees that which is bound under the sandy place.

After these signs, the three ..."

He opened his eyes again. "That's as far as it—what is it?"

Justin was staring at him. "The sandy place," he said. "That's really what it says?"

"*Chōrion amathon*," said Owen. "That's about the only way to translate that."

"The Sandy Place is what the Indians called Brooklyn," Justin said.

Owen's eyebrows went up. "I didn't know that. We got to the same conclusion, though."

"I bet," Justin said then. "And—" He stopped, realizing what else the verses implied.

"Yeah." Owen met his gaze. "The door by the stone-crowned hill—that's pretty much got to be Chorazin, where you opened the door. You know about the Shining Trapezohedron and how that got back to the Starry Wisdom church in Providence. And now this."

"But I had no idea what I was doing," said Justin.

"Of course not," said Belinda. She was smiling. "The Weird guided you."

Owen nodded. "A Weird isn't just a wish or a prediction. It's a work of sorcery, or something bigger than sorcery. And, yeah, it guides people."

Justin took that in. "Does it send people typewritten notes?"

A silence followed, and then Belinda said, "Owen, please. He's earned it."

"You're right, of course," said Owen. To Justin: "No, that wasn't the Weird. That was something else: the most closely guarded secret our side has. Only six people know about it, and there's good reason for that." He got up, and to Justin's puzzlement walked to a corner of the room, took what looked like a piece of chalk out of a pocket, and traced an odd set of angled lines and curves on the walls. He stepped back and murmured something under his breath.

Violet light spilled out of the lines, as though they opened out improbably on some other dimension of space. Justin stared as the violet light flowed into a small humanlike form—

And Owen's daughter Asenath, with her kyrrmi perched on her shoulder, stepped out of the light into the sitting room.

Justin gaped in stunned surprise. Asenath saw him and sent a worried glance to her father, who said, "It's okay, Sennie. I've told him."

Justin turned slowly to face Owen, still staring. "She—" he began, stopped, and then understood what he'd seen. "The stuff Keziah Mason did," he said. "She can do that."

Owen nodded. "That's the secret. The goddess Phauz gave her the gift of being able to travel through the angles of space. At first she just went to the Dreamlands, but about a year ago she figured out how to go other places in this world. Nobody's been able to figure out how she does it." He glanced at Justin. "And if the Radiance ever finds out that she can do it, they'll move heaven and earth to kill her."

"I bet," said Justin. "I won't breathe a word."

Asenath glanced at her father, caught some signal that Justin missed. "I'm glad you know, Mr. Martense," she said to Justin. "It was hard to stay hidden and still get you those notes."

Justin started laughing. "You typed those on your mother's typewriter, didn't you?"

She nodded. "Dad said it would be safer that way."

"The whole time I was in Red Hook," Owen said then, "Sennie kept in touch with me. She brought me food when I was in the tunnels, and kept track of you and Arthur and Rose after you got there. She let me know when the Radiance captured you—and she visited you there once, the one time they left you alone."

"I would have gotten you out of there if I could," said Asenath. "But I still haven't figured out how to take other people with me yet. Phauz says I have to learn a lot more first."

Justin nodded slowly, feeling dazed. "You put a spell on me there, didn't you?"

"A Word of Protection," Asenath said, nodding. "I hope it helped."

"You know," Justin told her, "I think it did."

* * *

As afternoon faded outside the window, Justin spared a glance around Jenny's sitting room. In the years they'd known each other, he'd never before been to her rooms, but she'd invited him and Belinda to spend an hour or two talking before dressing for dinner.

The sitting room looked like what it was, the place where a sorceress studied and practiced her art. Shelves full of old leatherbound volumes leaned toward each other as though whispering secrets. Delicate brass instruments Justin thought had something to do with astrology covered the top of a table against one wall, and a big ironbound trunk stood against another, its hasp sealed with a disk of lead carved with strange sigils. On the coffee table in front of him rested a tablet-shaped piece of black stone maybe six inches on a side, marked with little spirals and whorls that might be writing: a gift from Dr. Muñoz, Jenny had explained. Nearby, on a tall stand shaped like an Egyptian pillar, a jackal's head of tarnished silver, larger than life, gazed out into the room. Justin glanced at it once, and then again, and was sure the eyes had moved.

"We have no idea what happens next," said Jenny. The three of them had been talking about the Weird of Hali. "There are the three signs, if the letter you got from Dr. Muñoz is what we think it is, and the three treasures: the Ring of Eibon must blaze on another's hand, the Blade of Uoht must rise and fall in wrath, and the *Ghorl Nigral*, the Book of Night, must give up its last secret. Then, when the stars are right, four will join their hands where the gray sea meets the gray shore and open the way for the fifth. Then what was bound will be loosed, what was broken will be made whole, and an age that began in flame will end in darkness. When? We have no idea. What else might be involved? We're just as clueless. All we can do is see what happens."

Justin nodded slowly, but his thoughts were elsewhere. An hour earlier he'd talked with Rose and Arthur, told them about the plans he'd made with Belinda, and learned that they'd made plans of their own. "I'm a mountain girl, you know," Rose had said, smiling, "and New York City reminded me of everything I don't like about living close to towns. The people in Lefferts Corners were as nice as anyone I've ever met, but—" She shrugged. "I'd like to live where I can walk for miles and never see another person, the way I did when I was little."

"And I'm more than ready to try the same thing," said Arthur.

"Where do you have in mind?" Justin asked them.

"We're talking about the country north of Dunwich," Arthur replied, and Rose added: "It was so beautiful when we went there for deer season three years ago."

"Yes, it was," Justin agreed. Then: "Thank you, both of you, for being there for me these eleven years. It's been a really good time."

That got him a teary-eyed hug from Rose and a grin and embarrassed words from Arthur, and they'd made plans to stay in touch and get together come deer season that fall. Recalling the rutted and potholed roads he'd driven from Lefferts Corners, though, Justin guessed their parting of the ways would become permanent before too many years went by.

Abruptly he realized that Jenny and Belinda were both silent, and looking at him. He reddened and stumbled through an apology.

"Don't worry about it," Jenny said. "Rose and Arthur?"

He nodded. "One of those things." Then, with his lopsided smile: "Not just them. There's a lot to settle still. I've got my things in Lefferts Corners to get here, and my car—it's in a marina lot next to the Hudson River—and we need to find our new home, of course. There's a block of big Federal-era places on Benevolent Street Owen told us about, three floors plus cellar and attic, and we'll probably be looking at one of those first."

"That sounds really pleasant," said Jenny in a wistful tone.

Her expression, edged with old unhappiness, reminded Justin of the reading Owen had interrupted, and the conversation he'd had with Belinda after he'd left. A glance at Belinda showed that she'd had the same thought. He raised an eyebrow to ask the relevant question, and she beamed and nodded her agreement. "Jenny," he said, and when she looked at him: "You mentioned you were going to be renting a couple of rooms in Arkham."

'That's all I really need," said Jenny, visibly making herself smile. "A bed-sitting room—isn't that what the English call it?—and a study with bookshelves and room for conjurations."

Belinda nodded again. "Justin and I had an idea. We're going to have plenty of rooms to spare. Would you like to move in with us?"

The smile vanished from Jenny's face. She glanced from one of them to the other, and in her gaze Justin could read the wounds of misunderstandings not yet healed. "Seriously," he said. "I like your company, so does Belinda, Robin already thinks of you as an honorary aunt, and if we have more, I bet they will too."

Jenny's eyebrows went up, and she turned to Belinda. "The Black Goat's altar?"

"We've been talking about that," said Belinda, with a fragile luminous smile. "If Mom's willing, we're going to do it." Then: "Will you come live with us?"

Jenny drew in an unsteady breath and closed her eyes. "Thank you," she said. "Yes, please." She opened her eyes again. "The only time I've ever lived by myself was the three months between when my mom died and when I went away to my freshman year of college. It was pretty miserable, and I really wasn't looking forward to living alone again."

It was another moment of self-revelation, and Justin knew that it needed a response. "Then don't worry about it," he said, and reached out a hand. She glanced up at him, and put her own hand, thin and angular, in his. For good measure he reached out to Belinda. One of her arm-tentacles coiled around his wrist and forearm, and another reached out to Jenny, who took it tentatively in her other hand.

"Thank you," said Belinda. "The three of us can go house-hunting, then."

Justin blinked, and thought: the three of us. He glanced at Jenny and then at Belinda and began to smile. Daughter of Tsathoggua, daughter of Shub-Ne'hurrath, he needed them both in his life, each in a different way; though the fact baffled him in his bleaker moods, it finally made sense to him that they both needed him in their lives, each in a different way;

and he could sense that they needed each other, too, though there were dimensions to their friendship that would always be closed to him, and that was also as it should be.

We only think we understand the universe. That was true, Justin realized, but there was another side to it: the universe doesn't have to be understood. Somewhere in the tangled destiny the three of them had shared, somewhere along the winding path he'd taken through love and loss and death, his life had gone careening down a path he'd never imagined, and against all logic and expectation, it had finally come round right.

The universe doesn't have to be understood, he thought. It doesn't have to make sense. His smile broadened. Belinda was smiling too, and Jenny, who was watching them both, nodded slowly, and began to smile as well.

ACKNOWLEDGMENTS

Like the earlier novels in this series, this fantasia on a theme by H.P. Lovecraft depends even more than most fiction on the labors of earlier writers. The most important contributions were of course the three New York City stories written by Lovecraft himself, "Cool Air," "He," and "The Horror at Red Hook." Other Lovecraft stories, notably "The Lurking Fear" and "The Case of Charles Dexter Ward," also contributed their share, as did a variety of stories by Clark Ashton Smith and Robert E. Howard.

As New York City is very nearly a foreign country to me, I am indebted to David McCullough's *Brooklyn And How It Got That Way* for an introduction to the city's legends and lore, and to one of my readers, Brooklyn resident Jonathan Roberts, who kindly forwarded an abundance of information about the Red Hook neighborhood. Readers familiar with colonial Brooklyn will know already that Lady Deborah Moody and her improbably church-free settlement at Gravesend are matters of historical fact, though Agatha Sleght, the witch of old Greenwich, not to mention her strange daughter and her dealings with Lady Moody, are entirely my own inventions. The divination cards used by Justin Martense, on the other hand, are a variant of the Gypsy Witch cards, a traditional American cartomancy deck.

I also owe, once again, debts to Sara Greer, who read and critiqued the manuscript. I hope it is unnecessary to remind the reader that none of the above are responsible in any way for the use I have made of their work.